KINGZ OF THE GAME 4

Lock Down Publications and Ca$h Presents

Kingz of the Game 4

A Novel by *Playa Ray*

Lock Down Publications
P.O. Box 870494
Mesquite, Tx 75187

Visit our website @
www.lockdownpublications.com

Lock Down Publications
Like our page on Facebook: Lock Down Publications @
www.facebook.com/lockdownpublications.ldp
Cover design and layout by: **Dynasty Cover Me**
Book interior design by: **Shawn Walker**
Edited by: **Lashonda Johnson**

Stay Connected with Us!

Text **LOCKDOWN** to 22828 to stay up-to-date with new releases, sneak peaks, contests and more…

Thank you.

Submission Guideline.

Submit the first three chapters of your completed manuscript to ldpsubmissions@gmail.com, subject line: Your book's title. The manuscript must be in a .doc file and sent as an attachment. Document should be in Times New Roman, double spaced and in size 12 font. Also, provide your synopsis and full contact information. If sending multiple submissions, they must each be in a separate email.

Have a story but no way to send it electronically? You can still submit to LDP/Ca$h Presents. Send in the first three chapters, written or typed, of your completed manuscript to:

LDP: Submissions Dept
Po Box 870494
Mesquite, Tx 75187

DO NOT send original manuscript. Must be a duplicate.

Provide your synopsis and a cover letter containing your full contact information.

Thanks for considering LDP and Ca$h Presents.

Playa Ray

ACKNOWLEDGEMENTS

As always, I give high praises to God for for the abundance of blessings HE has bestowed upon me. To my grandmother, Mary 'Mom-Mom' Robinson, for giving birth to my mother Mary McCoy, who pretty much got on my beyond for leaving a lot of people out of previous acknowledgements; people we came up with. However, in the beginning I mainly focused on the ones who supported me on my journey to become a published author, which I was quite appropriate, if I may.

Now, without further ado, here goes: First, I want to acknowledge my sisters Alicia 'Twin' Flemister and Victoria Duffy. My niece Angela 'Angel' Cider. My son Rayquan 'Lil Ray' Nunn, and my brothers Bernard McCoy, Morris 'Boobie' McCoy, Christopher 'Chris' Pullins, Michael 'Tripp James' Pullins, Sandy 'Flip' Washington, Major Gramz (CEO of Drogue Apparel), Michael 'Poppo' Paige, Randal 'Big Ru' Jones, Raymond Clark, and Tommy 'Usher' Wright.

Others are Michael Morris McCoy, Vickie McCoy, Oscar ''Uncle Toot' Cobb, Tiesha, Cookie, Debbie Strachen, Natasha Nunn, Millicent Nunn, Shaneka Nunn, Nee-Nee Nunn, Krystal Bibbs, Melvin 'DJ Goldfinger' Bibbs, Kinnard Redding, Kinnard 'K. Redd' Redding Jr, Lisa Porter, Jermaine 'Moe' Porter, Melissa 'Lisa' Wright, Don Carlos 'Barlow' Wright, Eric 'New York' Ferguson, Antonio Lanier, Wayne Williams, Anthony 'Detroit' Spencer, Christopher 'Slick' Williams, Johnny 'Rain Man' Ware, Kadarius 'Bandana' Davis, Randy 'Chip' Johnson, Christopher 'Iceberg' Wilkerson, and Terri Willis.

A special thanx to my GED teacher, Cindy Reyes, and her aide Richard Hayes, for staying on me and encouraging me not to give up. Another driving force behind my becoming a published author is CEO Ca$h and his staff at Lock Down Publications. I claimed 2019 as my year and they made it happen.

Lastly, I want to take time to reflect on those who are no longer with me. J.L Jones, Mae McCoy, Kimberly McCoy, Tiberius 'TC' Hester, Allene 'Pee Wee' Porter, Delores Redding, June Bug, Freeman Sallahuddin, Sister Dyiah Sallahuddin, Alicia 'Lou-Lou' Dorsey, and Tanisha Oliver. Each and every one of you are forever loved.

"Wealth maketh many friends, but the poor is separated from his neighbor" Proverbs 19:4

ABOUT THE AUTHOR

Playa Ray was born Ray McCoy on November 23, 1979, in the city of Atlanta, Georgia. Introduced to the streets at the age of 9 years old, he witnessed and experienced a great number of things that have become play a prominent part in his ability to paint vivid pictures in his stories.

He is currently incarcerated, but makes great use of his time by writing. It his Playa Ray's wish to welcome you into the mind of a paragon. He thanks his supporters, and he promises you all that there is much more to come.

Facebook: Norris McCoy
IG: Norris McCoy
Email: Therealplayaray@gmail.com

Playa Ray

Chapter 1

Ray didn't know much about The Queenz, but he felt that in order for one of them to spot him in the dimly lit club at the Battle of the DJs, and call out his name, obviously, they were very familiar with him. Although he'd cut his hair and now wore trimmed sideburns connecting with his goatee.

That night remained unforgettable to him. He could not stop thinking about the encounter. It seemed like it was meant for her to spot him because if he'd perceived the scene correctly, she was already watching him before he looked up at the VIP booth, where The Queenz were stationed as judges of the event. Pondering this, Ray had Joe call Spenz to inform The Queenz of a meeting at the Grown Folks restaurant in Roswell, Georgia, at eight o'clock.

Now he was thinking they wouldn't show, considering the death of Spenz, who Ray was told one of The Queenz were dating. Spenz was like a friend to him. Therefore, he was also affected by the news. Joe had talked him out of going to the funeral and tried to talk him out of meeting with The Queenz. He was going to the meeting! Being that Poppo was over security, he appointed Hot Ru and Stone, two members of the Bloods gang, to the location at seven-thirty, to survey the area and monitor traffic. He had recruited a number of his gang affiliates to help with the running of the business, but most of them couldn't seem to let the street mentality go. All they wanted to do was throw gang signs and beef with rival gangs, in lieu of taking advantage of the large income that came with working for L.K.S.

Ray didn't mind working with Stone and Hot, who both seemed to be quite level-headed and more about getting money. He was just amazed by how gang banging had hit the South and rapidly increased. Now it seemed like everybody was affiliated with something.

"Call and see what the move is," Ray, who was seated in the back seat of the black Lincoln Town Car driven by Joe, told Poppo.

Poppo, who was seated in the passenger seat, called Stone, then informed Ray that The Queenz had arrived with their quad-man security team, leaving two outside in the parking lot.

"Tell them to keep an eye on the two outsiders," Ray said. "If they make a move, take immediate action!"

While Poppo relayed the message, Ray was thinking about this meeting he was on his way to, clad in a dark-blue suit that concealed his bullet-proof vest and Glock .40 in the holster on his hip. He was wondering how the meeting would go. He already knew they wanted to deal with him on the weed and Ecstasy pills. Whether he deals with them or not depends on how this meeting goes.

"Circle the lot," Poppo told Joe when they'd made it to the restaurant.

As Joe circled the lot, they spotted the black Mitsubishi Eclipse that Stone and Hot were occupying. Moving along, they saw two guys standing beside a black GMC Denali, sharing a blunt.

"That's gotta be them," Joe said.

"It is," Ray agreed. "Go ahead and park."

Once Joe parked, they all got out and made for the entrance, fully aware that they were being watched by the two watchmen. Upon entering the restaurant, Joe and Poppo made sure to precede Ray, to do a quick survey of the place, and provide cover for him, just in case they were walking into an ambush. Of course, Ray did his own overview. There was a light crowd. The two, hard-looking guys shared a table with only two cups in front of them, he immediately pegged as the other guards. Once he'd spotted The Queenz, who were all seated at a table, regarding him with expectant looks, that's when he realized who they were. He couldn't believe he'd forgotten about them.

Poppo and Joe chose a table close by. As Ray approached their table, The Queenz slowly stood and – to his surprise – were happy to see him; greeting him with hugs and tears. The touching ceremony lasted for almost two minutes before they bided him to have a seat. As Ray sat with them, he was wondering why they were wearing bullet-proof vests. Then he figured they were just being cautious, as Poppo was when he'd insisted that Ray wear his, which he knew they felt while they were hugging him.

"So, you were really at the Battle of the DJs that night, huh?" Shonda asked.

Ray nodded. "I was. Who spotted me?"

"I did," Sheila spoke up.

"And how'd you manage that?" he asked, taking off his round-brimmed hat.

"I don't know," Sheila answered. "I saw you when you came in. It was something about your posture and the way your men surrounded you that caught my attention. Then, when you looked up, I guess my instincts kicked in because I felt something. Besides, I've dreamed about you too much to forget your face."

Ray just looked at her, either she was crazy about him, or just plain crazy. Now he remembered her being at the hospital with him when he'd come down with the stomach virus and staying with him until he'd recovered.

"So, what happened?" Shonda asked. "The media claimed that all four Kingz were murdered that night."

Ray knew this was coming. He drew a breath, then lunged into his side of the story of that night, starting with how he'd come down with a cold, to how his Delta had broken down on the expressway and being picked up and driven home by Raymond.

"Sick or not," he resumed. "I was going to the event, but James insisted, I let Raymond take my place, and get some rest. I mean, nobody knew that was gonna happen."

"What about the Kingzmen?" Ebony asked. "Weren't they supposed to be following them?"

"I really don't know the full details," Ray answered, loath to speak on the Kingzmen, and what he felt about them. "Y'all still looking for a plug on the pills and weed?" he asked, hoping to change subjects.

"You said you didn't wanna deal with false-claimers," Shonda reminded.

"That was before I realized who y'all were."

"And when did you realize it was us?"

"The moment I walked in here."

"You mean, you forgot who we were?" Sheila seemed hurt.

"Not really," Ray managed. "I just had a lot going on, but I apologize for the remark if it hurt y'all feelings."

"What about, Spenz?" Theresa asked. "Did he know you were still alive?"

"Not exactly."

"He didn't know you were, L.K.S.?" Shonda inquired.

"No," Ray answered, still hating the fact that he didn't get the chance to reveal himself to Spenz before he died. "Which one of you were dating him?"

"I was," Theresa admitted.

"I offer my condolence."

She nodded.

"I can't stay long," he told them, after being signaled by Poppo. "Do y'all still need the product?"

"We do," Shonda answered. "And I was told that you have the best deals on the planet."

"Perhaps, I need a number to reach y'all."

As if by supernatural powers, Sheila produced a business card, handing it to him. "This is our business phone, but if you want my cell phone number, just in case—"

"This'll do," he cut her off, standing and donning his hat.

"I haven't even told you what we need," Shonda said, standing and the others followed suit.

"We'll discuss that when I call."

They all hugged him again. Then Ray made his exit, with Joe leading the way and Poppo bringing up the rear. As they made for the car, they noticed The Queenz' two outside men were now seated in the rear of the truck they'd been standing by earlier. Once inside the Lincoln, Poppo told his men to stand down.

On the ride back to Canton, Georgia, Ray settled into his thoughts. He was so ready to reveal himself, he was anxious to tell Joe to detour to Atlanta, and ride through every neighborhood that existed, but it was almost nine, and he had to let Joe and Poppo go, so they could get home to their women and kids. All he had to go home to was his two Rottweilers, Kujo and Bruno and him being in dire need of a sexual romp, didn't make his situation any better. Had he not had to meet with The Queenz, he would have called an escort service and been held up in a hotel room, right now, but being that he was about to relieve his security, he was going to have to hold out until he was able to make arrangements.

"You aight?" Poppo asked Ray, once they'd pulled into the driveway of Ray's house that was quite distant from any of his neighbors', and the only one with an electrical gate.

"Yeah," Ray answered. "Y'all go on home and do the family thing. Get at me around twelve. I got a few places I wanna visit tomorrow."

Entering the house, Ray activated his alarm. As he made for his bedroom to undress, he reflected on The Queenz again. Remembering all the things he'd heard about them, it was still hard for him to believe that these four women had built their drug empire without the support of a male figure, but then again, there's no telling what James had taught Shonda while they were together. Although she seemed innocent and sweet while working as their secretary at Kingz' BMWs, Ray could tell she was quite ambitious and inquisitive.

After a long shower, Ray donned a pair of pajamas, fed the dogs, then retreated to the living room to watch television until he was ready for bed. Instead of turning to the TV Guide channel, he used the remote and surfed through the channels, but it seemed as if every channel was a commercial, and it seemed as if every commercial was promoting sex, which broadly reminded him that he was in need.

"This is not gonna work," Ray said, turning off the TV, grabbing his cell phone off the table and dialing BJ's number.

"Talk to me," BJ answered.

"You busy?"

"Not really," BJ said. "What's up?"

"I need you to find me something nice," Ray told him.

BJ responded, "Shit, you caught me at a good time."

"Why is that?"

"Cause, I'm at a hotel right now with three of 'em," BJ informed. "We're waiting on Rick to get back with the beer and blunts."

Once he'd established which hotel they were at, Ray redressed, grabbed his keys, and entered his three-car garage. For some reason, before he climbed into his black 500 Mercedes Benz, he stopped to stare at his and James' BMW's, which he'd kept stored in the garage. His brain was trying to force his body to get into the Benz, but his body wasn't responding. Now, he was wondering if God was showing him a sign.

Playa Ray

Chapter 2

"Good morning!" Sheila, who was making breakfast, greeted Shonda, who'd entered the kitchen.

"Mmm-hmm," Shonda responded taking a seat at the table. "I can't remember the last time *you* cooked breakfast."

"Last Wednesday," Sheila replied, stirring the grits that accommodated pancakes, smoked sausages, and eggs that were already done.

"That came from a restaurant," Shonda accused. "You didn't cook it."

"It doesn't matter who cooked it," Sheila stood her ground. "I provided it."

"Whatever." Shonda looked at the business phone, seeing that they had no messages. "You seem to be in an extremely good mood. What gives?"

"Nothing," Sheila lied, knowing she'd thought about Ray so much, she'd slept in intervals last night. "A sistah can't be happy without there being a specific reason?"

Shonda just looked at her cousin. She knew damn well why Sheila was in such high spirits. She had only posed the question to see if Sheila would be honest. She didn't, so Shonda was going to pry it out of her. She waited until Sheila had fixed their plates and taken a seat at the table, before going on.

"Ray was looking good last night, huh?" Shonda asked, pouring syrup on her pancakes.

Sheila's only response was a wide grin that spread across her face.

"Heifer!" Shonda exclaimed. "I knew that was why your ass was floating on air!"

"I still can't believe he's alive!" Sheila said. "Last night didn't even feel real!"

"Yeah, it does seem like it was a dream," Shonda agreed, biting into one of her sausages. "And your hot ass was just throwing yourself at him."

"I was not!" Sheila protested.

"*But if you want my cell phone number,*" Shonda mimicked her cousin. "That's probably why he got the hell on!"

"That's not the reason," Sheila begged to differ. "One of his lieutenants signaled to him that it was time to go."

Shonda didn't bother to contend with that. Being who he was, he couldn't take the risk of being in one place for a long period of time, considering it's possible he could still have enemies, who could easily recognize him and take immediate action. This made her wonder what their next visit would be like.

After breakfast, Sheila and Shonda prepared the orders for the clients they'd be dealing with today. Once that was complete, Sheila made off to take her shower, and Shonda retreated to her bedroom to check her cell phone for messages. There was one from, Tino telling her to call when she got a chance. Figuring it was important, she dialed his number.

"Apparently you're not familiar with the time difference," he answered in a slight, groggy voice.

"What time is it up there?" Shonda asked, looking at her clock to see that it was 11:27 a.m.

"It's almost eight-thirty," he told her. "Ain't nobody up this damn early!"

"Boy, its Sunday! People go to church on Sundays."

"Well, you'll need *somebody's* God, next time you call me this early!"

"Fool, you left a message on my phone last night. Telling me to call you when I got a chance!" she reminded him.

"Hell, I didn't want shit," he admitted. "I was high and horny as fuck! I was hoping I could get a lil' phone sex,"

"From who!" Shonda exclaimed, knowing damn well she wasn't going to play with her pussy on the phone like she'd done when they were together, and he was incarcerated.

"Oh, it's like that?"

"Boy, you know better!"

"That's fucked up!" he told her. "So, how'd the meeting go?"

"What meeting?"

"With L.K.S."

"It went well," she answered slowly, figuring that Ant had told him about the meeting, but not sure how much Ant told him.

"Have you met him before?"

"I met him last night," Shonda answered cautiously, with the intent to throw a curveball. "He said he'd heard a lot about The Queenz and wanted to meet us. He also wants to deal with us."

"I thought y'all already made a move with, Vincent?"

"We did," she answered. "That was on a loan. King – I mean – L.K.S. will be our plug. Especially with the pills. That's what we really need."

Tino was silent, at the same time, Shonda was silently praying he didn't dwell on her almost saying King Ray's name. She still didn't know what he knew. She didn't think about it until now, but it was possible that one of the Queenzmen could have recognized Ray and relayed this to Tino.

How else did he know about the meeting? Maybe he was testing her to see if she would reveal what he may already know. Well, if that was true, then this would be the first test she intended to fail because she wasn't volunteering any information about Ray to him, or anybody else. As far as she knew, Tino could be one of his enemies.

"I heard he pretty much got the city on lock with the pills," Tino finally said. "He got niggas pushing that shit in damn-near every club, down South. Now that's what y'all need."

"What's that?"

"Some niggas to pedal the crumbs while y'all push the weight."

"And how do we go about finding—"

"Send Ant out there," he cut in. "He'll recruit some young niggas that wanna make some money."

Shonda had already thought of that, but she didn't have the guts to approach someone and ask them to stand on a corner and *pedal crumbs* for her. Come to think about it, The Kingz had a slew of street workers. She knew that if The Kingz could do it, then so could The Queenz.

****

Ray had managed to pull himself out of bed, a little after ten, feeling the same way he'd felt before he'd gone to bed last night. Had he not taken heed to the sign he was shown last night, he probably would have woken up in a hotel room with BJ, Rick, and three women. Or, he may not have woken up at all. It was better safe than sorry! Accustomed to feeding his dogs before himself, Ray donned a light jacket and initiated the task. After washing up, he made himself some breakfast. Once he'd eaten, washed the dishes, showered, and gotten dressed, he saw that it was only a few minutes after eleven.

He knew Poppo would still be in church at this time and being that Joe was over distribution, he would probably be out running errands and collecting money from some of their workers. So, with ample time to spare, Ray figured he'd peruse his books to make sure everything was accurate.

He entered one of his three guest rooms – which were all decorated as if someone actually lived in them – and took down his painting of George Washington Carver to reveal his safe. Once he'd applied the combination and opened the safe, he pulled the record book from atop the stacks of bills and carried it to the living room. It only took him twenty minutes to access everything, which was all in order. Then, he just leaned back on the sofa and watched the surveillance monitors, but his main focus was on one of the front gates, as he anticipated Joe and Poppo's arrival.

As he watched the monitor, he thought about the safe that was still in the warehouse on Fulton Industrial. He was only keeping up the payments on the place until he was able to get the safe or its contents out of there. Hell, he really didn't know if the safe was still there, because he hadn't been to the place since the last meeting, he'd had with his fellow Kingz, prior to their deaths. Well, today would be the first time, because the warehouse was his first destination, to make sure the safe was still there. Then, his mission to obtain Black's and Fred's keys to the safe would begin. He was already in possession of his and James', which he kept on his key ring.

Spotting the Lincoln when it pulled up to the gate, Ray grabbed the book and retreated to the guestroom, returning it to the safe. There was a remote to the gate, hanging from the visor of the Lincoln, so he didn't have to avail them. They both also had spare keys to the house and the alarm code, but by the time they'd made it to the front door, he was coming out.

"You got on a vest?" Poppo inquired.

"Nope," Ray answered, brushing past them, heading for the car. "My first stop is The Palace."

When Joe pulled the car up to the gate of the warehouse, Ray got out, removed the lock and chain, then pressed the button in the security booth to open the gate. He then climbed back into the rear seat of the Lincoln. As they neared the building, Ray wondered about the two rottweilers they'd had guarding the place. It's been a little over two years. If they were still here, then Ray was sure they'd died of starvation.

"Circle around first, Joe!" Ray said.

As Joe circled around, Ray surveyed the place, looking under the trucks, trailers, and loading docks. Seeing that the dogs weren't there, made him wonder who'd come by and collected them, but he didn't have to wonder for long, because Grip was the one who'd brought the dogs. Plus, he was the only Kingzman with a key to the gate, as well as the entry door of the building.

Joe parked in front of the building, they all dismounted and entered. Immediately, they were hit by a strong, ineffable stench.

"Shit!" Joe exclaimed. "What the fuck is that!"

"Don't tell me y'all left the dogs in here!" Poppo said, regarding Ray with his nose wrinkled up.

"Open the doors on the loading dock!" Ray said, knowing damn well it wasn't the dogs.

He used the edge of the carpet to prop the door open, while they made for the loading dock. The smell was impossible, but he had a job to do. Therefore, he headed for the office, where he used his key to get in. The office was the same as they'd left it, though Ray, for some odd reason, expected to see it in total disarray. The black oak table and leather chairs were still in good condition. The Mona Lisa painting was still sitting atop the boxed artifact. Remembering the hidden button, Ray pressed it, and the small door opened with a faint click, revealing the steel safe.

Being that Joe and Poppo knew nothing of the safe, Ray quickly closed the wooden door back, and took a seat in his chair, staring at the telephone in the center of the table that he knew was off, because he saw no reason to keep the bills up on it. Then, he diverted his eyes to the box. If he'd remembered correctly, there was over five hundred thousand dollars in the safe. He just couldn't get to it without the other two keys, which made him wonder what possessed James to even come up with such a contraption.

Poppo appeared at the office door. "Yo, check this out, Ray."

Getting up, Ray followed Poppo to the large, wooden door that was secured with a padlock and chain. This was the same room he'd never been in, nor asked James about. Hell, he had never seen James go into the room.

"This is where that smell is coming from," Poppo informed him.

Poppo was right because the stench was so prominent in this area, Ray thought he could actually see it seeping through the crevices of the wooden structure.

"You got the key to that shit?" Joe asked, who'd just joined them.

Remembering James' keys on his key ring, Ray pulled it out and duly recognized the slim, but slightly large key that was incontestably the key for this particular lock. He stuck the key into the lock, turned it to the right, and it snapped open. When he removed the lock and chain, it seemed as if the smell intensified, but when he dropped the items to the ground and pulled the door open, the mephitic odor swarmed them, along with a multitude of insects. Whatever Poppo had for breakfast, spewed from his mouth as they all rushed for the front door, gasping for fresh air. Once outside, they all found a spot on the Lincoln and clung to it.

"Man, I ain't never smelled no shit like that!" Joe exclaimed. "It's gotta be a dead body!"

Ray had never smelled anything like it himself, but he was hoping like hell it wasn't a dead body, because the handling of a carcass was not a part of his plans for today. After a good fifteen to twenty minutes, Ray was ready to face whatever It was he had to face and get it over with. Upon entering the building, he noticed that the smell was now less severe, due to the current of air flowing in through the open loading dock doors. As he stood at the threshold of the room, he noticed that the smell still lingered eminently in the air, but the smell immediately became extraneous, once his eyes caught sight of the contents of the room.

Ray remembered joking to himself that it was probably a torcher chamber. Well, it was definitely that. There was a small, Mayberry-looking jail cell; a wooden chair with straps that could probably be found in a mental institution; a heavy-duty battery charger that sat beside a tin tub; and a pillory that actually held a decomposed body.

'*Where the hell did James get all this shit?*' Ray wondered as he studied the remains that resembled the crypt keeper from the horror show '*Tales from The Crypt.*' He could tell it was male, by the type of clothing, which hung extremely loose, due to the lack of tissue and other 'ingredients' that makes up the body fat of human beings. Now he thought about the rats that had scattered when he'd first opened the door. The very thought of them feasting on the carcass, made him cringe. Perhaps they'd started on him before he could completely '*give up the ghost,*' seeing that he was vulnerable, and couldn't put up much of a defense. All he could do was scream and holler for help, but the gag in his mouth would have prevented anyone from hearing him, which had Ray feeling that the man was still alive and hollering for his life at the same time he was in the building.

"I say we lock this shit back up and get the hell on!" Poppo said over Ray's shoulder.

"Nah," Ray replied. "We can't leave this shit like this."

Poppo asserted, "Well, I'll get Stone and Hot to handle it."

"Nobody else should see or know about this."

"So, who are you gonna get to dispose of this body?" Joe asked.

Now, Ray turned to face them.

"Hold on!" Poppo protested. "I'm over security!"

"I'm over distribution," Joe chimed in.

"Exactly!" Ray was not in the mood for wisecracks. "Poppo, you *secure* the body, then accompany Joe as he *distributes* it to a secluded area, far away from here. Then, we need to stop by K-Mart and pick up some Pine-Sol, bleach, sponges, and mops."

Joe and Poppo grunted, but considering the salary Ray was paying them, they acceded to assist him with the task. After searching the building for some latex gloves, to no avail, Ray suggested they check the four eighteen-wheelers, where they'd found an unopened box in one of the rigs.

"Tell me you got the key to that lock, too," Poppo said, once they'd made it back to the room.

Ray had already analyzed the lock, which was the same as the one that was on the door. He figured the erratic-shaped key would unlock that one, also, but he could tell that the key wasn't needed. For, the guy's hands were now small enough to be pulled back through the holes of the pillory, without having to open it.

"We don't need the key," Ray answered. "But we do need to get this over with."

After donning several pairs of gloves, they all entered the room and were now standing over the cadaver. Ray didn't know about Poppo and Joe, but he had never touched a dead body before – which was probably why he'd absently donned six pairs of gloves – but he knew someone had to take the initiative. When he positioned himself behind the carcass that was on its knees in a half-praying position, he started to pull the body free, when he noticed something bulging from the back pocket of his pants. Figuring it to be a wallet, Ray gingerly pulled it out and examined the brown leather exterior of it.

Suddenly, his hands began to tremble, and his body perspired. He wouldn't dare look at his lieutenants, because he was sure they were watching him. Deliberating that, he maintained his composure and casually opened the wallet. Disregarding the bills and Magnum condom, his eyes went straight to the driver's license. As he stared at the picture, the jitters came back, unabated.

"Oh shit!"

Playa Ray

Chapter 3

It was well after six when The Queenz completed their runs for the day. Being that Ebony's mother had invited them over for Sunday dinner. Shonda dismissed the Queenzmen, and they made their way out to Ebony's mother's house, where Erica was already present. The food was already done, so everybody washed up and assembled at the kitchen table.

"So, how have you girls been?" Ms. Davis initiated the conversation.

"Everything's been good," Sheila answered.

"Theresa and Shonda, how are you two holding up?"

"Just taking it one day at a time," Theresa answered, figuring she was referring to the loss of Mario and Spenz.

"Did they ever catch anybody?" Ms. Davis wanted to know.

"Not that we know of," Shonda answered who'd already planned to one day go out to Bankhead and do her own investigation. "But you know how slow they are."

"Yeah, they are slow at times," Ms. Davis concurred. "I hope they find whoever did it. At least that would give you two some kind of closure."

"Mama, what did they say about your cat?" Ebony asked, hoping to take the attention off her friends.

"It's a kitten," she rectified. "I'm waiting for it to be weaned away from its mother."

"Mama, you're not gonna bring a cat home!" Erica interjected.

"Kitten!" she corrected again. "You're moving out. So, you shouldn't be worried about what I bring home."

"Moving!" Ebony exclaimed, looking back and forth from her mother and sister.

"Dang, mama!" Erica blurted out. "Can't I break my own good news?"

"You're moving out?" Ebony asked.

"In another week or so."

"You got an apartment?"

"Nope," Erica answered. "I'm moving in with my boyfriend."

There was a silence around the table. Everyone, except Ms. Davis, had stopped eating. Everyone, except Ms. Davis, knew who her *boyfriend* was, and Ebony already knew her sister was headed down another path of disappointment, considering the things Pam stressed about Ted. Ebony also knew there was nothing she could say to stop Erica.

"Hello?" Ebony answered her vibrating cell phone.

"How are you, Ms. Davis?" a familiar voice inquired.

"I'm good, Phillip," she returned. "How are you?"

"I can't complain. Are you busy?"

"Pretty much," she told him. "I'm having dinner with my family and friends."

"I guess I'm interrupting, huh?"

"Um—" Ebony looked around the table at everybody, who were now staring at her. "Not really, but can you call me back later?"

"Give me a time."

"Nine."

"Okay, I'll talk to you then."

"Alright." Ebony concluded the call to see that everyone was still watching her. "May I help y'all?" she asked smiling.

"Yeah," Ms. Davis answered. "We wanna know who that was that got you blushing like that."

"Yeah. Who was that, Ebony?" Erica asked, regarding Ebony with arched eyebrows.

Ebony scowled at her sister. "I know you didn't! I really think it's messed up how you never introduced mama to the man you're about to move in with! Where are your manners?"

"Slow your roll, *Queen*, Ebony!" Erica shot back, putting emphasis on Queen. "We both know what's done in the dark, always comes to light."

"Mama, the man I was talking to his name is, Phillip," Ebony prompted, disregarding her sister's attempt to daunt her. "He owns a limousine service. That's all I know about him because we haven't started dating yet."

"That's helpful," Ms. Davis said. "I will like to meet him before y'all decide to tie the knot. And when can I expect some grandchildren?"

"Some *who!*" Ebony and Erica exclaimed in unison, sparking laughter from everyone.

After dinner, The Queenz said goodnight to Erica and Ms. Davis, and were back in the Denali, driven by Shonda on their way to Riverdale to drop Theresa and Ebony off.

"I wanna call a brief Queenz meeting," Shonda said, now remembering the conversation she'd had with Tino, earlier. "I spoke to Tino, today. He said we should hire some foot soldiers to pedal the crumbs, while we handle the weight. I think it's a good idea because we can generate a little more money. Plus, we'll need some people on the streets to push the ecstasy pills."

"That sounds like a huge task," Theresa said from the back seat.

"It is," Shonda replied. "That's why I'll leave it up to, Ant. But I gotta know if everyone agrees with it."

"Go for it," Sheila said, yawning.

"It sounds like a plan," Ebony agreed.

"You don't have to ask me," Theresa chimed in.

Shonda didn't say a word, she knew what she had to do, but right now, she had to gas the truck up before hitting the expressway. Therefore, she pulled into Race Trac, parking beside a vacant gas pump.

"We need to get some credit cards!" Shonda stated, hating the fact that she had to walk inside and stand in line to pay for the gas.

"You want me to pay for it?" Ebony asked, who was the only one that owned credit cards.

"I got it," Shonda answered. "Y'all stay put. Should I bring y'all something back?"

"Three scratch-off tickets," Ebony told her.

Theresa said, "I'm good."

As her imperative, being that the Queenzmen were not present, Sheila dismounted and followed Shonda towards the store, where five, bandanna-wearing guys stood out front. They all had their pants sagging, sharing a blunt, and showing off gang signs.

"If you ever bring something like that home, I'll strangle you!" Shonda joked.

"I'll strangle myself!" Sheila avowed, regarding them with a disgusted look.

"That's gotta be jelly, cause jam don't shake like that!" one of the guys responded as they approached the entrance.

"Y'all thick as fuck!" another joined in.

"I'll eat both of y'all from the back!" a third one asserted.

Shonda rejected them as she pulled the door open and entered, followed by Sheila.

"Young, stupid-ass niggas!" Shonda muttered. "I bet neither one of them got over a hundred dollars in their pockets!"

The store wasn't as packed as they thought it would be. They grabbed a few junk food items and made for the check-out counter. Once Shonda paid for the junk food, scratch-off tickets, and gas, they made their exit.

"Damn, y'all didn't buy a nigga a drink?" one of the gang members asked.

"Suck my dick!" Shonda spat, fed up with these disrespectful, poor excuses for men, but kept walking.

"What!" the guy exclaimed.

"Bitch, I know you didn't just try my homeboy like that!" one of his friends spoke up. "Ol' once-a-month-bleeding-ass-slut!"

These guys were livid, but Sheila was shocked. She couldn't believe her cousin had actually let those words roll off her tongue. She didn't dare look back at them, as she followed closely behind Shonda. The goons kept ranting and raving; she could tell they were following them towards the truck. As they neared the truck, Shonda shoved her free hand into her pocketbook. Sheila did likewise. It was not quite dark, and the place was not quite packed. Sheila had the feeling they were going to have to bust their guns, flee the scene, and set the truck on fire while hoping like hell no one would be able to link them to the incident.

Apparently, Theresa and Ebony had been watching the scene, because as soon as Shonda and Sheila approached the SUV, they dismounted with guns drawn. Theresa was holding the Uzi that had taken the place of the AK-47 they ended up having to discard. Seeing this, Shonda and Sheila pulled their guns and turned to face the small mob.

"Shit!" one of them cried out as they stopped in their tracks.

"Nah, don't bitch-up now!" Shonda spoke. "I thought gang members were tough. Let me hear some more of that tough shit. I think somebody called me a bitch. Let me hear some more of that shit."

"Shit, you disrespected my lil homie, first," one of them asserted.

"Fuck that!" Theresa voiced. "Y'all wanna shoot this shit out, or what?"

The gang were now regarding Theresa – and her weapon – with looks of disbelief, as if they'd never been, or expected to be opposed in that manner. Shonda already knew Theresa was still pissed off about Spenz, as she was about Mario, so if Theresa planned on sending these clowns to the *upper room*, Shonda was all for it.

But clearly, the goons recognized that The Queenz weren't just ordinary bitches and gave in. One of the guys who seemed to be the leader apologized and pretty much ushered his crew back towards the store. Shonda knew they would cross paths with them again, but she wasn't worried. She was worried about Theresa. She'd noticed how violent Theresa had become since she'd been back from her basic training with the Army. She was really worried about Theresa.

****

It took over eight hours for Ray, Poppo and Joe to fully complete their task. First, Poppo had to drive out to his house for three blankets to wrap the corpse up in, before putting it in the trunk, and taking it out to Buford Highway to an abandoned building, where they set it on fire. After obtaining the cleaning supplies they needed, they returned to The Palace and got to work. First moving the pillory, battery charger, tin tub and chair with straps to one of the trailers at the back dock. Being that the small cell was bolted into the concrete floor, Joe drove out to RJP Customs, on Browns Mill Road – they'd opened another in Conyers – to retrieve a blow torch, in which they'd actuated to disassemble the cell, and tossed the steel in the trailer with the rest of the stuff. Then, they scrubbed the room from top to bottom, ridding it from dried blood stains and that horrid smell.

Now in the office, they were all assembled at the table, hungrily consuming their burgers and fries from Krystal's. Ray had worked up a huge appetite, also, but he was barely attacking his meal like his friends. He was too busy thinking about the body they'd found, and wondering what Steve could have possibly done, for James to bring him before The Kingz in court, which clearly never happened, due to the tragic incident. Now he was thinking about Precious. Logically, by now, she had already considered her cousin to be dead. They were too close for him to just up and disappear for over two years, and not call to say that he was okay.

'*What the hell could Steve have possibly done?*' Ray thought.

"So, what's your next move, Ray?" Poppo asked, pulling Ray from his abstract thinking.

"I don't know," Ray answered. "Why?"

"Cause, I really believe you should stay ducked off."

"Why?"

"It just seems like the right thing to do," Poppo told him. "You already got the game on lock. L.K.S. is the shit, right now. You don't have any visual beefs. Niggas can't touch what they can't see!"

"So, what's your point?" Ray asked, already knowing what he was getting at.

"That you keep it like it is," Poppo said. "Let me and Joe continue doing the footwork. If you reveal yourself, it could complicate matters, and bring heat from all kinds of directions. I already know why you wanna do it. Hell, if it was me, I would probably do the same thing. I just don't think it's a good idea, right now."

"He's right," Joe added, wiping his mouth with a napkin. "It's only three of us. If we come across some major heat—"

"I don't have y'all under contract," Ray cut in, not in the mood to hear anything other than what he had planned. "Y'all are free to leave, whenever y'all get good and ready. The only ties we have is RJP Customs. Hell,

I don't really care too much for that. I got bigger shit to handle, and I can do it by myself."

"Slow down, Ray!" Joe voiced. "You act like we're turning our backs on you. You know damn well it's not like that! You pay us well, but friendship outweighs any amount of money."

"Does it?" Ray asked, locking eyes with Joe. He didn't know where the sudden rage inside him had come from, but it was threatening to make a guest appearance.

The conversation was pretty much over. Ray asked to be driven home and was silent for the duration of the ride. Once they'd made it to the house, Ray exited the car without a word to either of his lieutenants. He entered the house and made it his business to feed his dogs before showering. After his shower, he donned a pair of pajamas and climbed into bed. Seeing that it was almost ten o'clock, he decided to go ahead and force himself to sleep, hoping it would ease the anger he was feeling.

Ray managed to sleep well, but the rage was still there, and it seemed to grow and become stronger by the day. Therefore, he remitted his plans of revealing himself, and continued doing what he'd been doing for the past two years, staying cooped up in his house, waiting for Joe, Poppo, BJ, and Rick to show up with the money they'd collected from his workers, so he could log it all into his books, and stash the money in his safe.

Periodically, he would journey to the 'Kingz Room,' where he kept a lot of James' things he'd gotten from James' house before he let his mother sell it. He even had the crowns, robes, and chains of all Kingz, which were draped over four mannequins that Poppo and some of his affiliates had stolen from a clothing store. It had taken him three months to receive their things from the Homicide Division, who were holding them as evidence. Considering the vast amount of dried blood, Ray had to hand-scrub the crowns and necklaces and pay a lump sum to a cleaner to perform special duties on the robs, that now looked brand new, with the exception of the multiple bullet holes. The only things he didn't have of Black's and Fred's, were their BMWs. He knew Nikki had Black's car and assumed Eric had Fred's. Well, he was hoping, because he really needed to get those safe keys off those keychains.

Now, it was Friday, and Ray was sitting on his living room sofa, watching the monitors. He was awaiting the arrival of Joe and Poppo, who he had called a meeting with, to discuss the new plans he'd devised. They hadn't had a decent conversation since Sunday. Therefore, he'd kind of been rehearsing what he was going to say to them, in an endeavor to control his anger, so things wouldn't take a wrong turn like they had Sunday.

"Yeah?" Ray answered his cell phone.

"Hey, my son!" his mother beamed.

"Hey, ma," he returned with no hint of excitement.

"You okay?" she asked.

"I'm cool. How's everything on your end?"

"Everything's fine and dandy," she told him. "Robert done built another room onto the house. Shoot, if he builds any more rooms, we may have our own home-made mansion!"

She was tickled by her own joke, but Ray hadn't laughed in so long, he didn't think he was even capable of doing such a thing. However, it was good to hear from his mother, who now resided in Birmingham, Alabama, with Robert, who opened his own body shop. After the tragic shooting, he immediately moved them and his grandmother – who resides in Mobile, Alabama – away from Georgia, until he could sort things out.

"Have you talked to the Hellraiser?" she asked, referring to his grandmother.

"Last night," he answered, mechanically.

"Ray?"

"I'm here."

"I know you miss your brother," she started. "I miss him, too. But you gotta move on, baby. He's in a better place."

'*A better place*!' Ray thought, feeling his anger increase by the second.

He couldn't believe his own mother was actually advising that he forget about his brother and move on with his life. Was that even possible? Did she really know what she was saying? Perhaps she was under the influence of some kind of illegal substance.

"I'll talk to you later, ma," he said abruptly and ended the call before she could protest.

Just then, he looked up at the monitor and saw the Lincoln pull up to the house. All Ray could do was shake his head. He was okay until his mother had called with her crazy suggestion. Now, on the count of her, his friends were about to enter *hostile grounds*.

What his mother had said, was the same thing Joe and Poppo were trying to convey to him. Maybe they were right. Maybe he did need to forget about The Kingz. Maybe he did need to forget about Raymond. Maybe he did need to forget about Sylvia. Maybe he did need to forget about the ones who had taken those people away from him and just move on with his merry little life. *Bullshit!*

The doorbell rang twice, which was to let Ray know they were about to enter. He didn't consider himself an actor, but now, it was either put up a façade, or let his anger surmount him, and cause him to lose his two best men. He couldn't chance the latter!

"Come on in, fellas!" he offered, when Poppo and Joe entered the living room. "Have a seat!" Once they'd taken a seat, he asked if they wanted something to drink, which they declined. "Okay," he continued. "I guess we can get started."

Chapter 4

It was Friday and Shonda could not believe that Ray had not gotten back with them about purchasing the product. She was starting to think he'd changed his mind about dealing with them, which persuaded her to consider his demeanor at the meeting last Saturday. Despite the tragedy of his comrades, he was clearly not the same Ray they'd known two years ago. It was typical of a person to take on a different manner, after encountering what he had, but Ray seemed a bit too detached. She also wondered about his mental state, because his lieutenants were treating him as if he was an elderly man.

But Shonda couldn't dwell on that for too long, because today was Ebony's birthday. She'd agreed to be treated to a nice restaurant in lieu of staying home or having a party. Therefore, Shonda had made reservations at the restaurant they'd dined with The Kingz, which was the first restaurant they'd dined as 'The Queenz'. But it was going to be a surprise to the others because she didn't intend to tell either of them. Plus, she'd ordered a stretched H-2 Hummer for the occasion.

Now, after showering and getting dressed, Shonda was standing at her mirror, applying eyeliner and listening to her TV that was turned to the news station. They were reporting on a charred corpse found in an abandoned building off Bufford Highway. At that time, Sheila knocked, then stuck her head in.

"I got those ready," she said.

"I'll be done in ten," Shonda told her. "Let me know when the Queenz men get here."

"They just pulled up."

Finishing with her cosmetics, Shonda grabbed her pocketbook, then she and Sheila exited the house, the Queenz men were already parked across the street. Shonda and Sheila climbed into the GMC, with Sheila behind the wheel. Their first stop was to pick up Ebony and Theresa. Then they were off to drop off product to some of their clients, and to their six workers, Ant had managed to hire, who resided in Perry Homes, Carver Hills, and East Lake Meadows.

He had hired two guys out of each of those spots, one would sell the cocaine and the other the weed. The packages they were receiving today, would be their first. Shonda didn't know what to think when Ant informed her that he had two workers in East Lake Meadows. The same East Lake Meadows she'd always loathed to drive out to, even to pick up Mario, when she was fiending for some dick. She was just hoping not to run into Trent.

After the last drop to their last client, it was their turn to follow the Queenzmen, being that Ant was organizing the drops to their workers. They started in Carver Hills, then migrated to Perry Homes, leaving East Lake as their last stop.

Now, as they pulled into the projects, Shonda could not stop looking around. For her not wanting to run into Trent, she was damn sure looking for him. And like the axion goes, '*If you go looking for something, you'll find it.*' She spotted him standing in his usual spot with his usual crowd. Plus, they were all warily scrutinizing the Queenz convoy as if they were expecting FBI agents to jump out, flashing guns and shields.

The Queenz men truck stopped a short distance away from where Trent and his friends were standing. Sheila stopped behind them and they all waited in silence for almost two minutes. Finally, two teenaged looking guys emerged from an apartment and approached the right side of the Queenz truck. Shonda rolled her window down.

"Travis and Quent?" she inquired.

"Yeah," they both responded.

She handed them their packages, "It's the same as we discussed."

As they were leaving out, Shonda watched Trent through the dark tinted window, thinking about the conversations they'd had. He really did seem like a decent man, which was probably why she now wanted to talk to him, to touch him, to make love to him. Shonda quickly shook those thoughts. She knew she was wrong for thinking like that after she'd just lost Mario, but they were just thoughts. Or were they?

After dropping off Theresa and Ebony, Shonda and Sheila returned home to change and prepare for Ebony's birthday dinner. Shonda still hadn't told her girls where they were going. She also didn't tell them they would not be accompanied by the Queenz men tonight, which she didn't feel there was a need to be. They were only going to dinner, then probably hang out at one of the houses for a few.

The pink stretched Hummer arrived shortly after seven o'clock. Sheila and Shonda, who were already clad in their evening dresses and heels, grabbed their pocketbooks and were out the door, headed for the limousine, where the driver- a well-dressed white man- greeted them, then helped them into the truck. Then it was off to Riverdale to gather Ebony and Theresa.

"You ordered a pink truck!" Ebony exclaimed when she climbed into the limousine ahead of Theresa. "That is so cute!"

"Just like that pink dress you got on," Shonda acknowledged, smiling at her friend, who was obsessed with the color.

When the stretch pulled up to the elegant restaurant in Rome, Georgia, Shonda did her best to ignore the parallel looks her girls were giving her but failed.

"What?" she asked, suppressing her smile. "This was the only place I could come up with on such short notice."

"Yeah, right," Theresa said, a smirk on her face.

"So, y'all wanna just go home?" Shonda asked.

"Hell no!" Ebony was not hearing that. "I did not get all cute for nothing! We made it to the restaurant. We got reservations, let's eat, damnit!"

As soon as the driver opened the door, Ebony practically climbed over Theresa's lap and dismounted the truck with a zeal of a paratrooper, leaving her girls laughing and the driver stunned.

"Um, if you want to," Ebony spoke to the driver. "You can drop them off and come back and pick me up."

"Girl, hold your horses!" Shonda said, nudging Theresa to dismount. "We're coming and quit acting all ghetto in front of these people's place of business!"

"Yeah," Sheila pitched in, climbing down behind Shonda. "Act your age and not your shoe size!"

"Whatever!" Ebony replied. "It's not summertime out here!"

Upon entering the restaurant, they saw that the same frail-looking older white man who was there on their last visit was still there.

"May I have your names, ladies?" asked the man, regarding them through the lenses of his rather small glasses.

"The Queenz," Shonda answered.

"Ah!" the old man exclaimed, smiling broadly. "I remember you all! Welcome back! I'm quite sure you all remember, Edward?" The Queenz exchanged glances. "He's the one—oh, here he comes now."

They looked to see Edward, the young waiter who'd served them on their last visit with the Kingz.

"Welcome back, Queenz!" he greeted with a slight bow. "May I show you to your table?"

"Yes, you may, Edward," Shonda said.

They followed Edward to their table, where he took the time to pull out each of their chairs for them.

"It's good to have you all back," Edward said, once the women were all seated.

"It's good to be back," Sheila replied. "So, how have you been?"

"I've been okay," he answered. "My wife and I just had our first child."

"Congratulations!" they all exclaimed.

"Thanks!" Edward replied. "I requested to be y'all, waiter. So, you are my only priority tonight. Take as much time as you need with the menus. Right now, I'm going to retrieve your breadsticks and wine."

When Edward left, the Queenz took in the restaurant. It still looked the same as it did over two years ago. There was a light crowd and soft jazz playing in the background, that made the atmosphere a lot more relaxing.

"Who's the birthday, girl?" Edward asked, upon returning with the breadsticks and wine that was sitting in a bucket of ice.

"I am," Ebony answered.

"Well, first, the Madeira is on the house," he told her. "Second, I was informed by the chef that you had pre-ordered a special dinner. He wants to know if you would still like that meal prepared."

Not knowing anything about this special dinner or what it consisted of, Ebony turned to Shonda.

"I'm not the birthday, girl," Shonda protested, biting into a breadstick.

Ebony wanted to poke Shonda with her fork. Instead, she turned to Edward. "Yes, I would still like that prepared," she told him.

"Yes, ma'am."

"What did I just agree to?" Ebony asked Shonda, once Edward left.

"Maybe you should've asked him," Shonda answered. "Ain't no telling what kind of live animals they got stored in the back."

Edward returned, poured them all a glass of wine, informed them that their meal was being prepared and collected their menus, then left again.

"I wanna leave him a five-hundred-dollar tip," Shonda told her girls. "Anybody want to pitch in?"

They all concurred on the tip. It took almost fifteen minutes for their special dinner to arrive, which consisted of squid, oysters, clams, yellow rice, and salad.

"What the hell is this?" Ebony said in a low tone, once Edward had served the last dish and made off with the empty wine bottle to retrieve another. "I don't see nothing special about none of this stuff!"

Shonda said, "You are so ungrateful!"

"You act like you've never had squid before," Sheila voiced.

"And you have?"

"Nope," Sheila answered. "But I'll be glad when somebody says grace, so I can get my grub on."

Sheila ended up blessing the food and they dug in. While they ate, Shonda thought about Trent. Now she could understand why she had those thoughts about him earlier. Hell, he was handsome and seemed to have his morals and principles in order. She really didn't care too much for light skin men, but she was done with judging men by their skin tone. She wanted to fuck Trent, but first, she has to find out if he and Mario had a reciprocal friendship. It would be downright slutty- not to mention, dis-loyal- of her, if they had. Thinking of Mario, she figured she would make that trip out to Bankhead tomorrow.

"Hello?" Ebony answered her cell that vibrated atop the table.

"Happy birthday again!" Phillip asserted.

Ebony smiled, "Thank you again!"

"Are you enjoying your dinner?"

"I think I've just ruined my taste buds!" Ebony told him. "Whoever thought squid should be a meal, should be chopped up and fed to the fishes."

Phillip laughed. "I agree. Do you have any after-dinner plans?"

"Not that I know of."

"I have a hotel suite," he told her. "I was hoping I could interest you in a night of relaxation. I'm pretty good with my hands if you're in the mood for a full body massage."

"Sounds interesting," she said, smiling and looking at her friends, who were looking as if they could hear both ends of the convo. Once she'd given him the location and he promised to send a limousine to pick her up, she concluded the call.

"What was that all about?" Sheila wanted to know.

"That was, Phillip," answered Ebony. "He has a hotel suite and wanted to know if I was interested in some relaxation and a full-body mas-sage."

Sheila arched an eyebrow. "Did he say a full-body massage or full booty massage?"

"He's not even like that."

"So, he's gay?"

"Stop, Sheila!" Shonda interjected seeing the evil look Ebony had cast upon her cousin.

"He's coming to pick you up?" Theresa asked, remembering Ebony had given Phillip directions to the restaurant.

"He's sending a limo," she answered. "I know I should've consulted with y'all first but—"

Shonda waved a hand dismissively. "Girl, we understand."

"I don't!" Sheila voiced.

"Shut up, Sheila!" Theresa and Shonda prompted.

"I ordered you a cake," Shonda told Ebony. "At least cut the cake before you run off."

"I can do that."

Shonda flagged Edward down and informed him that they were ready for the cake. He cleared the dishes off the table and made off. Moments later, he returned accompanied by three waitresses with a pink iced cake, singing the birthday song. Edward approached Ebony, who was smiling from ear to ear.

Ebony felt bad about leaving her girls after they'd been nice enough to accommodate her on her birthday, but Phillip's proposal was euphonious. Being that she'd only been with one man, since Charles, her womanhood would not allow her to turn him down. They had been talking for two weeks, which felt like two months, but the time span was impertinent. She was going to fuck him tonight!

The driver of the stretched Lincoln, who had given her an envelope containing a hotel key, pulled up in front of the same hotel Phillip had taken her to on Charles's birthday. She thanked the driver, then entered the hotel making for the elevator. Getting off on the eighth floor, she made it to suite number three, slid the key into the key slot and entered.

The room was breathtaking. The lights were low, *Barry White's 'Practice What You Preach'* was playing from speakers she couldn't see. Some kind of sweet fragrance permeated the air. There were rose petals all over the floor and bed, but no Phillip. She cleverly crossed the room to the bed where a sheet of paper was lying atop one of the pillows. It read: *Go to the bathroom*!

'So, that's where he is,' she thought picturing him naked in a tub full of rose petals.

Thinking this made her feel as if she shouldn't waste another second. She sat her pocketbook and the room key on the nightstand, laid her jacket over the back of the chair, then sauntered towards the bathroom. The door was closed, Ebony was about to knock, then figured it that would be silly. Therefore, she tapped lightly, then slowly ease the door open. There were more rose petals on the bathroom floor. The tub was filled with peach-scented bubbles and a sprinkle of rose petals. Phillip, clad in dress pants and shirt was sitting on the edge of the tub with a sponge in his hand.

"I offer the royal treatment," he spoke. "Do you accept?"

Ebony nodded. Phillip placed the sponge on the edge of the tub and stood. He had to take Ebony's hands and pretty much pull her into the bathroom, being that her legs had only brought her as far as the threshold. Grabbing her chin, he tilted her head up and planted his lips on hers. Her eyes automatically closed, her lips parted, allowing his tongue to find hers. By this time, *Stephanie Mills* was singing '*I Have Learned to Respect the Power of Love*', Ebony felt as if she herself was about to learn to respect the power of love.

She felt Phillip's hands grip her waist, pulling her closer. She wrapped her arms around his neck. Finding the zipper to her dress, he slowly unzipped it. Then he broke the kiss and looked into her eyes as if seeking her permission to proceed. Well, she decided to give him more than her permission. She kicked off her heels peeled off her dress, and let her panties fall to the floor. Phillip took a second to admire her body before taking her hand helping her into the tub.

"Did you plan on giving me a sponge bath?" she asked, regarding the sponge.

"Well, that was my plan but—" he stopped when she grabbed the sponge and held it out to him.

Ebony had never had a sponge bath. She assumed she'd be admitted into a retirement home by the time this moment arrived. Plus, she had been touching herself for far too long. It was time to let a man do what a man is supposed to do. Instead of receiving the sponge, Phillip said he'd be back, then left out, leaving Ebony a bit confused. When he returned with a bottle of champagne and two glasses, she placed the sponge back on the edge of the tub. He sat on the closed lid of the toilet, first filling both glasses, then sitting the bottle on the floor.

"That bubble bath has soothing solutions in it," he told her. "You may want to relax a while and let it take its course."

"Relax for how long?" She didn't expect to be delayed.

"I don't know," he answered. "I guess until you're ready. Until then, tell me about your day. Was it a birthday to remember?"

"Of course, it was!" she exclaimed, making a face. "I ate squid, that has to be the nastiest dish on earth!"

Phillip laughed as he sipped his drink. They talked for a good twenty minutes before Ebony felt as though they'd wasted enough time. It was time to get it on before she could come up with an affirmative way to convey this to him, he pulled his cell phone out and looked at the screen.

"I gotta take this." He kissed her on the forehead, then exited the bathroom, closing the door behind him.

Ebony could not believe this. Here she was, ready for the royal treatment Phillip had promised, and he was on the damn phone. At least she had the decorum to turn hers off and leave it in her pocketbook.

"Fuck this!" she mumbled, grabbing the liquid body wash and sponge.

So much for her pre-retirement home sponge bath. Ebony applied liquid soap to the sponge and went to work. She thought she was gonna kick back and let him do what he called her over to do. But now she saw that she was gonna have to take control. She may have given herself the quickest sponge bath in history. When she was done, she got out of the tub, making sure to let the water out. There was a large grey towel with the royal suite stenciled on it. She dried off with it, wrapped it around her, then exited the bathroom, leaving her dress and heels on the floor.

Phillip was sitting on the edge of the bed talking on his phone. She couldn't hear what he was saying, over *Karen White* singing '*Secret Rendezvous*', but he quickly disconnected as she approached.

"Why did you get out of the tub?" he sounded disappointed.

"Because I don't like to be put on hold," she answered, now standing akimbo.

"It was important."

"Nonsense!" She asserted with attitude. "The only thing that's important to you, right now, is me!"

Phillips eyebrows raised. "Oh?"

"That's right!" she replied. "Now stand up!"

His eyebrows dropped, and he looked as if he was going to defy, but he obediently stood, facing her.

"Strip!" she demanded, relishing every bit of this. "Take it all off!"

Phillip sat back down on the bed as if he was already through playing her game. Well, that's what she thought until he began taking off his shoes and socks. Then, he stood, locking eyes with her as he slowly unbuttoned his shirt. For a second, she thought he was going to break into a striptease. He tossed his shirt to the floor, then started on his pants. He didn't have the six-pack abs, but he looked as if he spent a little time in someone's gym, which reminded Ebony that she and Sheila had agreed to work out with Erica at the gym in Buckhead, tomorrow before she was to do Sheila's hair.

Phillip had taken off his pants, revealing a pair of black boxer briefs. By the bulge of his manhood, she could tell he was as ready as she was. He couldn't see how erect her nipples were through the thick fabric of the towel. When Phillip finally removed his underwear, Ebony was awed by the girth of his penis. She knew she was going to perform oral sex on him, which was probably why her jawbone started to ache, even though her mouth still watered.

"Now give me the royal treatment you promise. Or I'll go home and give it to myself!" she asserted, not believing she'd actually said it.

Well, she had indeed said it, Phillip, who seemed to not want to disappoint her, made his move. He took her hands in his, planted a kiss on her lips, and pulled her towards the bed. After relieving her of the towel, he laid her crosswise on the bed, then walked off. Ebony could not help but stare at his behind that appeared firm but hard and accommodated by cute little curly hairs. As he retreated, she was staring at his dick again. She had never seen a man with something that large between his legs.

As *Force MDs* sang '*Tender Love,*' Phillip with a can of whip cream and a small basket of strawberries, laid beside her, first spraying whip cream into her mouth and feeding her a strawberry. Then, he sprayed some of the cream on both of her swollen nipples and took his time licking and sucking them. Once he licked all the cream off, he sprayed more into her mouth, feeding her another strawberry. Then, he sprayed the cream between her breasts and all the way down to her navel. He fed himself a strawberry before starting at her navel and seductively making his way up to her breasts.

His mouth felt good, but his rock-hard penis pressed against her thigh was what really had her juices flowing. She couldn't wait to feel him inside her. Hell, she had to fight the urge to reach down and grab it, just to see how it feels in her hand. Once he cleared the cream, Phillip kissed her passionately for a few seconds. Fed her another strawberry, got off the bed and positioned himself between her legs. Ebony scooted herself a little closer, then placed the soles of her feet on the bed, and spread her legs to give him a full panorama of her close shave peach.

Phillip wasted no time, he got down on his knees and sprayed a large amount of cream around her vagina. He then took a strawberry and rubbed it against her labia, moving it in and out as if he was going to use it to make her come, that was not the case. He pulled it out and looked into her eyes before consuming it. She didn't know why, but she found that quite intriguing.

Now Phillip was licking the cream from around her vagina taking his precious time, which sent her anxiety into overdrive. Then, his mouth finally made it to her G spot. He used his thumbs to spread her pussy lips, then furiously attacked her clitoris, licking it, then sucking it so hard it hurt but felt good at the same time. Therefore, she moaned with both pleasure and pain.

Phillip must have felt her about to come because he released her clitoris, lifted her legs, and slid his tongue down the crack of her ass, licking and blowing on her anus, prompting her to come anyway. She was wondering if he noticed this stuff oozing out of her. She wanted to look but couldn't seem to straighten her eyes that had rolled up in her head. She just hoped he didn't plan on entering that hole, because she was definitely a virgin in that department.

Phillip stood, before Ebony could open her eyes to see what he was about to do next, he was between her legs, ramming every inch of his rod inside her, which kind of hurt, being that she had never had something that size in her. Plus, she knew damn well he wasn't wearing a condom. She wanted to protest, but the dick was so good, she just kept her mouth shut and hoped he didn't shoot off in her.

"Oohhh, shit!" she moaned as she reached the quickest orgasm she'd ever had.

Remembering how cute his ass looked, she wanted to reach out and hold onto it, but her arms were short, and he was pushing all the way in, and pulling all the way out, giving her every inch of his dick that seemed to fill up her entire insides. Therefore, she just grabbed his waist, and threw the pussy back at him, helping herself to another orgasm.

Seconds after her third release, Phillip pulled out and positioned her doggy style. Immediately he was back inside her, gripping her waist and pounding with purpose, touching spots he hadn't before. The only sounds that could be heard was her moaning, his midsection colliding with her ass, and *Sade* singing '*No Ordinary Love*'.

Philip brought her to another orgasm. Seconds after that, he pulled out and masturbated with his dick between her cheeks. Ebony looked back at him. He grunted as he shot off. Ebony had never experienced this before, but the warm liquid felt good oozing down the crack of her ass.

Chapter 5

"Look at this tired heifer!" Sheila said to Erica, referring to Ebony.

The three of them were at the gym, power walking on treadmills that were alongside each other. Ebony, who was in the middle had shut hers off and was leaning on the control panel.

"That was at least thirty minutes," Ebony said, panting.

Sheila checked her watch. "Girl that was thirteen minutes. Your sorry ass can't walk for twelve more minutes?"

"Hell, I can't walk for two more minutes!" she admitted. "I'm still exhausted."

"You should be," Erica said. "Why would you be out all night, sucking dick, when you know we made plans to come to the gym?"

"Cause, it was my birthday!" Ebony answered like a spoiled child. "And FYI, I ain't suck no dick, but he gave me the best sex I've ever had!"

Erica cut her machine off and faced her sister. "And how old is this dude?"

"Forty-two."

"He don't look forty-two," Sheila complimented. "And why do you keep ending up with these old ass men?" She had turned off her machine.

"It doesn't matter how old they are," Erica defended. "As long as they are financially stable and can get that dick hard enough to make the pussy skeet."

"Okay!" Ebony exclaimed, slapping high five with her sister.

"Y'all ready?"

They all look to see Dante, Erica's personal trainer, standing before them, clad in gym shorts and a tank top. He was dark skin, six feet one, bald and perfectly built as if he himself had invented the gym.

"This one cheated," Sheila told him, pointing to Ebony.

"It's only been sixteen minutes," he asserted, checking his watch.

"As far as I'm concerned, you all cheated. That's okay, we'll just move on to the squats."

"What part of the body does the squats work?" Sheila asked as they followed him to the area they were going to use.

"Your thighs and glutes," Dante answered.

"Isn't glute another word for butt?"

"Pretty much."

"But we already have thick thighs and fat butts."

He shot her a skeptical look.

Erica saw the look. "Don't mind her, she's single and desperate. Did I mention, single?"

"First, I need you all to stand in this starting position," he said, demonstrating the stance and clearly disregarding what Erica had said. "Now squat to this position and hold. Bring it back up. We'll do twenty-five of these, stop, stretch, twenty-five more."

While they exercised, Sheila couldn't help but stare at Dante. He wasn't bad on the eyes. Hell, he was the type a woman would look at, and immediately want to bed. Then, she thought about what Erica had said about him having three kids, by three different women, and driving a beat-up Honda that looked like it was on its last leg. This made Sheila smile to herself. It was crazy how women would fuck a man because of how he looks, end up getting pregnant, then come to realize he's in no position to take care of a child and is barely taking care of himself, which was one reason why Sheila didn't care too much for pretty boys and muscle heads. She didn't have time for conceited men. The only thing worse than a conceited man was a broke, conceited man.

Therefore, she quickly dismissed her thoughts of Dante and was now thinking about Ray. He wasn't all that cute, and he was definitely not built like Dante. Being that most women were fascinated by muscular men, they will probably pass him by, unless they were familiar with his personality. Although he'd slighted her and showed her his mean side when all the Kingz were still alive, she knew it was a façade. He's really a decent man, with a heart of gold. His personality surpasses his looks, and the looks of every Dante she'd encounter and will encounter in her life. She had let him slip through her fingers once and was determined not to let it happen again. She just wondered why he hadn't called them yet.

****

Shonda was glad Sheila had made plans to go to the gym with Erica and Ebony. Therefore, she didn't have to lie to her, or actually tell her what she had planned, which was to drive out to Bankhead to see if she could gather any information about Mario's murder.

When she'd gotten dressed and ready to leave the house, she realized she didn't want to go alone. So, she phoned Theresa and asked if she would accompany her. Theresa agreed, which was why she had the Denali parked in front of the house, waiting on Theresa to come out.

Shonda also wanted to drive out to East Lake to see Trent. That was the only way she could find out if he and Mario were mutual friends. That she did want to do alone. Plus, she didn't want him to see her in this truck, being that it was their company's truck and they now had two workers in East Lake, who they would be driving out to do business with. She was sure he wasn't aware of her being one of the Queenz, who she was positive he was highly conversant with. So, she would take that journey some other time.

"You had lunch?" Shonda asked when Theresa climbed in beside her.

"I can wait," Theresa told her. "Let's handle your business first."

Shonda didn't bother to contend. She put the truck in gear and made for the expressway. She got off on the Bankhead exit, and as she traveled Bankhead Highway, she attentively looked around as if she would actually spot Mario somewhere. Who she was really looking for was that *cavewoman* she'd seen him with. For some reason, she felt Mario was with her when he was killed. The only two people she felt could assist her with any information about her, was Montez and Dee, which was why she was now pulling up to Montez's house.

"Why here?' asked Theresa.

"I need to find out what I can about the woman Mario was with."

"Why?"

"I think she knows something," Shonda told her. "Maybe she was with him on that night."

Theresa nodded. "Okay, I'm with you."

They both dismounted and made for the front door, where Shonda knocked rather hard, to make sure she was heard over the stereo playing *D4L's Betcha Can't Do It Like Me*. Seconds later, the door swung open, and Dee, with a blunt in one hand and a beer in the other, was bouncing and singing along with the Bowen-Homes based rap group. Theresa and Shonda were laughing.

"Y'all don't know nothing 'bout my niggas up out that B-town!" he said, still bouncing to the music. "This that real Westside shit right here! Y'all come on in."

They entered the house where Montez was seated on the living room sofa with two females, who were also drinking beers and sharing a blunt.

"What's up?' Montez asked, looking puzzled.

"Sorry for the interruption," Shonda said. "I just need to speak to y'all for a brief second—in private."

Montez looked as if he was considering it, then passed his blunt to the girl beside him, and got up. "We can talk in my room," he said, leading the way.

Dee closed the door once the four of them were inside the room.

"What up?" Montez asked again.

"It's about, Mario," Shonda stated.

"The junkie who got killed about three weeks ago?" Dee asked. "The same one you asked about?"

Shonda almost glared at him but caught herself. "That's the one," she said.

Montez asked, "What about him?"

"I need to know about the—" She stopped and tried to figure out a way to say what she needed to say. "I saw him with a female," she tried again. "And from the looks of her, a blind man could see that she was strung out on something, if not everything."

"Olivia!" Dee blurted with certainty.

Shonda turned to him. "Are you sure?'

"There are not too many muthafuckas on Bankhead I don't know!" he boasted. "Her people stay in Bowen Homes. She be all up and down Bankhead, doing whatever she can to get a hit. Her main spot is Petro. She be fucking with them, truck drivers."

"Were she and Mario always together?" Shonda asked, already hating the answer.

"Hell yeah!" Dee answered. "Shit, you can pretty much say they were boyfriend and girlfriend. You must've known this nigga?"

"Is Olivia still around?" Shonda asked, ignoring his question.

"Shit, she came through yesterday and spent fifty," Montez informed.

"And where does she go to get high?" Shonda wanted to know.

"Hell, ain't no telling," answered Montez. "Smokers used to go to an abandoned house on Grove Street until that shit happened."

"They still do," Dee offered. "They don't care 'bout no dried-up blood. Hell, they'll sleep right in that shit."

"I appreciate the information," Shonda told them.

"It's all good," Montez said. "Just hook us up with a few extra grams on re-up day."

"Very funny," Shonda replied, and they all laughed.

When they re-entered the living room, Fabo was chanting, *"Girl, shake that Laffy Taffy."* One of the girls was standing, shaking her ass in the other's face. Yes, it was definitely some real Westside shit going on, Shonda thought as she and Theresa exited the house.

"You're not gonna beat the girl up, are you?" Theresa asked once they were back in the truck.

"Who, Olivia?" Shonda asked, regarding her friend. "Why would I do that?"

Theresa narrowed her eyes.

"She hasn't done anything," Shonda admitted. "I had feelings for Mario, true enough, but he's the one who chose to do whatever he did that brought that upon him. I'm just trying to see if I can find out anything about whoever killed him."

Theresa didn't respond. She had slipped into her thoughts of Spenz. She wished she could find out anything about whoever had killed him, but she wouldn't know the first place to look, or the first person to ask considering where it happened. She still hadn't heard anything about anyone being caught or his car being recovered.

Shonda turned the truck onto Grove Street, and it wasn't hard to spot the abandoned house. It still had pieces of yellow crime scene tape hanging on certain parts of the house and as she stared at it, it reminded her of something out of a horror movie. Probably because she knew someone had actually been murdered inside.

"Having second thoughts?" Theresa asked, pulling her from her reverie.

"No," Shonda lied, shutting off the engine. "You ready?"

"You armed?"

"Yeah."

"Let's go!"

They got out and slowly approached the house looking around. There were several kids out playing and riding bicycles. They didn't seem to pay Shonda and Theresa any mind as they made it to the front door that was closed but had no locks or doorknobs. Shonda paused for a second, before pushing the door open with her foot, reluctant to touch anything. They were hit by the aroma of urine, feces, alcohol, and mildew. Once inside, they instantaneously drew their guns.

There were four stained mattresses spread out on the living room floor, amid discarded needles, cans. Bottles, fast food bags, and plastic drug bags. No one was there, but that didn't stop Shonda from stepping over and around the trash to check the rest of the house, followed by Theresa. The kitchen was a mess, but empty. There being no windows on the house to parry the cool Autumn air, made the stench from the filthy bathroom more bearable. The first bedroom was connected to the living room, with two mattresses and trash strewn all over the floor. The door to the next room's door was closed, but like the front door, it had been stripped of its means of security. Again, Shonda used her foot to ease it open. This room was parallel to the others, but not unoccupied.

In fact, there were two occupants – one male, one female. The male was lying on his back on one of the mattresses, receiving oral sex from the female, who just so happened to be Olivia.

Yes, the *cavewoman* was doing what she had to do to get a hit of cocaine. The man was the first to spot Shonda and Theresa. He quickly grabbed his pants that were down to his thighs, and pulled them up, automatically snatching his penis out of Olivia's mouth. She was about to protest until she realized there was a viable situation. Clearly, they had considered the guns and did their best not to make any sudden movements.

Shonda pointed her gun at the man. "You, get out!"

The man who appeared to be in his mid-forties didn't waste any time. He got up, fumbling with his belt as he moved fast, sagely towards the door.

"How much was he paying you for the blow job, Olivia?" Shonda asked.

"Ten dollars," she stammered, a confused look on her face.

"I'll compensate you for that," Shonda told her. "I'll give you thirty, but first I need to ask you some questions."

"Are y'all detectives?"

"No."

"Well, who am I talking to?"

"Has Mario ever mentioned anything about someone by the name of Shonda?" she asked, then realized how silly it sounded.

"Oh!" Olivia exclaimed, eyes growing bigger than they already were. "You're the one who jumped out of the truck on him that day!"

"That was me," Shonda admitted, suppressing her smile. "Where were you on the day or night Mario was killed?"

"I was here," she answered, getting off her knees and sitting in the middle of the bed with her knees bent and her arms wrapped around her legs. "It was daytime, but we were both sleep, in this same bed. Two men came in with guns. They snatched him out of the bed and started beating on him. I was too scared to move. All I could do was watch and cry—" She paused to wipe tears from her eyes with the back of her hand. "—they were asking him about a kilo he had stolen. He told them he'd hid a kilo in your closet, but I didn't believe him, because he's always lying. He wouldn't tell them where it was, so they killed him. They shot him over there."

They looked to the corner where she nodded. The dried blood on the wall and carpet seemed to tell its own story, that corroborated hers.

Shonda's stomach churned, not from the sight, but from the fact that she knew who the blood belonged to. She quickly diverted her eyes.

"Did you know the guys?" Shonda asked. "Have you ever seen them before?"

"I don't think I've seen them before." Olivia looked as if she was trying to retain.

"After seeing them that day," Shonda persisted. "Do you remember what they looked like?"

"One was heavy-set and light skin," she answered. "The other one was dark and skinny."

"You didn't notice anything distinctive about them?" Shonda asked, now realizing she sounded like a real crime scene investigator.

"The only thing I can remember—" Oliva started, looking reflectively towards the ceiling. "Is the tattoo the big guy had on his arm. It was a dog with an arm in its mouth. It may have been a Pitbull."

"On which arm?" Shonda asked, feeling a bit relieved that she'd gotten this much information. When she didn't have anything in the beginning.

"I think it was his right arm," Olivia answered. "Right at his shoulder."

"Thank you very much, Olivia!"

Feeling quite exuberant, Shonda gave Olivia a hundred dollars, in lieu of the thirty she'd promised, and she and Theresa exited the house. Now, she was on the lookout for a heavy-set, light-skinned man, with a tattoo of a dog on his arm, with an arm in its mouth. Clearly, they were amateurs, because they didn't kill Olivia, a substantial witness, who could ID them to the authorities and send them to prison for the rest of their lives or give their descriptions to someone who had a better place to put them.

Playa Ray

Chapter 6

Monday had finally rolled around and Ray was ready to get the ball rolling. Joe and Poppo had talked him into putting his, *Return of King Ray* stunt on hold until they could come up with enough manpower. He made it clear to them that he had to pay visits to Nikki and Eric, though he didn't tell them why. They were familiar with Nikki because he had them case out her apartment in Avondale Estates. He was surprised she had maintained that residence, after Black's death. He figured she would have moved back to Florida with her parents.

Now, clad in a blue jean suit, Ray was in his stash room, marking off the names of some of his employees and customers on a notepad. As he placed their product in a small carry bag that was sitting on the bed. Poppo and Joe tried to talk him out of going with them on their run, but he wouldn't hear it. To appease their worries, he promised to remain in the back seat and not interfere.

"Yeah?" Ray answered his cell phone.

"You ready?' Poppo asked.

"I'll be out in ten," he said before hanging up.

Once he'd finished placing the product in the bag, he took the bag to his bedroom, tossed in his Glock 9mm with the extended clip, donned his blue fitted cap, grabbed his keys and made for the front door. After punching in his alarm code, he was out the door, headed for the black Lincoln Navigator Joe had traded the Town car in for. Climbing into the back seat, Ray extracted his gun from the bag, place it on the seat beside him, then handed the bag to Poppo, who was in the front passenger seat.

"That should be everything," Ray told him. "Still check it to make sure."

"Where to, first?" asked Joe, pulling out of the driveway and securing the electrical gate with a remote in the sun visor.

"Avondale Estates," Ray answered. "And what's the word on my mercenaries?"

"I'm still on it," Poppo said. "I wanted to recruit Hot and Stone, but you said you didn't want any gang members on the squad."

"I have my reasons for that," Ray told him. "What kind of progress have you made?'

"Not too much," Poppo admitted. "It seems like everybody is affiliated with something."

"Do you think you can make it happen?" Ray was beginning to doubt his friend's word.

"Of course," Poppo answered. "You gotta be patient and give me some time. It's not gonna happen overnight. I gotta interview these niggas to make sure these niggas are really 'bout that life. I may have to test a few of 'em. Just give me some time. I'ma make it happen."

"There's a shooting range at the warehouse," Ray said. "I want them there, twenty-four seven. Anybody can shoot a gun but being that they'll be part of an elite security team, they need to know how to do more than just shoot. I want accuracy!"

Ray couldn't believe how much he'd just sounded like James. Or maybe it just sounded that way, because he was still missing his brother. Yeah, that had to be it.

"Is that necessary?" Poppo asked.

"You don't think it is?" Ray countered angrily, thinking about the Kingzmen, who he still believed was responsible for the death of his fellow Kingz and would be the ones to come after him. The Kingzmen were highly trained and Ray would feel a lot better if his men had some kind of skills under their belts.

"Yeah, I guess you're right," Poppo concurred. "I've met niggas that were quick to buss their guns but couldn't aim worth a fuck, yo!"

They had finally made it to Avondale Estates. As soon as Joe pulled into the apartment, Ray immediately spotted Black's BMW. It still looked the same, except for the chromed wheels that had been traded for a pair of factory wheels. The gold crowns that had taken the place of the BMW emblems, stood out with eminence, which caused Ray to smile a little.

"So, how you wanna do this?" Poppo asked once Joe had parked.

"Y'all said she got a boyfriend, right?"

"Yeah," Joe answered. "But he be in and out, he don't stay there."

"Well, y'all need to make sure he's not in now," Ray said.

Joe replied, "I don't see his car."

"A'ight, let's go!"

As they dismounted, Ray didn't even bother with his gun, due to the extended clip. Plus, he didn't feel as if he would need it right now, because his lieutenants were strapped. Just in case they so happened to run into some unemployed thugs, who had nothing better to do than to jump in front of a hail of flying bullets.

When they'd made it to Nikki's apartment door, Poppo and Joe looked at Ray, as if to figure out who was going to knock. Ray took the initiative. As he knocked, he wondered how he was going to respond to, "*Who is it?*" To his surprise, there was no answer, the door just opened.

"Oh!" Nikki exclaimed. "I couldn't see your face, I thought you were—" Her eyes enlarged, and tears streamed down her face. "Oh, my God."

She threw her arms around his waist and wept, with her head on his chest. All Ray could do was hold her. He already knew his presence would induce this reaction. Now, he was wishing he would have left her alone, but he really needed that key.

"Can we step inside, Miss?" Poppo asked.

Nikki lifted her head, wiped her eyes and regarded Poppo as if he'd said something rude.

"That's my head of security," Ray told her. "They're both my lieutenants. Is anybody here with you?'

"No," she answered. "Come on in."

When they'd entered, Nikki locked the door and offered them something to drink, in which they declined. She and Ray took a seat on the living room sofa, while his lieutenants remained standing.

"So, what happened?" Nikki asked. "Nobody told me anything about the funeral. Was there a funeral?"

Ray had already known she was going to inquire about the death of her children's dad. He felt she had every right to know. Her question, "*Was there a funeral?*" Made him feel as if she was implying that the Kingz had falsified their demises and Black would soon reveal himself to her. Well, as much as he hated to rain on her parade, he once again, told his side of the story. When he finished, he studied Nikki, who looked as if she was still trying to digest his words. Her hair was now cut into a bob and dyed brown, and she appeared to have lost a great deal of weight.

"Somebody had been sending me money," she finally spoke, still looking engrossed. "Through the mail, but there was no return address. All it said was LKS. Was it you?"

"Yeah," Ray answered, hoping she didn't question his acronym. "And how are the kids?"

"They're doing good," she answered. "Lil' Keith just started pre-school. I've never told Nicole about her daddy because I didn't believe it myself. Like I said, I didn't hear anything about a funeral. Whenever she would ask, "*Mommy, where's my daddy?*" I would tell her I didn't know. I mean, I really didn't know."

Ray reached over and held her hand as she cried. He couldn't believe that, for over two years, she had been holding on to false hope. Now, he was really hating the fact that he'd shown up on her doorsteps. If it wasn't for that damned Frankenstein of a safe, he wouldn't be in her presence now, looking for a key she probably didn't—

That's when he'd spotted Black's keys on the table. The safe's key was what really stood out to him. Now, he was trying to figure out a way to obtain the key from her, without raising suspicion in either of them or prompting questions he didn't intend to answer.

"I see you still have his car," Ray ventured, picking the keys up, looking at them. "What happened to the rims?"

"I had to sell them last year," she answered, now regarding him. "I wasn't working, and the money Black had given me got low. The rim shop I sold them to had some BMW rims. They gave me a good deal. That's all I sold, I'll never sell the car."

"You shouldn't have to," Ray told her. "Can I have this key, right here?"

She shrugged, "I don't see why not. I don't even know what it goes to. What kind of key is it?"

"It's a key to a puzzle." He pulled out his keyring, showing her the other two belonging to him and James. "It goes with these two."

"I guess you need it more than I do," Nikki asserted. "Have you heard anything on, Connie and Felicia?"

"Felicia's doing okay," he said, taking the key off her ring. "I haven't heard anything on, Connie."

"Was Connie pregnant the last time you saw her?"

"Not that I know of. Why?"

"I think I drove past her, downtown, a few months ago," she told him. "She was holding a little girl that looked to be almost two years old. She didn't have the same complexion as any of Black's kids. She was lighter, maybe your complexion. Or, maybe it wasn't, Connie. So, what are you doing now?"

"I'm laying low for the moment," he told her. "Which reminds me, you can't tell anybody you saw me. No one is to know I'm still alive yet. I plan on resurfacing, but not right now. Can you handle that?"

She nodded. "Am I going to hear from you again?"

Once he'd gotten her number, Ray and his lieutenants were out the door. As they were en route to Bankhead Highway to see Eric, Ray thought about what Nikki had said about seeing Connie with a little girl who didn't share the same complexion as any of Black's children. Then, she offered that it probably wasn't Connie. He had already noted that she wasn't the same as he'd remembered. It seemed as if she'd lost her spirit, which was highly fathomable. It also seemed as if she was trying hard to retain her sanity, to keep from falling apart. She just seemed so frail to him, as if any little thing could induce her to break. Perhaps something like his abrupt visit, and his confirmation that Black was really dead. Thinking this, he pulled out his cell and called to check on her. He listened to the phone ring until her voicemail picked up, then tried again, getting the same results. Not wanting to jump to conclusions, he waited for a few more minutes just in case she was in the bathroom- and tried again. No answer.

"Get off on the next exit!" he told Joe, now feeling something was wrong.

Playa Ray

Chapter 7

Shonda had finally gotten around to taking that trip to East Lake Meadows to see Trent, although she was taking her time, attentively driving slow on the expressway. She was still unsure of what she was going to say to him. Now, she pulled her vibrating cell phone from the cupholder.

"Hello?"

"Dude still haven't hit y'all back?" Tino inquired.

"Who?'

"LKS."

"Not yet," she answered. "I don't know what's the hold-up."

"Well, I found a plug," he told her. "I don't know the nigga, but I was told he has the pills. I was also told that his shit was going for the high-high. I don't fuck with the shit, so I really can't comment on his prices. Do I plug you in?'

"Not yet," she answered. "I'ma give him another week to—"

"Another week!" Tino cut her off. "It don't take no week for shit like that! You either want the money or don't want the money. What, he gotta travel to the moon to get the shit?"

"You are so damn sarcastic!" Shonda asserted, laughing. "Let me handle this, please. If he doesn't hit us up in another week, I'll call and let you know."

"That's clever," he replied. "Y'all still holding up y'all end of the deal with, Vincent?'

"We're good on our end," she told him. "We should meet the deadline."

"That's how you do business," he said. "Well, I was just checking on you. I'll hit you back some other time."

Shonda finally pulled her Ford Mustang into East Lake, and around to where Trent usually hung out. As always, the local drug dealers were on their posts, but she didn't see Trent. She looked around and managed to see their two workers, who were holding down their spot. Then, one of the guys from Trent's spot made his way to her car.

"Whatcha need?' he asked.

Shonda cracked the window a little. "I'm looking for, Trent."

"Hold on."

The guy went to an apartment door and knocked. Seconds later, the door opened. Shonda couldn't see who he was talking to, but when he pointed towards the car, Trent stuck his head out the door. When Trent closed the door back, the other guy rejoined his group. Now, Shonda didn't know what to think. She didn't know if he was coming out or not. Hell, he could be in there with his girlfriend. She definitely didn't ponder that possibility. How could she be so naïve to believe that a man of his caliber would not be taken? Just when she was about to give in and leave, Trent emerged from the apartment, pulling a dark sweater over his head. Shonda had to force herself to stop smiling as he approached. She rolled her window down.

"What's up?' he asked.

"I came by to check on you," she said, letting it flow. "Did you go to Mario's funeral?'

"Nah," he answered, looking around. "Look, I really can't talk, right now. You gotta catch me some other time."

Shonda could see that he was a bit agitated, so she quickly jotted down her number and handed it to him. "Can you call me when you get a chance?" she asked. "I really do need to talk to you."

"I'll do that."

Trent walked off, and Shonda proceeded to turn her car around to leave. As she was doing this, she noticed Trent heading in another direction. As she slowly made for the exit, she watched from her rearview mirror as he approached two guys who were standing by a black Chevy Impala. The guy he was talking to was light skin, heavy-set and accompanied by a darker, much slimmer guy.

****

When they'd made it back to the apartments, Joe parked in the same spot. Ray had not conveyed to them that something might be wrong, but when he lunged from the truck, stuffing the 9mm in one pocket, and the extended clip in another, they were right at his heels, moving as if they could sense what he was sensing. Getting to the door, Ray knocked, waited a few seconds, then knocked again as he fought the volition to call out her name, lest he draws unwanted attention.

Not getting any answer, Ray tried the knob. It was unlocked, and he didn't waste one second. He pushed the door open, entering. The living room was empty. The keys were still on the table, along with Nikki's cell phone. Not knowing what to expect, Ray drew his gun and re-inserted the clip, which prompted his lieutenants to do likewise.

A quick glance showed that Nikki wasn't in the small kitchen. They slowly moved towards the bedrooms. The bathroom came before the bedrooms. Being that the door was closed, and the bedroom doors were open, Ray figured she had to be in there. He grabbed the knob, readying himself for the inevitable. When he finally turned the knob and eased the door open, he saw Nikki lying on the floor. Her body was twitching, and her eyes had rolled up in her head. Then, he saw the pill bottle lying beside her.

"Fuck!" he exclaimed. "Get her in the tub!"

He moved out of their way as they tucked their guns and entered the bathroom. Ray fought back tears as he watched them lift her into the tub.

"Force cold water down her throat and pump her stomach!" Ray told them.

"We can drown her like that," Joe protested.

"Or we can just sit here and watch her die!" Ray vented.

"Force cold water down her throat and pump her stomach. See if y'all can get somma that shit to come back up, while I call these people."

Ray re-entered the living room, where he placed his gun on the coffee table, grabbed Nikki's cell phone and dialed 911. As he waited for the lines to connect, he could hear Nikki choking and retching. He felt that, as long as he heard that, he knew she was still breathing. He just couldn't help but blame himself for all of this.

"Nine one one," the dispatcher came on. "What's your emergency?"

"My friend has taken a large number of pills," Ray answered as formal as he could. "She needs medical attention right away!"

"Sir, what is her condition?"

"She's dying!" Ray raised his voice, almost calling her a bitch. "You need to be sending somebody over here!"

"What's the address?"

"Um..." Ray looked to the open door at the apartment number and was able to tell her the name of the apartments also.

"Paramedics are en route, sir," said the dispatcher. "Can you stay on the line?"

"Nope."

Ray hung up, closed the front door, placed the phone back on the table, grabbed his gun and went back to the bathroom, where his lieutenants were looking like a pair of *ghetto paramedics* as they attempted to flush the medication out of Nikki, who was barely putting up a struggle, being that the drug had already numbed her senses, and was gradually taking its course.

"She threw some of it up," Joe said still forcing water down her throat while Poppo pumped her stomach. "I don't think we can get all of it."

"We won't be able to get all of it," Ray agreed. "I called nine-one-one. They got somebody coming."

Now they were looking at him.

"I'll be the one to stay," he answered their inquisitive looks. "Y'all just—" He stopped when he heard someone knocking at the front door. He knew damn well he'd just gotten off the phone with them, so there was no way in hell they were already at the door. Saying nothing, Ray made for the door, not knowing Poppo was behind him until he'd gotten to the door and peered through the peephole at some dark-skinned man with cornrows.

"Is this her boyfriend?" Ray asked Poppo in a low tone, stepping back for him to take a look.

Poppo peered through the hole. "That's him."

"Stay in the kitchen," he told Poppo. Once Poppo was out of sight, Ray opened the door, with his gun concealed behind his back, "You're looking for, Nikki, right?"

"Yeah," he answered, a cautious look on his face.

"And you are?"

"I'm Ace," he stated with authority. "Her boyfriend!"

"Well, come on in, Ace!" Ray asserted, maintaining his cordiality façade. As soon as he entered, Ray closed the door and put the gun up to his face.

Ace raised his hands in surrender. "Hold on, man!"

"Go to the bathroom," Ray demanded. "Move!"

By this time, Poppo had emerged from the kitchen. They followed Ace to the bathroom, where Joe was still trying to save Nikki, who was still gagging from the rush of water that irritated her throat.

"I got some out," Joe informed, only regarding them with a quick glance.

Ray nudge Ace in the back with his gun. "Step in!"

Entering the bathroom, Ace automatically picked the pill bottle up off the floor. "Don't tell me she tried this shit again!" he said, facing Ray.

"Again?" Ray couldn't believe what he was hearing, although his assessment of her mental state was necessary.

"We gotta roll out," Poppo interrupted. "Right now!'

Ray heard the faint sound of sirens and realized Poppo was right. He was kind of glad Ace had shown up, because he really didn't have the patience, right now to deal with the authorities and their barrage of questions.

"Look," Ray started, ejecting the cartridge from his gun and returning them to his pockets, "An ambulance is on the way. I gotta go, but when she's revived, tell her, I'll be by the hospital to check on her later."

"And who do I say?"

"LKS."

With that, Ray and his men were out the door. As they made for the truck, Ray thought about how Ace had looked when he'd mentioned his pseudonym which people were highly familiar with. Clearly, Ace was one of those people. He was hoping Nikki didn't tell him who he really was before he got a chance to publicize his own existence.

An ambulance pulled into the apartments as they were exiting, which brought Ray's mind back to Nikki. He couldn't believe she had actually pulled a suicide stunt *again*, according to Ace. He couldn't help but take the blame for this one. He assumed that Black's death had caused the first attempt, but considering Ace's inflection, it appeared that they were together at that time, which left a passel of questions in his head. Questions he intended to ask Nikki when he visited her in the hospital later.

They had finally made it to Hair Masters, the barbershop on Bankhead, that was owned by Eric. Joe pulled the truck into the small plaza and parked. Ray didn't see the Chevy Caprice, so he assumed Eric had bought another car.

"I'ma need one of y'all to see if he's in there," Ray said. "He's a tall, brown skin dude, and may still have long hair. His station is the first one."

"What do I tell him?" asked Joe.

"That you're an old friend of, Fred's," Ray answered. "And you need to talk to him in private. Once you get him outside, I'll do the rest."

Joe dismounted and entered the barbershop.

"We may have to put our run on hold," Poppo said.

Ray looked at his watch. "Y'all might be a lil' late, but I don't think y'all should put it on hold. This shouldn't take long."

Joe emerged from the barbershop, alone and climbed back into the truck.

"He don't work here," Joe stated before Ray could ask. "He still owns the place, but he works at Posh BMWs."

'*Posh BMWs*?' Ray thought. What would possess Eric to even *think* about changing the name? Perhaps he had a perfectly good explanation for it. Well, Ray couldn't wait to hear what it was, which was why they were now on their way to Marietta, Georgia.

When they'd made it to the dealership, the first thing Ray noticed was the sign that pretty much let people know that it was no longer *Kingz BMWs*, but to Ray, it would always be that.

"Park in front of the building," Ray told Joe. "I already told you what he looks like. Approach him as if you're trying to buy a car."

As Joe got out and made for the entrance, Ray looked around for Eric's Chevy Caprice and didn't see it. He was absolutely sure that the white four-door BMW on chrome wheels belonged to Eric, and the cherry red BMW coupe belonged to Sharonda.

"Y'all can still make it happen," Ray told Poppo, who'd looked at his watch, clearly worried about making the drops on time.

"It's always better late than never. They know it's coming."

"I'll call 'em as we go," Poppo avowed.

"As long as you—" Ray started, then stopped, when he saw Joe emerge from the building, followed by Eric, who was clad in a suit and tie, and now wore his hair cut low. When they approached the truck, Ray lowered the rear window. Eric regarded him but didn't look at all surprised.

"It's about time," Eric asserted. "I was wondering when you were gonna show up."

Chapter 8

It took a few seconds for Ray to realize what Eric said. He stated that he was wondering when Ray was going to show up as if he knew for sure Ray was still alive. *But how*? Ray didn't want to jump the gun and believe Eric had something to do with the demise of his own brother, but the thought had come to him, unabated. Fred and Eric were close, but that didn't mean shit these days! Brothers were turning on each other for no-good bitches.

"Step into my office," Ray told Eric, sliding over and placing his gun in his lap.

Ray didn't have to ask Poppo for privacy. He took the initiative, getting out as Eric climbed in beside Ray.

"So, you knew?' Ray asked, studying Eric for any signs of betrayal.

"I called Fred that night," Eric answered. "I needed his permission to grab a pistol from his closet. He said y'all were on the way to the DJ battle at that time. Then, I thought about this nigga who was trying to cop a pound and asked about you. That's when Fred told me you were at home, sick. But you did right by laying low. Shit had gotten outta hand in the streets and all fingers pointed to y'all as the initiators."

"I heard the same thing," Ray said, checking his watch, remembering that his lieutenants had runs to make. "Do you have Fred's car?"

"The BMW?"

"Yeah."

"It's at the house," Eric answered. "I had to go and get all of his shit from mom's house after she died."

"*She died*?" Ray wasn't expecting this news. He loved their mother as if she was his own. He was hoping like hell she didn't get caught up in something they'd created.

"She died a few days after the funeral," Eric told him. "Do you need Fred's car?"

"Nah," Ray answered. "He had a key that belonged to me."

"A key?"

"Like these," Ray said, pulling out his keyring, showing him the other three keys to the safe.

"I don't remember seeing a key like that," Eric replied. "But I got all his stuff at my house. You can swing through later and look through everything if you want."

Ray was considering this, but at the same time, he was wondering how could, Eric not seen the key if he was in possession of Fred's car, which meant he was in possession of Fred's keys. The oddly shaped key was not that hard to spot. Now, he was wondering if his old friend was trying to lure him into a trap and perhaps, finish the job.

"You still stay in the same spot?" Ray asked, checking his vibrating cell phone to see B.J.'s number and ignoring it.

"Nah," Eric answered. "We copped a nice spot out here in Marietta."

Once Eric had given him the address and he vowed to stop by later, Ray and his lieutenants were on their way.

"There's been a change of plans," Ray told his lieutenants. "I'ma let y'all make the runs without me. Just drop me off at the crib. I'll get up with y'all, later." His phone vibrated again. "Yeah?"

"We got a problem," B.J. asserted.

"Not now, B.J.," Ray said, feeling as if he'd picked the wrong day to come out of the house. "What is it?'

"It's Trent," B.J. answered. "He approached me, not too long ago, about that business me and Rick handled."

"Which business?"

"The bird that flew West," B.J. coded.

Ray had to think for a second. "Okay. What about it?"

"He claims he's the one that handled it," B.J. informed. "He said LKS needs to come on with that."

"So, who really did the job?" Ray asked, remembering that B.J. would lie to God.

"Come on, Ray!" B.J. said. "This *me* you're talking to."

"Exactly!" Ray replied. "So, who did the job?"

"You want proof?"

"Or my money back."

After being dropped off at home, Ray called Grady Memorial Hospital, to see if Nikki was housed there. Once they'd confirmed that she was in the Recovery Unit, he set out to feed his dogs. Completing that task, he donned his bulletproof vest, grabbed his two-shoulder holsters that held two Glock 40s, and a light jacket. He put on the jacket and carried the holster out to the garage, where he climbed into his Mercedes Benz.

On his way to Atlanta, Ray's mind was on Eric. The thought of him having something to do with the termination of the Kingz had subsided when Eric explained the phone conversation he'd had with Fred, on that night, which was how he knew Ray was still alive. But this key thing had him reconsidering that thought. If he had *all* of Fred's belongings, then there was no way he had not encountered the funny shaped key. Well, Ray did vow to use himself as bait, to draw the culprits who murdered The

Kingz. If Eric proved to be one, Ray just hoped he was the one who comes out on top.

Getting to the hospital, Ray parked, put on his gold-rimmed, non-medicated glasses, pulled his hat lower over his eyes and got out. Entering the building, he approached the information desk, hoping he didn't look like he was about to stick the place up, while at the same time, hoping not to be noticed by anyone who knew him. Once he found out where Nikki was located, he made for the elevators, feeling out of place. He had not been anywhere near any crowded places, in over two years.

Making it to Nikki's room, Ray entered to see Ace sitting in a chair beside her bed. They appeared to be engaged in conversation before he walked in. Now, they were both regarding him as he stood beside the bed, opposite of Ace.

"How ya' feeling?" Ray asked her.

"Better," she answered in a composed tone. "You found me?'

"Yeah." He looked at Ace. "Can I talk to her in private?'

Saying nothing, Ace kissed Nikki on the forehead, then left the room, closing the door behind him. Ray took a seat in the chair, removing his hat.

"You know I'm surprised at you, right?' Ray said to Nikki, who responded by looking to the ceiling.

"What made you attempt something like that? And from my understanding, it's not the first time."

She was silent for a moment, before speaking, "So, he's really dead?"

"That's no reason to take your own life, Nikki," he told her, trying to contain his anger. "And you didn't even think about those kids before you attempted that selfish ass stunt. They didn't ask to be here! They've already lost their dad. Why deprive them of both of their parents? They need you, Nikki!"

"I know," she said, wiping tears from her eyes. "I love my babies."

"Well, act like it!" He stood. "I gotta go, but I'll be checking on you. And my number is in your phone. If you get depressed, reach out to me, before you do something stupid. Okay?"

She nodded.

"And I'm still, LKS."

"Okay."

He kissed her on the cheek, donned his hat, then exited the room. He was glad to see Ace seated outside the room, because he had one more question to ask, and Ace was the one he intended to get the answer from.

"So, you're LKS?" Ace asked, standing.

"Yeah." Ray eyed him for any signs of a threat. "You must be one of my clients."

"Nah," said Ace. "But I used to work for a dude who used to deal with you."

"Who,"

"Spenz."

That's when Ray recollected his lieutenants, informing him that Spenz had two guys working under him at the club, while he D.J.'d.

Now, Ray had another question for Ace, "Have you heard anything on his murder."

"Man, nobody's heard a thing," Ace answered. "Spenz didn't have any enemies, as far as I know. But I still got my ears to the streets."

"That's what's up," Ray posed his initial question. "So, this is not the first time Nikki has pulled this stunt."

"Nah."

"How many times?"

"Once, that I know of," Ace answered.

"What drove her to it?"

Ace drew a breath. "Well, like I said, I worked for, Spenz. Nikki knew what I did, and where I did it at. But she was constantly accusing me of messing with one of the dancers. Eventually, I got tired of it and called it quits. I was about to leave her apartment. Before I could get out the door, she grabbed a bottle of sleeping pills and was forcing 'em down her throat. I rushed her and knock 'em out her hand. She had swallowed some, but not enough to kill herself."

"Do you love her?" Ray wanted to know.

"I wouldn't be here if I didn't!"

"She's a good woman," Ray told him. "You just have to be patient with her she's been through a lot."

Ray didn't plan on sermonizing Ace; it just came out at the spur of the moment. But he had to assure himself that his friend was in good hands. Well, as far as he was concerned, she was. Therefore, he left the hospital feeling as if he'd completed one task for the day and was off to complete another.

Ray had already given Eric's address to his lieutenants, but when he pulled up to the house, he called and let them know he'd arrived. He'd already told them that if he didn't call them at ten o'clock to let them know he was alright, they were to storm the house and kill everything that didn't look like him.

Taking off his jacket, Ray put on his holster, then slipped the jacket back on, leaving it unzipped knowing he no longer needed the hat and glasses, he dismounted, leaving them in the car. And just as he figured, the white and red BMWs did indeed, belong to Eric and Sharonda. He also noticed another car sitting off in the grass. It was covered, but by the shape of it and the small portion of the rims he could see, he knew it was Fred's BMW.

"Hey, Ray!" Sharonda greeted him, upon opening the front door.

"What's up?"

"Nothing," she answered. "Come on in, Eric's in Fred's room."

'Fred's room?' Ray thought as he entered. Then, he assumed that Fred's room was probably something like the Kingz room, where he kept a lot of their things.

"So, you knew I was still alive, too?" Ray asked her.

"Eric told me you were not in the limo that night," she answered, locking the door back. "But I didn't believe you were still alive until he told me you came by the dealership, today."

"I see y'all doing good," Ray said, looking around, also changing subjects.

"We're doing better," she admitted.

"How's the baby?"

She smiled. "Which one?"

Ray just looked at her.

"I had another one," she informed. "Lil' Eric, he just finally went to sleep. Erica's in the living room, watching cartoons. They're doing fine, though."

"That's good," he told her. "I guess you have to show me to Fred's room, huh?"

"Yeah."

As Ray followed her, he subtly unlatched his guns. He didn't get any vibes off Sharonda, but she was not the one he was worried about. He was just hoping Eric didn't have any tricks up his sleeve, because he did not plan on dying tonight.

They made it to the room, where the door was closed. Sharonda knocked, stuck her head inside and informed Eric of Ray's arrival. Ray couldn't hear Eric's response, but Sharonda pushed the door open and stepped inside. When Ray entered, he immediately noted that this was actually Fred's room. Eric had actually taken everything from Fred's room at their mother's house and transferred them here. Plus, everything was set up in the same fashion. The only unbefitting items were the two soft cushioned chairs that sat on each side of a small wooden table. Eric was seated in one of the chairs.

"Have a seat, my friend!" Eric said, indicating the chair across from him.

Ray complied. On the table were two drinking glasses, a fifth of Cognac and a chessboard. By the arrangement of the chess pieces, he could tell Eric had been playing a solitary game.

"Drink?" he offered, pouring himself a glass.

"Nah."

"I guess you still don't drink, huh?"

"Nah."

"Well, like I said," Eric continued, "I got all of Fred's stuff, and I haven't seen that key. I don't allow nobody in this room, but you're more than welcome to look for it."

"Did you check the car?" Ray asked, looking around the room.

"Man, I thoroughly checked everything," Eric stated. "You know, to make sure I wasn't in possession of something I didn't know about."

Eric seemed sincere. Plus, how possessive he seemed about the room, made Ray feel as if he didn't have to search it. But he knew all Kingz kept their safe keys on their keyrings. So, if Fred's key wasn't on his keyring, then that means someone had taken it off. But who?

"The key was on his keyring," Ray said.

"I have all his keys on my keyring," Eric told him. "Are you sure he had your key?"

"I may have misplaced it," Ray said to keep Eric from inquiring the significance of the key. "You haven't heard anything?"

"On that?"

"Yeah."

"The streets are real hushed about that," Eric answered. "Nobody's saying shit."

"What you think about, Norris?"

"What, you think he had something to do with it?"

Ray just looked at him.

"Fuck, no!" Eric let out. "Shit, he was fucked up about that shit."

'*He didn't try to commit suicide*,' Ray thought, but asked, "So, you don't think he was jealous of us?"

Eric took a sip of his drink. "Why would he be jealous of y'all? This nigga got cake on top of cake. He was proud of y'all if anything."

Ray nodded, but he wasn't ruling Norris out as a feasible suspect. "So, why'd you change the name of the dealership?" he asked, changing subjects for the moment.

"For the sake of the business," Eric answered. "I figured whoever burned it down, were no friends of the Kingz. And by changing the name, they would think it was owned by somebody else."

That's logical," Ray agreed.

"And speaking of which," Eric told him. "Being that the dealership is technically yours—"

"Is it still in, Sharonda's name?" Ray wanted to know.

"Yeah," Eric rejoined. "I'm the manager, she's the secretary. Plus, we have two salesmen. We'll sign it over to you, whenever you're ready."

"We can discuss that some other time," Ray said. 'Are you still in contact with the hood?"

"Nothing's changed on that end," Eric told him. "We still club and throw get-togethers at the barbershop on Saturdays. Hell, even Norris may stop through every blue moon. We still got that hood love. And speaking of love, ya' girl is sick."

"My girl?"

"Trina," Eric answered. "And this is not a rumor. She was fucking with a nigga who was already known to have that shit. Then, when she got sick, it was confirmed."

"I'm not surprised," Ray responded, and really wasn't because Trina would fuck any and everything that had a dick. "What happened to, Bobby?" he asked, remembering they were engaged to be married."

"Man, she married that nigga and tossed his ass to the side," Eric told him. "He went out bad anyway, for even thinking about marrying a hoe who done fucked damn near every nigga in Atlanta!" He took a drink from his glass, then his expression changed as if he was trying to remember something. "Fuck! You know what? Fred did mention something about a key. Before I got off the phone with him, I think he said to tell you that Lisa had the key or some shit like that."

"And who the fuck is, Lisa?"

"I don't know," Eric answered. "I was in a rush I didn't even ask."

"Are you sure he said, Lisa?" Ray asked, wondering why some bitch would have his key to the safe.

"I'm positive."

Playa Ray

Chapter 9

It was Friday, the day B.J. planned to validate his and Rick's partaking in the termination of the man who'd conned Ray's lieutenant out of a kilo. By going in half with another man, but only producing two hundred dollars and the rest in counterfeit bills, which was his half. Ray had put a bounty on both their heads, but Trent exonerated himself, claiming his half was legit and his business partner had pulled that stunt on his own accord, without the backing of him. Now that his partner was dead, Trent's claiming that he's the one who'd taken the hit and was now anticipating his money. But Ray had already paid B.J. and Rick who'd already reported the guy's demise, claiming they were the ones who'd burned him. Well, today, somebody better present some substantial evidence, or there won't be any confusion as to who pulled the trigger.

Now, Ray was seated in the back of the Ford Expedition, Joe had rented, as they were en route to meet B.J. and Rick on Bankhead, where they claim they had a witness who could prove their involvement. Ray was a bit skeptical about this because he couldn't believe they'd killed this guy and intentionally left a witness behind, which did not sound right to him at all.

Ray shook his head, he would just have to make some kind of sense of the situation when he arrived. Now, he reverted to his thoughts of trying to figure out who the hell this Lisa bitch was, who had Fred's key. For him to relay this message to Ray through Eric, then it was obvious that Ray was somehow familiar with her. But the only women Fred was seeing before he died, was Yvonne, Theresa and some dancer at Strokers, whose name may have been Cherry. Yvonne was dead and Ray had only once been introduced to Cherry.

Perhaps he'd said, Theresa instead of, Lisa?

"That them?" Poppo asked, pulling Ray from his thoughts.

They had made it to Bankhead and were driving down Grove Street, approaching the black Honda Civic B.J. said they would be in, which was parked on the side of the street.

"Yeah, that's them," Ray answered.

Joe parked behind the Honda. Ray unlatched the two Glocks in his holster, before getting out. Getting to the Honda, he climbed in behind B.J., who was in the front passenger seat.

"So, who is this bitch?" Ray asked, keeping his eyes on their movements, just in case they'd intended to try something flakey.

"Some junkie, bitch," B.J. answered. "We murdered the nigga in that house across the street. She saw the whole thing."

"Where is she now?" Ray regarded the abandoned, rundown house that still had pieces of crime scene tape attached to it.

"She's in there," he answered. "Her and some dude."

"So, what's the plan?"

"Wait until the dude comes out."

"Some plan," Ray muttered, checking his watch to see that it was one-thirty and keeping in mind that his lieutenants had to meet with his ecstasy pills supplier at three.

"There he is!" Rick announced when an older man emerged from the house and made his way up the street.

"I'll handle this," Ray told them. "Y'all stay put."

Ray got out and as he crossed the street headed for the house, he dialed Poppo's number on his cell.

"Talk to me!" Poppo answered.

"Watch them, niggas!" Ray told him. "If they make a move toward the house, ring me up!"

"Should I put 'em on ice?"

"I'll do it," Ray answered, knowing Poppo would be glad to do it himself, being that Pollo was a Blood and B.J. was Folk.

Approaching the front door, Ray fastened his phone back onto his hip. Seeing that the door was void of doorknobs and locks, he pushed it open with his foot and entered, pulling both Glocks out. Just as he'd expected, the house reeked of urine, feces, alcohol, and mildew. Plus, there were several stained mattresses, discarded needles, cans, bottles, plastic drug bags and other trash cluttering the living room floor. But there were no sign of the woman that was supposed to be there.

Ray has known B.J. ever since he was nine years old, but that didn't hinder him from feeling as if he was walking into a trap as he moved about the house. That thought subsided, when he made it to one-bedroom, where a female was sitting upright on a bare mattress, wrapped in a blanket, with her arms around her legs, rocking back and forth, with her back bumping against the wall. He quickly concealed his guns behind his back. She showed no acknowledgment of his presence, as she continued rocking, staring at the wall and moving her lips as if she was talking or singing to herself.

"You got a minute?" Ray finally spoke, startling her.

"Huh?" She stopped rocking and was regarding him with enlarged pupils.

"You got a minute?" he iterated, crossing the threshold, but keeping his hands behind his back.

She cocked her head to the side. "Are you a cop?"

"Detective," he said, taking advantage of her query.

"Is this about, Mario?"

Ray wasn't familiar with the guy's name but went along with it. "Can you tell me how it happened?" Once she'd told him the same story, she told Shonda. He asked, "Do you remember what the two guys looked like?"

"One was light skin and stocky," she answered. "The other one was dark skin and smaller than the other one."

"How well do you remember their faces?"

"Real well."

"Can you pick them out of a photo line up?"

"Yes."

As he evaluated her, Ray could tell she was a real decent female, who obviously had chosen the wrong path. He thanked her, backed out of the room so she wouldn't see his guns, and re-holstered them as he crossed the living room to the front door. She had given him the confirmation he was looking for and sealed her fate because he was going to have to convey this to B.J. and Rick. If they had grown any brain cells since the last time they'd been inside that house, then they would make it their last visit.

When Ray approached the driver's side of the Honda, Rickrolled the window down. "I wouldn't be surprised if the whole U.S. Army was looking for y'all niggas!" he told them.

"Why'd you say that?" B.J. asked

"Y'all underestimated her," Ray answered. "She can pick y'all out of a photo line-up, blindfolded. Y'all need to handle that!"

"What about, Trent?" Rick wanted to know.

"I'll handle that," he answered, then retreated to the Ford, climbing in. "To the crib!"

Joe made a U-turn as B.J. and Rick were exiting the Honda, Ray knew what they were about to do, and he really felt sorry for the frail-looking woman, but it had to be done. He couldn't take the chance of them getting arrested and throwing him in the mix.

Not to say that they would, but who knew?

****

At Shonda and Sheila's house, which was the stash spot, the Queenz were all seated at the kitchen table going over their books and preparing orders for the clients they were to meet with. Plus, Ant had recruited more workers in Allen Temple, Summer Hill, Mechanicsville, and Grady Homes.

"Everything's adding up," Shonda said, looking through the record book, while the others were packaging the orders. "Our profit fluctuates, but it's generally increasing. We'll meet Vincent's deadline, and probably be able to cop those BMW convertibles by next year."

Ebony smiled. "We'll be riding like some true Queenz, then!"

"We should try our hands at real estate," Theresa voiced. "Queenz Realtors."

"Now that's fly," Sheila said, slapping Theresa a high five.

"Shit, we got the money," Theresa said.

"All Queenz agree?" Shonda asked.

"Hell, yeah!" they all exclaimed in unison, then burst into laughter, right as the business phone rung.

"Queenz," Sheila answered through muffled laughter.

"Is Queen, Theresa in?" a familiar voice asked.

"Who is this?" Sheila asked, hoping that one of their clients weren't using this phone line to try and hook up with Theresa.

"LKS."

"Oh!" Sheila exclaimed, happy to hear from him. "We've been waiting to hear from you. She's here, but you can talk to either of us. This is Queen, Sheila."

"I need to talk to, Theresa," he told her.

Frowning, Sheila reluctantly held the phone out to Theresa.

"Who is it?" Theresa asked.

"LKS," she answered. "He asked for you."

Sensing the mild hostility in her friend's tone, Theresa opted for speakerphone. "I'm here."

"Theresa?"

"Yeah."

"It's LKS," Ray announced. "I need to ask you a question."

"Okay."

"Did Fred give you a key?"

"A key?"

"A vending machine key."

"Fred didn't give me any kind of key," she answered.

"James had one of those keys," Shonda said.

"We all had one," Ray said. "I was just looking for, Fred's."

"He didn't give me any key," Theresa restated.

"Are you still gonna deal with us on the pills?" Shonda took advantage of the opportunity.

"Yeah," Ray answered. "My shipment comes in today. How much are y'all trying to spend?"

"Five hundred, at the least," Shonda told him.

Ray was quiet on the other end for a few seconds, before saying, "A'ight, I'll hit y'all back later with the destination."

After getting off the phone with Ray, the Queenz finished their orders and were out the door, headed for the GMC Denali, where Sheila and Shonda climbed into the front seats. The Queenzmen were already parked across the street.

"Where to, first?" Sheila, who was driving, asked.

"We'll cover Atlanta, first," Shonda told her. "Grady Homes."

"What time will we stop by the salon?" Ebony wanted to know.

"We should do it around closing time," Shonda answered. "That should give the girls enough time to get their rent money up."

"We gotta have some kind of license to do real estate, right?" Ebony asked Theresa.

"Huh?" Theresa snapped out of her reverie. She was thinking about Ray, wondering why he'd asked her about receiving a key from Fred.

"Do we have to have some kind of license to do real estate?" she repeated.

"A real estate license," Theresa answered.

"We should get our own office building," Ebony said, pulling her ringing cellular from her pocketbook. "Hello?"

"Hey, sexy!" Phillip's voice came through the other end.

Ebony blushed. "Hey, yourself. How are you?"

"I'm good," he answered. "I was hoping we could get together, tonight."

"It's possible."

"I got a room at the same hotel," he told her, "But I can't spend the night."

Ebony almost asked why but caught herself. She had never asked Phillip, but she was quite sure he had a woman and probably kids at home, which was why he'd always opted for a hotel room and never invited her over to his place. It was okay because she was going to enjoy the moment while it lasted.

"Okay," Ebony agreed. "We can do that."

"Should I send a car?"

"I'm out on errands, right now," she told him. "I don't know when I'll be done. I'll drive myself and just call you when I'm on my way."

"That'll work, I'll see you then."

"What you got going on?" Shonda asked when Ebony concluded her call.

"That was, Phillip," she answered. "He wants me to meet him at a hotel, later."

"Should we drop you off?"

"I'll be okay."

"You don't know that." Shonda turned in her seat to face her friend. "At least take Hakeem with you, that's what he gets paid for."

"Alright," Ebony agreed.

It was well after five when the Queenz finally completed their rounds, but Ebony had called Khandi before five and told her they would be a little late picking up the rent money, which was why Khandi was still at the salon when they arrived. They entered the salon as Khandi's last customer was leaving.

"Y'all look good." Khandi beamed. "Let me wash my hands, and I'll get that for y'all."

They stood around as she journeyed to the bathroom to wash up. When she returned, she retrieved a wad of bills from her purse and handed it to Ebony.

"So, how are the new girls doing?" Ebony asked.

"Michelle, went to school for this," Khandi answered. "So, she's the best stylist here. And Tammi is still learning all the styles, but she's doing good."

"Well, we appreciate you for doing a good job," Ebony told her.

"No problem," Khandi replied. "Oh, Drama Queen came by Wednesday and got her wig propped up."

"Who?" Ebony asked, feeling as if she already knew the answer.

"Pam," Khandi answered. "She was all jeweled up. Hell, her outfit looked like she'd stolen it from your closet. She said, she had gotten her real estate licenses and was doing real estate. Plus, she was in that new convertible Cadillac."

Ebony's day was going well, she was not going to let this news bother her. She had already expected that Charles was going to upgrade Pam like he'd done her.

When Poppo and Joe returned to Ray's house, after receiving the shipment of ecstasy pills, they all sat down and sorted out the orders for their workers and customers. Ray had even remembered to set aside the Queenz order for tomorrow. He'd already left a message on their phone, with the destination, time, and how much money to bring. Plus, he told them to leave their Queenzmen at home.

Once they were done, Ray looked at his watch and saw that it was after eight o'clock. He knew that his friends were about to leave, and he was once again, going to be sitting at home alone, trying to keep himself from climbing the walls from boredom.

"Whatcha got planned for tonight?" Poppo asked.

"One of my homies from Savannah is up here for the weekend," Poppo answered. "I'ma meet him at Club Three Twenty-One."

"On business?" Ray wanted to know.

"Nah," Poppo answered. "This will be on some reunited type of shit."

"What about you, Joe?"

"I'll be at home with the wife and kids tonight," Joe answered. "I might do a little hanging out, tomorrow night."

"Shit, I'm trying to hang out tonight," Ray said. "Poppo, swing back through and pick me up. I guess I'll be hitting Club Three Twenty-one, too."

"Are you sure?" Poppo asked. "You know that's pretty much Bloods territory.

"Are you gonna swing back through or what?"

When they left, Ray fed his dogs, freshened up a little. He didn't see any need to change clothes, but he did change artillery. In lieu of his twin Glocks, he opted for his Glock nine with the extended clip and donned his fitted cap and glasses.

Poppo showed up in his Lexus, shortly after ten and they were on their way. Being that Poppo's from New York and a big *Jay-Z* fan, he had one of *Jay-Z's* CDs playing. *Jay-Z 'Song Cry'* was playing when they pulled into the clubs parking lot. As Poppo eased along, in search of a parking spot, Ray with his gun in his lap was looking around. He saw that a lot of guys and girls were wearing bandanas of different colors. He was about to ask Poppo why he wasn't wearing his flag or the color, but thought against it, feeling it wasn't his place to question his friend about something he didn't know the significance of.

Poppo found a spot, Ray tucked his gun under the passenger seat before they dismounted and made for the line, which felt a bit awkward to Ray because he'd gotten used to walking right inside the clubs with his fellow Kingz. While they waited in line, Poppo dapped up some of his affiliates. Ray was watching the women but keeping a wary eye on every group of guys that entered his line of sight, hoping no one was planning to pick this exact time and place to settle personal beefs.

It took almost fifteen minutes for them to make it inside the club. When they did, Ray followed Poppo to a table in a corner, where a dark skin guy was sitting with a white female. They were both clad in red sweatsuits with burgundy bandanas tied around their heads. If Ray didn't believe that Tupac was dead, he would swear he was looking right at the guy. All he was missing was a nose ring. But this wasn't Tupac. Poppo introduced him as O.Y.G. Ray Murda, a.k.a Murda Ru, and the female as his Ruby Alicia.

"And this is the dude I work for," Poppo concluded the introductory. "LKS."

"The Ghost!" Murda Ru said, regarding Ray.

Ray just looked at him.

"That's what they call you round my way," he went on to explain.

When they sat down, Alicia held the blunt she was smoking, out to Ray. When he shook his head, she passed it to Poppo.

"You don't smoke?" Murda Ru asked Ray

"Nah."

"Drink?"

"Nope."

"I already know my dog want a cup," he said, pouring Paul Masson into a plastic cup for Poppo.

"So, what brings you to the A?" Poppo asked.

"Shit, I had to get away from the spot for a minute, Derrty," Murda Ru answered, sipping from his cup.

"Laws on ya' back?" Poppo asked, passing him the blunt.

Murda Ru laughed. "Not this time. It's some ol' bullshit hood to hood beef going on. Some East and West shit. Niggas act like they want some drama, but they ain't prepared to bring it how I'ma bring it. Ya' feel me?"

As they conversed, Ray surveyed the atmosphere. In doing so, he spotted a female, who was out on the dance floor, grinding her ass on some guy with a black flag hanging from his back pocket. He figured he spotted her because she had on some loud orange pants. She was thick, and the way she was grinding on dude, was turning him on. Being that he hadn't had sex in almost two months, he was tempted to cross the floor, procure her fine ass from dude, and have Poppo drive them to the nearest hotel, pronto! But he knew he couldn't just pull such a stunt, so he just enjoyed the view, until Poppo announced that he was ready to go.

"Man, don't get into no shit while you up here," Poppo told Murda Ru as he and Ray stood to leave.

"I'm coolin', Derrty," Murda Ru replied. "As a matter of fact, y'all need to go ahead and put me on the team. You didn't tell, LKS how I got my name?"

"I'll see what's up," Poppo said, dapping Murda Ru and Alicia up.

"P-Funk!"

"P-Funk!" they shot back.

Once they made it outside, Poppo said, "I do wanna put the lil' homie on the team. I've seen the nigga in action. He's nothing nice on the gunplay tip."

Ray didn't reply. His attention was on the three guys that were coming their way, as they neared the Lexus. They all had red bandanas tied around their necks, so Ray didn't assume them to be any threat, being that Poppo was their blood brother. But he was wrong. Before they could reach for the door handles of the car, one of the goons rushed up on Poppo and the other two rushed up on Ray, all brandishing handguns.

"Y'all niggas know what it is!" the one who approached Poppo asserted. "Come up off everything. Especially the keys to the whip!"

"*Blatt*!" Poppo sounded with his mouth, causing Ray to regard him with an inquisitive look.

"Nigga, you bang?" the same guy questioned Poppo.

"I'm O.G., Poppo," he replied. "I bang Denver Lane Blood Gang. What you bang?"

"Shit, I'm O.Y.G, Capone Ru," he shot back. "I bang Treetop Piru." He looked over to Ray. "What you bang?"

"He don't bang," Poppo answered for him.

"Y'all pat that nigga down," Capone Ru commanded the other two.

"Stand down," Poppo barked.

Now, the two were looking back and forth from Poppo to Capone Ru, not knowing which one to obey. Ray was thinking about his gun under the passenger seat

"What, you're saving civilians?" Capone Ru accused Poppo.

"You're oppressing civilians?" Poppo countered.

This was when Ray realized he was going to have to exclude Poppo from his mission because it was obvious they were going to continue bumping heads with his fellow gang members. He did not want Poppo to lock horns with his Blood Brothers for trying to protect his real friend.

****

"I gotta go sexy."

Phillip kissed Ebony, pulled himself out of her, and got out of bed. She watched him as he gathered his clothes off the floor, and made for the bathroom, with a condom that was glossy wet with her juices, still clinging to his penis. Ebony was exhausted but with good reason, because Phillip had sexed her for over two hours, nonstop. She still didn't get a chance to suck his dick, like she intended, being that he was all over her as soon as she entered the room. She had been thinking about his size and wondering how much of it could fit into her mouth. Well, he didn't give her a chance to find out.

Minutes later, Phillip emerged from the bathroom, fully dressed. As he stood by the bed, putting on his watch, Ebony looked at his left hand. Just as she'd suspected, he was married, but the ring wasn't there. All she could see was the ring impression the ring left. Ebony didn't tend to question him about it, because like the saying goes if you can't give them satisfaction, they'll find it somewhere else.

"You can stay here for tonight if you want to," Phillip told her as he donned his jacket. "Just drop the key off at the front desk when you leave."

"I don't plan on staying." She got out of bed, approached him and pressed her nude body into him. "Don't I get a kiss before you go?"

As he gripped her waist, she wrapped her arms around his neck and tilted her head up, with her lips meeting his. Tongue meeting his. It was brief, but before breaking the kiss, he grabbed two hands full of her ass. After bidding him goodnight, she grabbed her clothes off the floor, then sauntered towards the bathroom. Getting to the bathroom, she looked back to see that he was regarding her with extreme lust in his eyes. This made her wonder about his wife. What was she like? Did they have children? How long have they been together? Does she suspect him of cheating? These were questions she might never know the answer to.

After washing herself and getting dressed, Ebony exited the bathroom and was not surprised to see that Phillip was gone. She didn't mind staying here tonight, but she figured if she was going to sleep alone, then she'd rather do it in her own bed. Therefore, she grabbed her things and left, not forgetting to leave the key at the front desk.

As she exited the building and made for her car, she looked around for Hakeem's car, then remembered she'd sent him on his way, after he followed her here. She climbed into her car and drove out of the parking lot, listening to *Mariah Carey's 'Don't Forget About Us'*. When she made it to the expressway, she put the car on cruise control, and let her mind drift.

For some reason, she started thinking about Charles' daughter, Robin and realized she really missed the little girl. She really believed, she would watch Robin grow into a woman and be there for her whenever she needed someone other than her mother and father to talk to. But Charles had stripped her of that when he left her for Pam.

Her thoughts were interrupted, when the high beams of a vehicle, illuminated the interior of her car from behind. The lights were so bright, she couldn't decipher who or what it was, through either of her mirrors. She could tell the vehicle was extremely close. Therefore, she deactivated her cruise control an accelerated a little. She tried the rearview mirror again and saw that the vehicle had another set of bright lights on its roof.

Immediately, Ebony was hit with a Deja Vu. This was the same kind of truck that they were attacked by on Theresa's birthday, upon leaving the club that night. Of course, she was scared, but they don't bury the scared. Therefore, she grabbed her gun from her pocketbook on the passenger seat, just as the black H2 Hummer was approaching the driver's side of her car.

Ebony was thinking of trying to outrun them, but she didn't think that her Infinity conveyed that kind of horsepower. She looked over at the truck and couldn't see the occupants for the dark tinted windows, but could sense them watching her, which gave her the only idea she could come up with.

Maintaining her current speed, with her left hand on the wheel, she raised her gun and pointed it at the truck, with the barrel rested on the window. Immediately, the H2 decelerated. Ebony's heart was beating triple time now. She knew for sure it was about to get ugly, but when she looked in her rearview, she saw that they had switched off the high beams and we're gradually dropping back. She didn't trust this, but she watched until they dropped out of sight.

Playa Ray

Chapter 10

"That's why you should've made Hakeem stay his ass in the parking lot until you came out!" Shonda vented, after Ebony informed them of her encounter with the mysterious truck, last night.

It was Saturday and the Queenz were on their way to Conyers, to meet with LKS, without the Queenzmen as he had instructed. Skeptical about the request, Shonda insisted they all wear vests, and be prepared to go down fighting, in case, Ray planned to use this meeting for anything other than what it was intended for.

"I didn't know what time I was gonna leave," Ebony, who was driving, now replied. "I didn't wanna leave him out there all night."

"You could've left him out there all year," Shonda insisted. "He gets paid to protect you. As a matter of fact, no Queen is to make any solo ventures without physical protection."

"I agree," Sheila, who was seated in the back with Theresa, chimed. "We could've lost you last night, Ebony."

"But y'all didn't," Ebony said, with a hint of attitude. "Can we please talk about something else?"

"This is serious, Ebony," Shonda said, looking over at her friend.

"I know," she replied. "But I made it through the ordeal, it's over."

"For now," Theresa stated. "We need to find out who they are before this shit gets outta hand. It's clear that we've been targeted by somebody we don't even know."

"For now, we just have to be extra careful," Sheila announced.

Shonda was in her thoughts, she knew it was possible that they could be targeted by somebody they didn't know. It was also possible that they could be targeted by somebody they did know, which was why she was precarious about Ray's request to show up without their Queenzmen. But she still couldn't think of any reason why he would want to harm them.

"Is this it?" Ebony asked, pulling the Denali into the parking lot of a small, abandoned building that still had a sign that promised *the best soul food on the planet.*

"Yeah, this is it," Shonda answered, pulling her gun from her pocketbook.

"Lock and load! Roll the windows down and keep an eye on the building. Anything moves, shoot to kill!"

Ebony and Sheila drew their guns as Theresa grabbed the Uzi from the rear compartment of the truck. They all lowered their windows, despite the cool air, and watched the building. Hearing the sounds of another vehicle pulling into the parking lot, they all looked back to see a black Lincoln Navigator with tinted windows. It parked three car spots from the right side of the GMC.

"Did he say what they were driving?" Sheila asked.

"Nope," Shonda answered, trying to see through the dark windows. "But this gotta be them."

It was confirmed when the driver's window rolled down. LKS's lieutenants were regarding them with expectant looks.

"We don't have all day," said the one with the ponytail, who was the driver.

Shonda knew what she had to do. "Ebony, watch the store! Sheila, watch the rear! Theresa, watch me. Trust nothing."

That said, Shonda placed her gun back into her pocketbook and dismounted. When she made it to the Lincoln, she pulled the rear door open, expecting to see Ray, but he wasn't there. Knowing that the deal had to be done, she climbed into the back seat, closed the door and rolled the window down, so Theresa could see her.

"Let me see the money," Ponytail demanded.

Shonda pulled the wad from her pocketbook and handed it to him. As he counted the money, Shonda glanced over at the other lieutenant, who had a handgun in his lap, and appeared to be surveying the area. Once Ponytail counted the money, he handed Shonda a large Ziploc bag containing a large number of multicolored pills, which reminded her of Skittles

"Those are double stacks," he told her.

"Okay," she replied, not knowing what the hell that meant. "So, how do I get in touch with him when I'm ready to re-up?"

"He'll contact you."

Saying nothing, Shonda rolled the window back up, stuff the pills into her pocketbook, got out, and return to the GMC.

"How's my, King?" Sheila asked once Shonda was back in the truck.

"He didn't come," she answered. "To the stash house, Ebony."

Shonda had called Ant and told him to meet them at the house. So, when they arrived, he was already parked in front of the house. They all assembled at the kitchen table as Ant explained to them the essentials of the pills. Moments after he left, Theresa and Ebony headed home, taking the truck. Shonda and Sheila retired to their rooms to dress down, being that they didn't plan on leaving the house tonight. They prepared and ate dinner together, then assembled in the living room to watch *Set It Off*. In the middle of the movie, Shonda's cell phone rang. The number on the screen was unfamiliar, but she answered it, anyway.

"Hello?"

"What's up?" A familiar voice asked.

"Who is this?"

"Trent."

"Oh!" she exclaimed. "What's going on?"

"Not too much, "he answered. "What you doing?"

"Watching, *Set it Off* with my cousin."

"So, I guess I'm interrupting, huh?"

"I've seen it over a hundred times," she replied, not wanting to end a call that she had been anticipating. "What you got going on around your way?"

"Shit, it's slow motion on my end," he told her. "I was hoping for some company."

"And who were you hoping to visit you?" she asked, concealing her excitement, knowing she was going to get some dick, tonight.

"I mean if you can't—"

"Who said I can't?" she cut in. "Don't be making assumptions."

Trent laughed. "Shit, my bad. So, you'll slide through?"

"Mmm-hmm." She looked over at Sheila who was regarding her with furrowed eyebrows.

"You know where I be posted at."

"A'ight."

"And where do you think you're going?" Sheila asked when Shonda ended her call.

"To the moon," she answered, getting up and heading for her room, walking fast.

"Uh-uh, heifer." Sheila chased behind her. "What happened to physical protection?"

"I got condoms," Shonda joked, looking through her closet for something to wear.

"So, you're just gonna break the rule you made, for some dick?" Sheila asked, flopping down on the bed.

"The rule was really made for you and Ebony," Shonda stated, now regarding her cousin. "I'm more worried about you and her. I already know Theresa can hold her own. My fear level is zero, so I'll flatline some shit with no hesitation."

"So, you'll be alright?"

"I should be," Shonda answered. "Y'all won't have to make funeral arrangements for me. If anything, y'all might have to bond me out."

After getting dressed and kissing her cousin on the cheek, Shonda was out, making sure to arm the alarm and lock the front door behind her. Then, she was in her car and on her way to East Lake Meadows, wondering why Trent had called her, all of a sudden, and wanted her to come over.

'*Of course, he wants some pussy*,' she thought.

But she was contemplating if she should give in to his whim or string him along like a puppet for a while. Yes, she figured, she would string him along until she found out how close he and Mario was. Then, she would consider the proximity of their friendship.

Shonda pulled into East Lake and drove with caution. She didn't like coming out here in the daytime. So, she was being extra careful, being that it was dark out. She pulled around to where she knew Trent would be. As always, he was on his post, accompanied by two other guys, which seems to be the only somebody's out. Shonda parked before she could figure out if he wanted her to get out. Or if he was going to come and get her. He was on his way to the car, as his friends set off in another direction.

"For a minute, I thought you stood me up," Trent said when he slid into the passenger seat.

"I stay in Norcross now," she informed him.

"I didn't know that," he said. "I guess you done moved on up like the Jefferson's, huh?"

"Pretty much."

"That's what's up," he told her. "You said you needed to talk to me about something."

"Yeah, I did," she answered, almost forgetting her sole purpose of this visit. "It's about, Mario."

"I'd already figured that. What about him?"

"First, I wanna know how the deal went bad," she answered. "Second, I wanna know who he supposedly stole from. Then, I wanna know how close you two were."

"You really wanna know?" Trent asked, looking into her eyes.

"Yeah, I do," she answered, returning his gaze. "In that order."

Trent sighed. "I guess I can tell you. Hell, everybody else knows. Mario asked me if I wanted to go in half on a key with him. Of course, I was with it. We got in touch with—"

His words were cut off when the driver and passenger windows, simultaneously, came crashing in and guns were shoved in their faces by three masked men, two on the passenger side and one on the driver's side.

"Cut the car off," the one on the driver's side commanded, while the other two were ordering Trent to get out.

Shonda did as she was told, thinking about her gun in her pocketbook between the seats.

"Now, gimme the keys," the same one demanded.

"Hell no," Shonda protested. "If you're gonna take the car, take the car. But I'm not giving you my keys. Fuck that!"

She looked over to see Trent getting out of the car with his hands up. She watched as they escorted him to a dark-colored van that was sitting behind her car. The third man joined them. Once they'd forced Trent into the cargo area of the van and climbed in behind him, the van sped off.

'*What the fuck just happened*?' Shonda thought, looking around seeing that people were coming out of their apartments.

Now, she was wondering if someone was sending out a grave message to them, by harming people close to them, which was the same thing the Kingz had gone through before they were murdered. Shonda had a lot of things running through her mind, but right now, she had to get the hell away from East Lake Meadows. There was no way in hell she was going to call for a tow truck. That would definitely trigger the police if they weren't already on the way. She was not in the mood to answer questions she really didn't have answers to. Plus, she didn't want Trent's neighbors to think she was complicit to his abduction, which is how she would perceive it if she was on the outside looking in.

"Fuck this," she said to herself, starting her car, glad that she didn't give up her keys and speeding out of the parking lot like a getaway driver.

****

At the warehouse, Ray was in the office, seated, staring at the Mona Lisa painting, although his mind was elsewhere. He had gotten a call from Poppo, informing him that he and his men were on their way with *that*. Ray didn't doubt his head of security, which was why he'd been patiently waiting at the Palace for almost two hours. He'd even pulled the wooden chair with straps from the trailer.

Once Poppo called again and informed him that they were out front, Ray went out to the loading dock, where he'd stationed the chair. Being that the loading dock was only constructed for tractor trailers, Ray left the door open for them. He had never seen Trent, but he was pretty sure that the man who was blindfolded with a red bandana and escorted by Poppo, Stone, Hot Ru and Murda Ru, had to be him. Poppo ordered his men to strap him into the chair and to put their masks back on.

"No need for the masks," Ray stated, knowing Trent wouldn't be able to identify anyone after tonight. He stood in front of Trent.

"Take the blindfold off!"

Stone snatched the bandana off and wrapped it around his hand.

"Do you know who I am, Trent?" Ray asked him.

Trent studied Ray's face for a few seconds. "Nah."

"I'm LKS," Ray told him. "I was told that I owe you money. What do I owe you for?'

"I took that hit."

"What hit?"

"Mario," Trent answered. "The nigga that ran off with—"

"Can you prove it?" Ray cut him off.

"Man, I knocked the nigga off," Trent insisted.

"That's not what I asked," Ray said, ready to get this over with.

"Can you prove it or not?"

"To be honest," Trent started. "I can't prove it, but—"

"Off this clown," Ray commanded, as he turned and made for the office to retrieve his jacket.

He exited the office and before he reached the front door, he heard three rapid reports from a gun, indicating that Trent was no more.

Chapter 11

Shonda still couldn't believe what happened to Trent, last night, which had her thinking about the incident with Clarence and wondering if the same guys who'd kidnapped Trent, were the same ones who murdered Clarence in front of her. If this was so, then it was viable that they had some professionals after them.

She hadn't told the other Queenz that she was with Clarence when he was murdered and didn't plan on telling them about Trent. But considering Ebony's close encounter the other night, Shonda knew she had to bring it to their attention and see if they could make some kind of sense of these encounters, which was why she'd called a Queenz meeting and they were all now assembled at the kitchen table of the stash house.

"I already figured you were with Clarence when that happened," Sheila said after Shonda spoke on both events.

"How?'

"I saw blood on the bathroom sink when I got home that night," Sheila answered.

"That doesn't mean—"

"I heard the message he'd left on the phone about not getting his order," Sheila cut her off. "I saw the news. They said he was murdered in Kroger's parking lot, on Howell Mill Road. The same place we meet him. It wasn't hard to put two and two together."

"I see," Shonda regarded her cousin with admiration.

"And they told you to find another occupation if you didn't want to end up like your boyfriend?" Theresa asked.

"Yeah."

"Clearly they couldn't have thought Clarence was your boyfriend?" Theresa said.

"Why not?"

"Because," Theresa started. "Why would you have to make a drop to your boyfriend in a place like that?'

"Well, who else would they—" That's when it dawned on her. "Oh, shit, King James, they were talking about, King James!"

"So, the same people that killed the Kingz, are after us?" Sheila asked as if she was surprised.

Theresa knew where this was going. "Sheila don't be so quick to jump to conclusions. Shonda, what do you suggest? Should we fold?"

Shonda was quiet, she had got into the drug game for a reason, whatever that was, and did not intend to fold because somebody couldn't stand the fact that they were being rivaled by women.

"What do you suggest, Queen Theresa?" Shonda asked.

"I'm in it for the long run," Theresa insisted. "Fear is not an option. It's a choice and I don't fear nan' nigga."

Shonda nodded her approval. "Queen, Ebony?"

"I'ma ride with my girls," she replied.

"And last but not least," Shonda started. "Queen Sheila?"

"Queen shit," Sheila exclaimed. "It's ride or die."

"That's what's up." Shonda nodded, looking around at her girls. "I broke my own rule last night, but from now on, we don't ride, unless we have physical protection. I don't believe in hiding, so if ever y'all feel like y'all wanna go to the club or a bar, I'm all for it. We'll just have to be careful. Right now, we have a lot of product to get off. Especially a large bag of ecstasy pills. Let's get this money."

The Queenz did just that. All week, they were all work and no play. The cocaine and weed was moving at a steady pace, but they were catching hell with the pills. It seemed as if most pill poppers had their own dealers. LKS was thrown into the equation, whenever someone felt the need to mention their supplier's name.

Now, it was Friday afternoon and Sheila and Shonda had just made it back home from making drops with Theresa and Ebony, who had dropped them off. Sheila went inside the house, while Shonda checked the mailbox. There was a letter from the Dekalb County Superior Courthouse, but she didn't open it until she made it to her bedroom and flopped down on the bed. The legal documents stated that she had a court date, next month. Instantly she thought about Lieutenant Anita Mallery, who she'd assaulted at the Dekalb County Jail, along with Captain Shaw who'd dropped his charge against her. She already knew Mallery was going to pursue hers.

"Shonda!" Sheila yelled out from somewhere in the house. "Telephone."

Shonda didn't hear the business phone ring, but she got up and went into the kitchen, where Sheila was standing with one hand poised on her hip and the phone's receiver in the other, held out to Shonda. Plus, Sheila was pouting, so Shonda could pretty much guess who the caller was.

"Queen Shonda," she announced through the mouthpiece of the phone.

"It's LKS," Ray's voice came back. "You got a minute?'

"How may I help you?" Shonda assumed formality for the sake of Sheila, who was still regarding her with that look she found funny and cute at the same time.

"We need to meet," he told her. "I made reservations for two at The Enchanting, in Smyrna. Eight o'clock. Can you make it?"

"Is this a business date?" she asked, trying her best not to look at Sheila.

"Yes, it is," he answered. "And you don't need your guards."

"That's one of our rules," she told him. "I can't move without physical protection. But I'll only bring one of our men."

"That's fine," he accepted. "Do you know where the restaurant is?"

"Yeah."

"I'll see you then."

"Alright." Shonda hung up the phone and headed for her room.

"A business date!" Sheila exclaimed, following behind her.

Shonda rolled her eyes as she entered her room. "That's all it is, baby."

Sheila smacked her lips, "Y'all gotta go on a date to discuss business?"

"I guess he wants to talk to me about something important," Shonda said, now regarding her cousin, who was leaned against the threshold of the door, with her arms folded over her chest, still conveying that funny, but cute look.

"Besides, maybe I can find out something about the people who are targeting us. So, this date could be beneficial."

"Mmm-hmm." Sheila stormed out of the room.

Shonda felt sorry for her cousin. She'd always been aware of the feelings that Sheila has for Ray, but now, she was showing signs of distrust towards someone who wouldn't dream of hurting her in that way, or any other way. Shonda knew she would have to have a talk with Sheila, but it was not going to be tonight, which was why she remained in her room until seven twenty. She'd already called Ant and Shelton. Ant was going to accompany her, and Shelton was going to sit outside the house until she returned. She showered, then searched her closet for an evening dress. She tried to find one that didn't bear too much cleavage but realized she didn't possess one.

After finding something to wear, she grabbed her keys and pocketbook, then made for the front door, realizing Sheila was still in her bedroom, with the door closed. Not willing to entertain any thoughts of Sheila right now, Shonda reset the alarm and locked the door behind her as she made for her Ford Mustang that was now painted yellow with a black racing stripe running along the hood and trunk. Across the street, Ant and Shelton were standing outside their cars, talking. Seeing her, they did some kind of handshake, then got into their cars.

Getting to Smyrna, it didn't take long for Shonda to find the restaurant. It also didn't take long for her to find a parking spot, being that the parking lot was almost empty.

"How long do you plan on being in there?" Ant, who parked beside her, asked when she got out of the car.

"I can't say," she answered. "This is a business meeting, so there is no telling. But if you plan on venturing off, try not to go too far."

Shonda didn't want to leave him in the parking lot like that, but he gets paid to protect her. Plus, she'd promised her girls, she wouldn't break the rule again. So, sticking to her guns, she turned and strutted towards the entrance of the restaurant.

"Your name, ma'am?" a young white female sitting at the front desk, inquired.

Shonda had forgotten about this part. She was about to state her full name, then realized Ray didn't know her full name. Therefore, she went with what she knew best. "Queen Shonda," she asserted.

"Right this way, ma'am," the female said, leading the way. "Your date is already here."

Indeed, her date was already seated at their table. Unexpectedly, Ray pulled out her chair for her, which had her feeling as if this was not a business date after all.

"Moet?" Ray asked once he'd taken his seat.

"Sure," she answered.

Ray pulled the bottle of Moet out of the bucket of ice and while he poured them both a glass, Shonda surveyed the restaurant to see that there were only three other tables occupied by couples.

"Thank you," Shonda took a sip from her glass. "So, what's the reason for this meeting?"

"You wanna order something to eat, first?"

"Perhaps."

Ray flagged down a waiter and after they placed their orders, asked, "How are y'all doing on the X?"

"Is that a trick question?" Shonda asked, figuring he already knew they were catching hell.

Ray appeared dumbfounded. "Why would that be a trick question?"

"It's moving kinda slow," she answered. "It seems that LKS has that on lock."

"Nonsense," Ray said, sipping his drink. "You just have to know where to look and who to connect with."

"That's why we chose, LKS," she told him. "We were hoping he could point us in the right direction."

"Perhaps," he said, as the waiter placed their food on the table. Once the waiter left, he said, "The Queenz are doing really well, from what I hear. And I respect their grind to the fullest. But I guess I can help them expand."

"You would really do that?"

"If I'm your supplier."

"Deal," Shonda prompted, pretty much excluding Tino and his ex-girlfriend discount. "Is that what you called me out here for?'

"No," Ray looked down at his food as if contemplating, then said, "There's a dancer at Strokers."

"Felicia?"

Ray seemed surprised. "You know, Felicia?'

"I've met her," Shonda explained. "Black's baby's momma. What about her?'

"I wasn't talking about her," Ray said, then told her who he was talking about and what he needed Shonda to do.

"I can handle that," Shonda told him.

"When?"

"Tomorrow night," she answered. "But you'll also have to do something for me."

****

The following day, the Queenz were out on their runs, accompanied by the Queenzmen. Making it to Bankhead, Shonda turned the GMC onto Cedar Avenue and up to Montez's house. Approaching the front door, they all noticed the bright orange sticker on his car's windshield that read: *Funeral* and exchanged glances. Shonda knocked, seconds later, Montez opened the door. He was wearing black dress pants, a white dress shirt that was untucked, and no shoes.

"Come on in," he told them. "I just got back, I was hoping I could change clothes before y'all got here."

"Whose funeral you attend?" Shonda asked once they'd entered.

"Olivia's."

"Olivia's!" Shonda and Theresa both exclaimed.

"The smoker?" Shonda asked, hoping like hell he wasn't talking about her.

"Yeah," he confirmed. "Somebody killed her in that same house, last Friday. City workers came by, yesterday and knocked the house down."

"You mean to tell me somebody actually killed that nice lady?" Shonda asked, feeling sorry for Olivia.

"Shot her in the head, twice," Montez replied.

"Where's Dee?" Sheila asked.

"He went home to change."

"Did he go, too?" Shonda wanted to know.

"Hell, it seemed like the whole city went," he told her. "I've never seen that many Drop Squad chains in one place."

"Why were they deep like that?" Shonda inquired.

"Her brother is one of the head niggas in Drop Squad," he informed. "They stormed every house on Grove Street, looking for answers. I hate it for whoever did that shit."

'*Me too*,' Shonda thought.

Especially if they were the same ones who killed Mario. Perhaps they realized they'd made a fatal mistake leaving Olivia behind, after killing Mario in front of her. Now, she was wondering if those were the two guys, she'd seen Trent approach in East lake meadows, two weeks ago. The news was still reporting that he was missing, after being possibly abducted.

After leaving Montez's home, the Queenz made their last two drops, dismissed the Queenzmen and retired to Zaxby's. Where they were now dining.

"So, when are you gonna tell Tino about the change of plans?" Theresa, who was seated beside Shonda, asked her.

"Huh? Oh." Shonda had heard Theresa, although she was thinking about the conversation they'd had with Montez, earlier. "I guess I'll tell him whenever he calls."

"He won't be too happy about that," Ebony, who was seated across the table with Sheila, pointed out.

"He'll get over it," Shonda replied. "It's all business."

"I gotta use the restroom," Sheila announced.

Shonda was supposed to escort her but being that she had been waiting for a moment to speak with Theresa, she implored Ebony to accompany Sheila.

"You got plans tonight?' Shonda asked Theresa, once they were alone.

"Not that I know of," Theresa answered. "What's up?"

"I gotta handle some business. And where I am going, I'd rather take you, than Ant."

"I don't even care what it is," Theresa said. "Count me in."

Shonda knew she could depend on Theresa. She dropped Theresa and Ebony off at home, then she and Sheila made for their own. She didn't tell Sheila what she was up to, but she did tell her she and Theresa were going out tonight and Ebony was going to keep her company. Again, Shonda opted for her Japanese wig and black eyeglasses. While she was standing at her dressing mirror, doing a last-minute inspection of herself, Sheila appeared in the doorway with her arms folded over her chest.

"Did Ray even mention my name, last night?" she asked.

'*Oh Lord*,' Shonda thought, but said, "We were discussing business, Sheila. But you did come up in our conversation."

Sheila smacked her lips.

"You did," Shonda insisted.

"What y'all say about me?"

Before Shonda could come up with something, the doorbell rang. She was relieved because she didn't want to tell Sheila how her name came up and what was said about her, at least, not yet.

"You gonna get the door?" Shonda asked Sheila who was still standing there as if she had not heard the doorbell.

After seconds of wavering, Sheila made for the front door. Shonda quickly grabbed her things and made it to the living room, just as Ebony and Theresa were entering the house. Within minutes, they were in Theresa's car on their way to Club Strokers.

"Now, I'm curious," Theresa said as she drove along the interstate. "What's at Club Strokers?"

"I have to find out some information about a dancer who works there," Shonda answered. "If she still works there, but this shouldn't take long."

Making it to the club, Theresa pulled her Oldsmobile into the half-filled parking lot. After about six minutes of waiting in line, they entered the club and automatically looked towards the D.J. booth to see who'd replaced Spenz. He wasn't familiar to Shonda, so she didn't regard him but for a few seconds, before looking around for Felicia, whose assistance she was going to need. Well, it didn't take long for her to spot the blonde, who was on stage, already down to her G-string and heels, working the pole, while a group of men tossed bills at her.

Along with Theresa in tow, Shonda approached the stage, pulling a twenty-dollar bill from her pocket, waving it at Felicia. Seeing her, Felicia walked over and squatted down in front of Shonda, with her legs spread eagle.

"I gotta get me one of these," she said, fingering the bang of Shonda's wig.

Shonda planted the bill in Felicia's G-string. "We need to talk."

"I'm almost done," Felicia told her, then returned to her dancing.

Shonda and Theresa grabbed drinks from the bar and found a table where they sat and surveyed the club. Once the song playing ended, they watched Felicia gather her bills and clothes off the stage and disappear through the dressing room door. It was almost twenty minutes later, when she emerged from the dressing room, wearing a black leather G-string with top and knee-high boots.

"Lap dance or table dance?" Felicia asked, standing in front of Shonda.

"Neither," Shonda answered. "Is there a dancer here by the name of, Cherry?"

"She used to dance here," Felicia answered, then regarded Theresa. "Aren't you one of the Queenz?"

"I'm Queen, Theresa," she answered with a hint of an attitude.

"And which King were you fucking?"

"That's none of your business."

"Felicia!" Shonda intervened.

"Why can't she just answer the question?" Felicia was now standing akimbo. "You want me to help you, but she can't answer one simple question?'

"She dated, King Fred," Shonda answered. "Now, what happened to, Cherry, did she quit?'

"She quit dancing," Felicia said. "She's a bartender now."

"Where?"

Felicia nodded towards the bar. "Over there. The bitch with the red hair."

Shonda looked over at the bar. The bitch that Felicia was referring to, was the one who'd fixed their drinks. Now, she had to find out if her name was Lisa and if Fred had given her any kind of key. After thanking Felicia and telling Theresa she'd be back, Shonda made her way to the bar, where Cherry was wiping down with a rag.

"Cherry!" Shonda called her name as if they were old friends. Cherry looked as if she was trying to remember Shonda. "We've never met," Shonda clarified. "But I was dating, King James at the same time you were dating, King Fred."

"Okay," she replied with a *so-what* attitude.

Shonda retracted her tone, for the sake of her mission. "Can I ask you what your full name is?"

"You can," Cherry answered, "But I'm not going to tell you."

'Strike two,' Shonda thought. "Well, did Fred give you any kind of key or keys?"

"No, he did not."

"Okay, thank you." Shonda returned to their table. "Let's go."

"Is it her?" Theresa asked as they made for the exit.

"She wouldn't tell me her real name," Shonda answered. "But she said Fred didn't give her any keys."

"Did she seem convincing?'

"Nope."

"And what's with this, Felicia, bitch?"

"That's Black's baby momma," Shonda told her. "I think she's trying to find out who was fucking him. Which got me wondering what she'll do to Ebony if they ever bump heads."

"Please," Theresa said. "That bitch don't want those problems."

"I hope not," said Shonda.

"So, what now?" Theresa asked once they were back inside the car.

"I guess we head on home."

"Now, that doesn't sound like the Queen Shonda I know," Theresa declared. "The Queen Shonda I know wouldn't fold that damn easy."

Shonda eyed her friend. "I'm almost scared to ask this, but what you got stirring up in that evil mind of yours?"

"Shit, we wait until that red-headed bitch comes out," Theresa said. "And we make that hoe tell us what we need to know."

That's exactly what they did. They'd waited for almost five hours for the club to close. While waiting, Shonda reflected on what Felicia said about knowing every car of the club's employees and hoped like hell Cherry exited before her.

She did.

"You ready?' Theresa asked, donning the ball cap she'd had in the trunk.

"Let's do it," Shonda replied. "And no bloodshed."

By the time they'd dismounted, they saw Cherry climbing into a dark-colored Lexus mid-sized SUV. The truck started, but before she could make a move, they were at her driver's door, Theresa tapping on the window with the barrel of her gun.

"Don't try no stupid shit!" Theresa told her. "Roll the window down." She did. "Gimme your license."

"My driver's license?'

"Nah, your real estate license," Theresa sassed. "Bitch, gimme the damn license."

Shonda looked around, while Cherry dug into her pocketbook for her license, handing them to Theresa.

"Monique Karen Stevens," Theresa said for Shonda to hear. "Now, did King Fred give you any keys?"

"Nope," Cherry answered, snatching her license out of Theresa's hand. "Now, if y'all don't mind, I have a husband and child to get home to."

Cherry rolled her window back up, backed out of her parking spot and raced out of the lot as if her husband was timing her arrival.

Chapter 12

It was November thirteenth, two thousand five and Sheila was pretty much in a good mood, being that it was her birthday, which now made her twenty-seven years old. Plus, the girls had gotten together and planned her a birthday bash at Club Central Station, in East Point and managed to book *Ludacris, Lil' Jon, the Eastside Boys*, and *Young Jeezy* to perform, with an opening act from Vika, an underground female rapper.

Today, was also Shonda's court date. She didn't want anyone to go with her, but Theresa insisted, considering their physical protection rule. Sheila figured Shonda didn't want them to come because she planned to meet up with Ray somewhere, being that they'd been communicating a lot and privately on the phone which angered Sheila. She knew Shonda was aware of the feelings she had for Ray, yet and still, she paraded around as if nothing was amiss.

Sheila didn't plan to dwell on that. She'd promised herself she would have a wonderful birthday, no matter what, which was why she was now at the Mall of Georgia, in search of a birthday outfit that didn't resemble anything she already has. Now, for the fourth time, she emerged from the small dressing booth, in an orange, long-sleeved dress that showed off every curve of her body, with matching low-cut, kitten heeled boots. Shelton, who was seated just outside the booth, was her only audience.

"What about this one?" she asked him, turning so he could get a full view of her body, in which she knew he was enjoying.

"I like it," he said, seductively eyeing her body as he'd done the first three times.

"Shelton, you like everything I try on," she accused, thrusting her hands on her hips.

"That's because you look good in everything you wear," he replied, looking into her eyes through his black-framed eyeglasses.

Sheila already knew Shelton wanted her, which was why she always felt safe around him, knowing he wouldn't let anyone harm her. He seemed like a nice guy, but she planned to keep it strictly business. So, disregarding his compliment, she retreated to the booth, disrobed and re-donned her jean suit. After paying for the dress and boots, they left the boutique and headed for the Chic-Fil-A restaurant within the mall, where they now shared a table.

After minutes of enjoying their meal in silence, Shelton said, "You gotta be a strong woman to go without a man, as long as you have. Most women couldn't do that."

"That's because most women don't have self-restraint," Sheila told him. "They let their hormones overpower their minds and end up laying with any and every man, for the pleasure of a nut, which is unladylike. A Queen has standards."

"Could you see yourself messing with somebody like me?" he asked.

Sheila almost choked on her chicken sandwich and had to use her lemonade to help swallow the piece that was lodged in her trachea.

"Boy, don't you have a woman at home?" Sheila asked, already knowing the answer.

"She has other men," Shelton told her.

"You don't know that for sure," she said, knowing how quick people would make those accusations against their mates.

"Trust me," he said looking into her eyes. "I know what I'm talking about."

"So, why are you still with her?"

"I guess until I find somebody else." He reached over, placing his hand on top of her hand that was resting on the table. "Somebody like you."

Sheila didn't know what to think, but her heart was fluttering and being that she hadn't been with a man since Andrew, her hormones had come alive, full force. Now, she was looking at Shelton in a new light. Who knows? Depending on how she was feeling after her party tonight, he might get lucky. It's not like Ray has any interest in her.

****

"Girl, I wanna come to the birthday bash," Khandi, who was doing Ebony's hair, said. "But sixty dollars a lil' too steep for my purse."

"Why didn't y'all book T.I. with his sexy ass?" Tammi asked, who was washing a customer's hair.

"He's on tour," Ebony answered. "He was the first one we called for."

"Y'all still got a mean line-up," Michelle said. "Luda, Lil' Jon and Jeezy's gonna have that thing stupid crunk. Shoot, I might stop through."

"I know y'all paid a grip for this party," Khandi asserted. "What about food and alcohol?"

Food and alcohol are free."

After Khandi finished with Ebony's hair, she chatted with the girls for a good twenty minutes, then made her exit. Being that she'd already bought Sheila's birthday present and had enough time on her hands, she drove out to her mother's house, where she used her key to let herself in. She found her mother mopping the kitchen floor.

"Oh!" her mother exclaimed, noticing Ebony. "I thought you were Erica and her boyfriend."

"What boyfriend?"

"Ted," she answered. "The one who—"

"They're on their way over here?" Ebony cut in, hoping like hell she wasn't about to blow their cover, being that Ted still didn't know they were sisters.

"They were already here," Ms. Davis answered. "They went to that fish place up the street to get us something. Have you met him?"

"Yeah, I've met him," she rejoined. "Look Ma, I just stopped by for a minute. I have to prepare for Sheila's birthday party. I'll see you Sunday, for dinner."

"Okay, baby."

Ebony kissed her mother, then made the quickest exit she'd ever made. She started her car, but as she was pulling out of the driveway, Ted's Escalade turned onto the street. Seeing this, she detoured and drove to the other end of the street, which was a dead end, where she parked, to wait for them to enter the house. As the truck pulled into the driveway, her cell phone rang. Erica's number was on the screen.

"Hello?"

"Beauty and brains," Erica prompted. "I guess we got lucky and ended up with both, huh? Oh, the Queenz are having a birthday bash tonight, at Central Station. I guess it's one of their birthdays. Me and my boyfriend are going. You wanna join us?"

"Are you serious?" Ebony asked, watching them as they carried food and drinks towards the house.

"Of course," Erica answered. "And don't worry. When it comes to playing poker, I'm that bitch."

Making it home from court, Shonda removed her court clothes and chose to walk around in her panties and bra, until it was almost time for the Queenz meeting that would be held before they set off for the club. Shonda was searching the refrigerator for something to snack on when Sheila entered the kitchen with a shopping bag.

"Girl put some clothes on," Sheila said. "What if Shelton would've come in with me?"

"I guess he would've had something to talk about with the rest of them," she answered, closing the refrigerator, facing her cousin. "You ready for tonight?"

"Yeah."

"The girls are gonna bring your gifts over when they come," Shonda confirmed. "Like I said, you'll get mine at the club."

"Okay," Sheila replied. "So, what happened at court?"

"My lawyer asked for a continuation."

"Did Mallery show up?"

"You know that bitch showed up," Shonda answered, shaking her head. "I had to summon all the willpower, not to charge that bitch like a raging bull and choke her ass out. That's why I didn't want you to come. I didn't need you catching the same charge I'm trying to beat."

The Queenz meeting was at nine. Shonda and Sheila had donned their party clothes and pulled out their tiaras. Theresa and Ebony showed up in the white stretched Cadillac Escalade, driven by one of Phillip's employees and escorted by Queenzmen. Phillip was with them but being that the Queenz were about to have a meeting, he had to wait outside with the others.

"Happy birthday, heifer!" Ebony said, upon entering the house, handing Sheila a small gift bag and kissing her on the cheek.

"Thank you," Sheila said, looking into the bag at some expensive perfume.

"I had this made for you," Theresa said, unrolling a large, white beach towel with Mickey Mouse in a suit and crown and Minnie Mouse in a dress and tiara. "It's you and Ray," she added, sparking laughter from the others.

"We need to go ahead and start the meeting," Shonda said, looking at her watch.

Once Sheila had taken her gifts to her room, they all assembled at the kitchen table.

"Alright, Queenz," Shonda started, looking around at her girls, who all looked like some true royal bitches with their tiaras on, "Like we all know, this party has been highly broadcasted. So, if anybody is really after us, this would be their chance to try and pull something off. We all had a choice to wear our bullet-proof vests. Sheila's the only one who chose not to. Pocketbooks are not allowed in the club, but we're taking ours in, be watchful at all times. Trust nothing! Drink, but don't drink to the point where you lose focus on what's going on around you. I want y'all to have fun because we spent too much money not to. But don't lose focus. Any questions?"

"Should we tell our men about the black truck?" Theresa asked. "That way they'll already be on point, just in case these guys decide they wanna pull that scare tactic shit, tonight."

"I wanna tell them," Shonda started, "But I feel we should keep that to ourselves for the time being. I trust them to do what I pay them to do, but you never know who's behind what these days. Especially in the drug game. But if y'all feel otherwise, we can call them in here right now and put them on point." After no one spoke, she said, "Shit, let's get our party on."

****

Ray couldn't believe he'd let Shonda trick him into attending Sheila's birthday bash. Well, it was pretty much his fault, because when he'd sent her on that mission to Club Strokers, although she didn't report back with any useful information, this was what she'd wanted in return. But she really wanted more than that. She was intentionally trying to hook him and Sheila up with each other, telling him how crazy she was about him and that she had not been with a man in a year. Each time they talk, she would always talk about Sheila.

Sheila did seem like a decent female. Plus, she was fine as hell! But he didn't want to get attached to another female, which was why he opted for the likes of escort services and massage parlors. But a deal was a deal, which was why he was now seated in the back of the Lincoln Navigator, driven by Joe and trailed by BJ and Rick, in BJ's Chevy Impala, as they pulled into the packed parking lot of Club Central station. Ray had entertained the thought of assuming his crown, robe, and Kingz necklace and attending the party as King Ray, but thought against it, feeling that this might not be the right time and not wanting to put the Queenz lives in jeopardy with his selfish stunt.

Once they parked, they made for the entrance, where Ray used the *Special Guest* pass Shonda had given him, to get in. The bouncers didn't frisk them, which was good, because they were all carrying. When they entered the club, the crowd was rocking their heads and singing along with Young Jeezy's *Bottom of the Map*. Above the stage, was a large banner that read: *Happy Birthday Queen Sheila!*

Approaching the VIP booth, Ray saw that the Queenz were out of their seats, grooving to the music. But who really caught his eyes, was Sheila in that orange, snug fitted dress that broadly showed off her ass and hips, which did something to him, sexually. They noticed him as their men stepped in front of him to block the entrance of the booth.

"Let him in," Shonda told them.

Once they'd cleared the way, Ray told his squad to stand by, then entered the booth. Once again, they greeted him with hugs. That's when he noticed another man sitting on the long sofa, who nodded at him. Ray nodded back.

"Am I allowed to give you a birthday present?" Ray asked Sheila, who was smiling from ear to ear.

"You already did," she answered, prompting laughter from everyone.

Ray didn't expect that one, but he did manage to smile. He pulled a small jewelry box from his pocket, handing it to her. The girls gathered around as she opened it and marveled at the diamond tennis bracelet. Taking the initiative, Ray pulled the bracelet from the box and fastened it around her right wrist.

"Happy birthday," he told her.

"Two times," Shonda added, nudging her in the side with her elbow.

Thank y'all!" Sheila said, wrapping her arms around Ray's neck as he wrapped his around her waist.

Her body was so soft and warm, Ray couldn't escape an erection to save his life. Feeling this, he unwrapped his arms. Sheila only loosened her arms and was now staring into his eyes. Ray saw it coming and did nothing to prevent it. She pressed her full, soft lips against his and he automatically parted them to allow her tongue to probe his mouth for his tongue. As he closed his eyes and clamped his hands on her waist. For a second, it felt as if they were the only two people on the planet until the other Queenz began cheering.

"Go, girl!"

"Claim your King, girl."

This caused them to laugh, breaking their kiss. Sheila was happy, but she wasn't the only one. Shonda had been constantly beating Ray's ears up about how good of a woman her cousin was and asked him to, at least, consider taking her out. But, after seeing this, there was no doubt in her mind that the connection was already made.

"You do plan on staying for a while, right?" Shonda asked Ray.

"Of course, he does," Sheila prompted, grabbing him by the hand and pulling him towards the sofa. "I'll make sure your men are fed."

She did just that, the caterers set up a large dining table in the booth and piled it with myriad party-friendly dishes. Sheila saw to it that their men, as well as Ray's men, were fed. During the course of them getting their grub on, Ebony introduced Ray to Phillip, making sure to refer to him as LKS.

"Bullshit!" Phillip exclaimed. "The LKS?"

"That's me," Ray answered, now noticing he looked vaguely familiar.

"I didn't even think you were real," Phillip admitted. "I mean, I didn't think you were one person. I thought it was some kind of organization."

"It's just me," Ray told him.

"I need some fresh air," Sheila said into Ray's ear. "Go outside with me."

Before Ray could muster a yay or nay, she stood, pulling him up by his hand.

"And where the hell y'all going?" Theresa inquired.

"I need some fresh air," Sheila answered. "We'll be right back."

"You're going outside?" Shonda was skeptical. "Did you hear anything that was said at the meeting?"

"Every word." Sheila grabbed her pocketbook. "I'm on point. Plus, I'm well protected."

Shonda didn't know what her cousin was up to, but she could tell her mind was already made up. So, reluctantly, she gave in. Besides, she didn't believe that Ray would let anything happen to her. Plus, she assumed his four-man squad was heavily armed and ready to handle anything that even looked as if they wanted to try something. Thinking this, she looked over at Ray's men as he and Sheila were leaving the booth. There his two lieutenants and—

'*Oh, shit*!' She thought.

She couldn't believe she was actually looking at the two guys Trent had approached in East Lake Meadows. The same two guys who were probably responsible for killing Mario and Olivia.

Happy birthday!

"Oh, thank you, Ted." Ebony had told them that he and Erica were coming, so Sheila wasn't surprised. "Y'all having a good time?"

While they were talking, Ray was hoping she didn't introduce him. He didn't want too many people to know that LKS was in the building. As far as he knew, LKS may have more enemies than King Ray.

After conversating with Erica and Ted, they proceeded on. They were just beyond the exit, when Andrew entered the club, blocking their path.

"Hey, Sheila," he greeted. "You know, I've just recently found out you and Shonda are a part of the Queenz? And I'm still surprised."

Before Sheila could do or say anything to him, Shelton stepped between them. That's when she realized, she'd forgotten all about Shelton and his feelings for her, when Ray showed up. So, she was sure he'd witnesses the kiss and perceived how happy she was around him. Now, she was feeling a bit sorry for Shelton, although he had a woman at home, whether she was a slut or not.

"Shelton, you should be with the rest of the Queenz," Sheila said to his back.

He turned to face her. "I'm going by the rule, you know you can't—"

"I have physical protection, Shelton," she cut him off, unable to look in his eyes. "Get back on your post."

She saw the menacing look he'd given Ray, before storming off. Ray had also seen it, in fact, it was not the first time. While they were in the booth, Ray had periodically caught the nigga sizing him up. Clearly, he had a *Love Jones* for Sheila's fine ass and Ray couldn't blame him. He just better stay in his place.

"Andrew, I don't have anything to say to you." Sheila turned on him with malice. "And you should already know this."

"I understand that," he said, apologetically, nodding to Ray. "This ya' man?"

"Yes, it is," she answered with much attitude.

"You got you a good woman," he told Ray, before disappearing into the crowd.

"So, who was that?" Ray asked Sheila, once they'd exited the club and began crossing the parking lot.

"The last man I was with," she answered, taking his hands in hers. "I caught him in the sixty-nine position with another skank."

"Straight up?"

"Yep," she answered like a small child. "In my bed."

Shonda didn't tell Ray about this, perhaps, it was none of his business. He couldn't help but think of Sylvia and how he'd caught her mouth around another man's dick. Now, he felt, he could relate to Sheila a little more, seeing that they both have sustained similar ordeals.

"Is the party over already?" the white male driver of the Queenz limousine, asked once they approached, being that he was already standing outside the truck.

"Of course not," Sheila answered. "We just need a little privacy, if you don't mind."

"I sure don't."

The driver opened the rear door for them. While helping Sheila into the truck, Ray couldn't help but look at her ass, seeing that she was wearing a thong. As soon as he climbed in beside her and before the driver could fully secure the door, she was all over him, gently kissing him on the neck, then moving her mouth to his ear, first nibbling on his earlobe, before sticking her tongue in his ear and licking it in a circular motion. Ray was so turned on his manhood threatened to burst through his pants. Sheila must've sensed it because she reached down and gripped it through his jeans.

"Can I have this, tonight?" she whispered in his ear.

"What's with you and this bodyguard of yours?" Ray wanted to know before he agreed or disagreed to do anything with her.

"Shelton?" she asked, releasing her grip on his penis.

"Whatever his name is." Ray glanced out at his men, who were standing beside the truck. "Do y'all have something going on?"

"You mean, sexually?"

Ray just looked at her.

"No, we're not having sex," she swore, holding his left hand in both of hers. "He has a crush on me, but that's as far as that goes. There will never be anything between us."

"Well, you need to make sure he understands that."

"Do I detect jealousy?" she joked, a smirk on her face. Ray did not find it funny. "Okay, I'm sorry, my King," she cooed, kissing him on the lips. "Now, can you answer my question?"

"Don't you have to confer with the other Queenz?"

"I can do that, right now." Shonda pulled her cellular from her pocketbook and dialed Shonda's number.

"That pussy ought to be on fire, with your hot ass," Shonda boomed through the phone, over Lil' Jon and the Eastside Boys, 'Bia'.

"It is," Sheila replied, smiling casting a glance at Ray. "Thank you for the present."

"You're welcome, baby," she answered. "How long do y'all plan on staying out there?"

"That's what I was calling about. I plan on spending the night with, Ray."

"Whaattt!" Shonda exclaimed. "He's gonna give you some birthday dick, too?"

"And you know I'm in dire need of that," Sheila pointed out. "Will y'all be alright without me?"

"We should be,' answered Shonda. "We got enough protection. Plus, I got Sistah Soulja, with her trigger-happy ass."

Sheila laughed, knowing she was talking about Theresa.

"You just enjoy yourself," Shonda told her. "I'll let the girls know what's up."

"Okay, I love you."

"Love you, too."

Upon leaving the club, Ray dismissed B.J. and Rick, letting them go their way. Now, Joe was pulling the truck up the front of Ray's house.

"Will you need us, tomorrow?" asked Poppo.

"I shouldn't," Ray answered. "What's on the agenda?"

"We got those two coming in from New York," Poppo informed. "We'll meet them at the bus station and get them situated. Other than that, it's regular transactions."

"Handle that," Ray told him. "I should be here when y'all show up."

Ray dapped his friends, then he and Sheila dismounted. Entering the house, he re-activated his alarm and locked the door back.

"This is nice," Sheila complimented, looking around the place. "You're gonna give me a tour de France?"

"Yeah, if we were in France," he answered, now realizing his sense of humor was returning.

Sheila didn't laugh, instead, she crossed her arms over her chest and assumed the look Shonda told him about, which he also found to be cute.

"I'll tell you what," he began, suppressing a smile. "You can stand right there all night, with that same cute ass look on your face. I'm going to bed."

"Unh-unh, Ray," she whined, wrapping her arms around his waist and resting her head on his back as he began to walk off. "I wanna see the house."

Ray was smiling now, which was something he hadn't done in a long time. There was no doubt he was really fond of Sheila and enjoyed being in her presence. He felt more at peace around her.

"This is the living room," he promulgated, once they'd entered the living room, with her still clinging to his back.

"You need a maid," she said, removing her arms from around him and studying the cluttered coffee table.

"Whatever," he said, exiting the living room and making it to the first bedroom, which was his stash room, although everything was stashed away and out of sight. "This is the guest room."

"You be having guests over?" she asked, peering inside the room.

"You my first guest."

"Well, too bad I won't be sleeping in there, either." She pushed him towards the Kingz room, where she gasped at the four human-like figures that stood along the far wall, wearing crowns, robes and Kingz necklaces. "Are those statues?"

"Mannequins."

Ray had never allowed anyone in this room, which is why he'd immediately taken offense, the second Sheila crossed the threshold. But he had to tell himself she didn't mean any harm, and she wouldn't take or break anything. He cut the light on for her, then leaned against the door jamb, while she looked around.

"Wow!" she exclaimed, approaching the mannequins and physically examining the robes and necklaces. "These are real bullet holes, huh?"

"Yeah," he managed, still trying to contain his anger.

"A bullet had gone through here, too?" she asked, fondling James' necklace, where a bullet had perforated the lower part of the "G".

"Yeah," he answered, now hating that he'd brought her to the house, in lieu of taking her to a hotel. Finally, she left the mannequins alone and slowly moved about the room, touching and looking at a lot of things belonging to James, which was most of the stuff in the room. Then, she approached the dresser that was partially cluttered with other miscellaneous items and picked up some small object.

"I remember this," she said in a hushed tone, showing him the half-heart pendant, he'd recently added to the room. "The doctor gave this to me and told me to give it to you when you woke up. They said you had it in your hand when they found you at the cemetery. There's another half to this, huh?"

"Yep."

"Sylvia has it?"

Now, he was really hating the fact that he'd brought her here. All night, she'd had his mind at ease and far away from those past tragedies. At the moment, she was doing the total opposite. Perhaps she'd sensed it, because she replaced the pendant on the dresser, crossed the room and wrapped her arms around him.

"I'm sorry, baby," she said, looking into his eyes. "I had no business—"

"Are you done here?" he cut her off, feeling another erection arise.

"Let's go." She grabbed his hand and led him towards the next room, which was his bedroom.

Ray stopped at the door. "Look, go on in and make yourself comfortable. I gotta feed my dogs."

"You got dogs?"

"Yeah."

"Do they bite?"

"They got teeth," he replied, making his way towards the kitchen.

"You are so sarcastic," she said to his back, smiling.

Entering the bedroom, Sheila expected to see a large, wooden bed with curtains hanging around it, like the Kingz and Queenz she'd seen on TV, but it was far from it. She didn't have to turn on any lights, because the room was illuminated by the same array of monitors, she'd seen in the living room. Taking off her tiara, she placed it on the dresser along with her pocketbook, then moved over to the stereo, looking through Ray's CD collection. Opting for the *'Best of Keith Sweat'*, she put it on and sat on the edge of the bed to relieve her feet from her boots, as *Keith Sweat* set the mood with *'Don't Stop Your Love'*.

Once her boots were off, Sheila crawled to the middle of the bed and laid down on her back, with her hands interlocked behind her head. Ray told her to make herself comfortable and she did just that. *Keith Sweat* had her mind at ease. Now, all she was missing was her King. Seeing movement on one monitor, she looked up and saw Ray petting two, rather large dogs. He also appeared to be talking to them. Maybe he was telling them to keep their barking to a minimum because he was about to have sex and didn't need any disturbances, she humored herself with the thought.

Ray disappeared from view, so she assumed he was on his way in. Moments later, he entered the room. She watched as he took off his jean jacket, revealing his double gun holster, which he took off and placed on the dresser. When he'd taken off his shirt, she smiled to herself, thinking about Donte, Erica's personal trainer. Ray was slim and nowhere near as muscular as Donte, but when he'd taken off his pants and was down to his boxer briefs, she told herself that the bulge in his underwear was all the muscle she needed him to have. Plus, he's a King—her King

Ray switched the track to number three, *'Make It Last Forever'*, before climbing into bed and positioning himself between Sheila's legs. He showered her with a long passionate kiss, before reaching under her dress and relieving her of her orange thong, tossing them to the floor. After peeling her dress off and relinquishing his underwear, he kissed her again, then moved his mouth down her neck, kissing and nibbling, before moving down to her full breasts. She moaned as he took his time licking and sucking her dark, fully erect nipples. He spent a few seconds on her navel, before moving down to her love mound. She automatically spread her legs wider, to invite the sensation she hadn't felt in a long time. Seconds after Ray began licking and sucking her clitoris, she was having a hard time keeping her legs open. It felt so good, she had pretty much clamped his head between her thick thighs. That didn't stop him, seeing that he had this kind of effect on her, prompted him to insert two fingers to double the pleasure.

"Ooh, stop—stop! Please stop!" She pulled him up by his ears and kissed him in the mouth, tasting her own juices. "I was about to come, lay down."

Ray dismounted her and laid down on his back. Now, it was her turn to treat him, but she didn't adhere to his routine. Instead of kissing him all over, her mouth went straight to his dick. Her eyes were closed, as one hand gripped the bottom half of his rod and her mouth gripped the top. Sheila moved at a pace that seemed to be in sync with *Keith Sweat* as he crooned '*How Deep Is Your Love?*' She kept at this for a good two minutes, before pulling it out and licking around the tip, while looking into his eyes. Ray couldn't bear much more of this foreplay. Hell, he was already stimulated to the fullest extent. Now, he was ready to lay pipe on Sheila's fine ass and find out how deep her love was.

Before she could go down on him again, he gently pulled her up by her shoulders and she laid on top of him, pinning his rock-hard penis between them. As they locked lips, Ray gave in to his urge to grip her ass, which happened to be the softest cheeks he'd ever encountered.

"You got condoms?" she finally asked.

Ray pulled a Magnum from the drawer of the nightstand. Sheila grabbed it out of his hand and took it upon herself to put it on, using her mouth. Then, she mounted him, using her hand to guide him inside her, but taking her time, being that her stuff was tight, due to a long period of non-use. Ray could tell she hadn't been penetrated in a while because she was fitting him like a latex glove.

While she rode, she was doing all she could not to go all the way down on him. Ray wasn't hearing this, which was why, with his hands clamped on her waist, he was assisting her, while thrusting his mid-section up, making sure she felt every inch of him inside her.

"Mmm!" Sheila bit down on her bottom lip as she reached her first climax.

Once the fluid escaped her body, she slowed her momentum, unable to keep her initial pace. Feeling the curtailment in her movement, Ray rolled her onto her back, mounted her and didn't plan on cutting her any slack. He found her entrance and rammed his dick inside her. Shelia gasped and gripped his waist, in an attempt to restrict his deep thrusts. She moaned, he was in her stomach now. Seeing that she couldn't stop this assault, she wrapped her legs around his waist, dug her fingernails into his back and welcomed her second orgasm, which came as quick as the first one.

Ray could tell when she was at the peak of her climax because she dug her nails deeper into his back and tightened her grip around his waist. Once she'd released, she loosened her nails and released her grip around his waist, lowering her legs back to the bed. Ray didn't miss a beat, he lifted her left leg and kept pounding. This time, he had enough room to go all the way in and pull back as far as his dick would go without slipping out.

He maintained his stride until he was close to reaching his climax. Then he pulled out and pulled her into the doggy style position. Wasting no time, he slid his penis back into her extremely wet and warm vagina, gripped her waist and was back to business. Now, they were both moaning. He thought he would keep her in this position for a good fifteen minutes but seeing the way her soft, well-rounded ass vibrated against his mid-section, brought him to his climax within sixty seconds.

Chapter 13

"My King?"

Ray awoke from his sleep to see Sheila standing over him with a plate of food and a glass of orange juice. Plus, she was wearing one of his t-shirts he knew wouldn't fit him the same, seeing how it stretched around her ass and hips.

"You trying to poison me, already?' he joked.

"I'll never hurt, my king," she promised. "Here."

She placed the glass on the stand, Ray sat up as she handed him the plate that contained cheese grits, cheese eggs, bacon, and four buttermilk biscuits, already severed and laced with strawberry jelly. He was about to ask her how she knew he preferred cheese in his grits and eggs, but she was already strutting out of the room, with her ass looking as if it wanted to bounce from under the shirt.

"Damn," Ray said to himself, shaking his head, then realized he was still naked under the covers, with an early morning hard-on.

Seconds later, Sheila re-entered the room with her own plate and glass of juice. She sat her glass on the stand before taking a seat on the edge of the bed.

"I don't know why I didn't ask you if you liked cheese in your grits and eggs," she said.

"Yeah, you should've asked me if I was lactose intolerant."

"I already know you're not lactose intolerant."

"How?"

"Cause you went mayhem on the squeeze cheese and Ritz crackers, last night," she pointed out, smiling.

"Was I that noticeable?"

"Uh-huh," she answered. "I wanted to feed your dogs, but they don't look too friendly."

"Well, it's a good thing you didn't go out there."

"Why?"

"Cause, all that ass you got back there—" he started, "Would've been enough rump roast to last them a whole week."

"Shut up." She laughed along with him.

After they'd eaten, Sheila set off to wash the dishes, while Ray showered. While she showered, Ray had gotten dressed, fed his dogs and went out to the garage to start his car, so that the console would be warm when it was time to leave. As he sat in the living room, waiting on Sheila, he decided to call Nikki.

"Hello?" she answered.

"Did I wake you?"

"LKS?" she asked, indicating that Ace was nearby.

"Yeah," he answered. "I called to check on you. Is everything alright?"

"Everything's fine," she answered. "The kids are in school. Ace and I are on our way to pick up his grandmother and take her to her doctor's appointment."

"Well, you got my number," he said as Sheila entered the living room, clad in her orange dress, with her pocketbook hanging off her shoulder. "Call me if you need anything."

"Okay," Nikki replied hanging up.

Now, he regarded Sheila. "You ready?"

"Yeah."

Returning to his bedroom, Ray donned his shoulder holster before putting on his jacket. Then they were off to the garage, where his Mercedes was still running.

"It seems like you held on to everything your brother had," Sheila stated, eyeing the BMWs.

"Yeah, I guess so."

Ray just watched her as she stood there marveling at the two cars as if they were some antique collector's items. Once she was done, they climbed into the Benz, where '*Toni Braxton's I Love Me Some Him*' was in mid-play.

"Ooh, play that back!" Sheila exclaimed like a small child. "That's my song."

"Correction," Ray said, pressing the button for the garage door. "That's my song."

"Re-correction," she came back. "That's our song."

"That's not even a word," Ray challenged, backing out of the garage.

"It is in my book," she countered. "Now, could you please start the song over?"

Ray started the song over, knowing she was going to sing it to him. She didn't sound anything like Toni Braxton, but she was doing way better than what Sylvia had done with Janet Jackson's hit.

When they'd made it to her house, Sheila handed her cell phone to Ray, who logged his number into it, then handed it back.

"So, where do we go from here?" Sheila asked. "I don't do one-night stands and I don't just give myself to anybody. I have very strong feelings for you. I know, I'm all the woman you'll ever need. And don't tell me you've heard that before, because I know you have. Talk is cheap. That's why I'm asking for a chance to demonstrate my love."

Ray leaned over and kissed her passionately. He'd felt everything she'd said and there was no doubt in his mind that she meant every word.

"We'll talk about that tonight," he told her. "Call me around nine."

"Okay."

They kissed again before she got out and sauntered towards the house. Ray waited until she was inside, then pulled off. He didn't have any definite plans, but he didn't plan on going straight home. He was going to drive around for a while, but first, he needed to fill up on gas. Therefore, he pulled into the first gas station he encountered. It wasn't crowded, but he had his credit card, so there was no need for him to go inside the store.

Pulling up to the gas pump, he pressed the button to release the door of the gas tank, before getting out. After unscrewing the gas cap and activating the pump with his card, he inserted the nozzle. While the tank was filling, he did a quick look around for any potential threat. People seemed to be going on about their day, without a care in the world. No one seemed to notice him, so he shoved his hands into his pants pocket, leaned against the car, and watched the digits on the pump.

"Oh my God!" he heard a female cry out. "Ray?"

Ray looked to his right and couldn't believe his eyes. He'd never even thought of running into Precious again. Considering he knew far more about her cousin's disappearance than she did, this was indeed an unwelcomed encounter.

Shonda was so tired from last night she didn't even hear Sheila when she'd entered the house. But she was wide awake when Sheila came bursting through her bedroom door, telling her that some unknown man had called their business phone, trying to cop a few kilos. Shonda lunged out of bed and followed Sheila to the kitchen, where the phone's receiver was lying on the table. She picked it up.

"Queen Shonda," she announced.

"Hello, Queen Shonda," the guy spoke with an accent. "I'm Alex, I was referred to you by, LKS."

"And why would he refer you to me?" Shonda tested, to see if this was some kind of drug operational sting.

"Is this line safe?" he asked.

"As far as I know."

"Well," he started. "LKS told me that he had some difficulties with his last shipment. He said I should contact the Queenz, who are close friends of his."

She took a seat. "And he gave you our number?"

"Yes."

"What does LKS look like?"

"Unfortunately, I'm one of the unlucky ones," he replied. "I've never gotten a chance to meet him, face to face. But we're on good terms, as far as business goes, I can assure you."

Shonda did not know what to make of this, but she knew she had to make some kind of executive decision. "So, what are you seeking, Mr. Alex?" she asked, knowing how she was going to play it.

"Three lovely ladies," he answered. "I prefer them young, somewhere around eighteen."

Shonda was impressed by his lingo, but she still had to play it safe. "Call us, Saturday. We have to get verification on you, first."

"What time?"

"Twelve pm."

Shonda hung up and looked at Sheila, who was clad in black jeans and a t-shirt, standing with her hands on her hips.

"I hope you got knocked up, last night," she said, rubbing Sheila's stomach. "Or did y'all even do the booty?"

"You know we did the booty," Sheila replied, batting Shonda's hand away. "And, no, my husband ain't got me pregnant, yet."

"Seems like somebody has high hopes," Shonda said, standing. "So, y'all made it official between y'all?"

"Not quite," Sheila answered. "We'll talk it about when I call him, tonight."

"It's official," Shonda assured her cousin. "Right now, I gotta get my ass ready for business."

Shonda left the kitchen, proud of her accomplishment with the joining of Queen Sheila and King Ray. She entered her bedroom with the intent to get her things ready for her shower, but the ringtone, *50 Cent's 'Just A Lil 'Bit'*, on her cell phone, hampered those plans.

"What?" she answered.

"Damn," Tino exclaimed. "First you cross me out to do business with another nigga. Now you just talking to a nigga all kinds of ways. Just tell me not to call you no more. I can respect that better."

"Don't play that reverse psychology shit with me, Tino," she said. "What the hell do you want?"

"I'll be in Georgia, this weekend," he told her. "Would we get a chance to fuck around?"

"Hell no!"

"Oh, it's like that?"

"You should've been fucking me when you had me, Tino."

"I was fucking you."

"You were fucking other women, too."

"Now, why are you bringing up old shit?' he asked. "Yeah, I fucked other women. But don't act like another nigga didn't have his nose all up your ass when I wasn't around."

"I'm 'bout to get in the shower, Tino," she informed, sick of his shit at the moment.

"I thought Kingz and Queenz were supposed to be loyal," he asserted.

"What's that supposed to mean?"

"How would King James feel—" he started. "If he knew you were fucking his brother? I mean, King Ray is still alive, right?"

Playa Ray

Chapter 14

"Wow!" Precious exclaimed after Ray had given her the rundown of the night the Kingz were murdered. "So, had you not been sick, you would've been in the limousine that night?"

"Yeah."

Despite their split, Ray knew from the moment Precious spotted him, she was going to hit him with a deluge of questions, which was why he'd suggested they assemble at the Chinese restaurant that sat across the street from the gas station.

"It hurt me to my heart when I heard that," she said, regarding him with those hazel eyes he still found appealing. "Did they charge anybody for it?"

"Don't nobody know shit," he answered, feeling the anger within him resurface. Now, he had to change the subject. "So, what have you been up to?"

"Working," she answered. "I'm the manager of a Small Business Association firm. Other than that, I—" She paused as if she'd just remembered something, then said, "They recently found Steve's body—" Ray swallowed. "In an abandoned warehouse," she went on. "He had been set on fire, but the autopsy showed that he had been dead beyond two years before that happened. I'd already assumed he was dead because he disappeared right before that happened with the Kingz."

"The autopsy showed he'd been dead for that long?" Ray asked, not knowing what else to say or do.

"That's what they told my mom," she answered. "He could only be identified by his dentals. For somebody to set his body on fire, after he'd already been dead for over two years, they had to be real sick in the head."

'*Not really,*' Ray thought.

The Queenz accompanied by the Queenzmen had already made three drops and had two more to go. Shonda who was seated in the passenger seat of the GMC that was driven by Ebony had just informed Ebony and Theresa about the call they received from Alex and was now dialing Ray's number.

"Talk to me," Ray answered.

"Alex," Shonda said, hoping he would catch on.

"He's legit," Ray told her. "Big spender, real consistent."

It wasn't any of her business, but she had to know. "Was something wrong with your last shipment?"

"Nope, I'm just keeping my word." He hung up.

"He's legit," Shonda told her girls. "being that we only have three kilos left, we'll make sure he gets those."

"So, we should be straight after we pay Vincent next week, right?" Theresa asked.

"That's no doubt," Shonda answered. "Plus, we got LKS behind us."

"Oh, I gotta call from, Tino, today. He was talking real reckless."

"He's always talking reckless," Ebony asserted.

"Nah," Shonda replied, shaking her head. "This was different. He asked me how would King James feel if he knew I was fucking his brother?"

"What!" Theresa let out.

"Who—Ray?" Sheila asked.

"Why would he let some shit like that come out of his mouth?" Theresa asked, casting a glance at Sheila, who looked as if she was ready to open a can of whoop-ass on Shonda.

"I don't know why he said that shit," Shonda answered. "But somehow he knows Ray is still alive."

"Well, don't forget that Ant used to be his lieutenant," Ebony pointed out.

Shonda replied, "I've always kept that in mind. To be honest, I don't even trust the Queenzmen. I really wanna let them go."

"Even if one of them did recognize, Ray," Theresa said. "Why would they tell, Tino, that you were fucking him?"

"Is it true?" Sheila asked, feeling betrayed.

"Sheila," Theresa spoke up. "You know Shonda wouldn't do no shit like that to you!"

"Were you there?" Sheila turned on Theresa with raised eyebrows.

"Cut it out, Sheila." Shonda turned in her seat to face her cousin. "You know damn well I wouldn't pull no shit like that!"

"Queenz meeting," Ebony intervened.

"Present," Shonda said, turning back around in her seat.

"Present," Theresa said.

Sheila smacked her lips, "I'm here."

"Go on, Queen Ebony," Theresa prompted.

"Y'all need to Queen up," Ebony stated. "We have some very important issues on our hands. We need to figure out how we're gonna handle them. Now, it's obvious that the Queenzmen has been relaying all kinds of information to, Tino. Why? We don't know, but now, I'm feeling like Queen Shonda, I don't trust them. Maybe we should let them go."

"I agree," Theresa stated. "We really don't need 'em. What you think, Queen Sheila?"

"Let 'em go," Sheila answered, thinking about the way Shelton had been behaving lately.

"I wanna reconsider that," Shonda said. "Maybe we shouldn't let them go just yet. I think we should use them to our advantage."

"Ooh baby, I'm coming," Erica cried out as Ted pounded her from the back, which was her favorite position.

They both exploded at the same time. Spent, Erica collapsed on the bed, as Ted pulled the condom off and left the room to dispose of it. Erica had been to the clinic today and couldn't wait to get home to tell Ted the good news. Ted had been so caught up in his work, she didn't get a chance to. Now, as she climbed up under the blanket, awaiting his return, she figured as soon as he climbed into bed, she would just flat out let him know that she was pregnant with his child. But as soon as he'd entered the room, there was a knock on the front door.

"I might have to put a closed sign up on the door," he said, donning the jeans he'd taken off. "I'll be back, baby."

He exited the room, closing the door behind him. Erica just shook her head and looked up at the screen of the TV. Had the remote not been sitting atop of the dresser, which was out of her reach, she would've turned the TV on. But she was too comfortable to move. Besides, she didn't need anything else to distract her from making this announcement to Ted.

She heard the sound of the front door closing and thought Ted was on his way back until she heard him talking to someone. Curious, she got out of bed and eased the bedroom door open, just enough for her to peer out and into the living room, where three men were standing around Ted. One of the men had his back to her. She could only see the side of the man's face, who was doing most of the talking, but she could see the full features of the one facing her direction. His coat was unfastened, and she could see a small portion of his medallion that hung from his necklace. She didn't have to see the whole medallion to know that it read *Drop Squad* or to know they were all Drop Squad members.

"Nigga, Drop Squad made you," she heard the guy in the middle say. "How the fuck could you turn your back on us? You can't shop with us, then turn around and shop with somebody else. We don't rock like that, Ted. When niggas do shit like that, it pisses the big dogs off and takes food out of our kid's mouth."

"It ain't even like that, Rico," Ted said.

119

"Bullshit," Rico objected, pushing Ted down onto the sofa, which prompted the others to draw their guns on Ted, pretty much assuring him what would happen if he attempted to defend himself.

Rico moved closer and was standing over Ted with a large pocket-knife in his hand.

'*Oh, shit!*' Erica thought as she watched the scene, hoping that it didn't go beyond what she was seeing at the moment.

"You know this was an OG call, right?" Rico said, and before Ted could respond, jammed the large blade into his throat.

Erica gasped, tears streamed down her face as her heart rate quickened. It seemed as if her heart had abruptly stopped when she heard Rico tell his men to search the house. That's when she realized that she didn't have much longer to live. There was nowhere to hide and basically nothing for her to do, but she was going to prolong the inevitable for as long as she could.

She eased the door back shut and turned the lock on the knob. As she looked about the room, her mind seemed to calculate a thousand solutions, but nothing was clear to her. She was still completely naked, and she knew she didn't have enough time to put on half of a pair of pants and try to escape through the window. Therefore, she moved on instinct. Erica grabbed her cell phone off the dresser, dialed 911, pressed send and slid it under the bed. then, she pulled her diary from her pocketbook, turned to the page that was marked: *November 14, 2005*, where she had already been writing, pulled the pen from its clasp and began to write just as someone was fumbling with the doorknob. But she didn't get a chance to finish what she was trying to write when the door was kicked in. She just quickly closed the diary and slid it close to her pocketbook, as one of the men entered the room.

"Damn!" he exclaimed, sexually eyeing her body. "Y'all check this out."

"Ooh, shit," the second goon preceding Rico, exclaimed, when he'd entered. "That nigga be having some bad bitches."

'What you want us to do with this?" the first goon asked Rico, who was leaning against the doorjamb.

"Whatever," Rico answered with a shrug. "Just make sure we don't end up on America's Most Wanted."

Erica had been watching Rico the whole time. After saying what he'd said, he gave her a once over, then left the room as if he was going to search the rest of the house. Erica didn't know what was about to happen, but they were in for a rude awakening if they thought she was going to be an easy target.

She quickly sized them up as the second goon closed the door and the first one slowly approached her, both with their guns to their sides.

"You might as well make this easy, bitch," the first guy said, gripping his crotch. "Your fine ass is gonna—"

He didn't see it coming. Erica's right arm moved like lightning and her fist caught him square on the chin, instantly knocking him out. Before his body could make a complete negotiation with the floor, Erica was stepping over him and lunging at the other guy, who'd raised his gun in the air as if to strike her with it. His reaction didn't stop her momentum one bit. She assailed him like a mad Russian. Being accustomed to fighting men, he made her feel as if she was fighting another woman, from how he was flailing his arms wildly, in an attempt to defend himself. He was failing, successfully, because all her punches were connecting and truth be told, she was wearing him out. Clearly, Rico heard the commotion and rushed to his friend's aide, but Erica didn't see, nor hear him enter the room as she fought for her life. But she did see a sudden flash of his knife's blade, before it perforated the side of her neck, crushing her windpipes.

Playa Ray

Chapter 15

Medical examiners held Erica's body for a week, before releasing it into her family's care, so they could make proper funeral arrangements. Now, as the funeral was underway, the reverend was conducting his eulogy. Shonda and Theresa were consoling Ms. Davis. Phillip was consoling Ebony and Ray, who'd never thought in a million years he'd be attending a funeral on his birthday, was consoling Sheila. Being that the service wasn't broadcasted, the only other attendees were the Queenzmen, who sat on the back rows and Ray's lieutenants who were accompanied by Hot and Stone. They were seated on the third row, behind Sheila and Ray.

After the service, they all followed the pallbearers out of the church, where the hearse and police escorts awaited. There was also a black guy leaning against a black Ford Crown Victoria, wearing sunglasses and a blue windbreaker with the letters FBI across the chest. He grabbed a large brown paper bag off the hood of the car, crossed the street and approached Ebony, who was being escorted by Phillip.

"Ms. Ebony Davis?" he asked. Ebony just looked at him. "These are Erica's things," he went on, handing her the bag. "They were at Teddy Jefferson's place. And I offer my condolences."

"Thank you," Ebony's voice was barely above a whisper.

Once everyone climbed into their vehicles, they followed the hearse and convoy of police to the burial site, where the reverend did his final eulogy. As Erica's casket was being lowered into the earth, Phillip asked Ebony if she needed to stay with him for the night.

"I have to stay close to my mom, Phillip," she told him. "She needs me more than anything, right now. I do thank you for being here with me."

"Always," he said, kissing her on the forehead. "If you need anything, give me a call."

"Okay."

Ebony always felt a sense of security, whenever she was with Phillip, which was why she'd really wanted to take him up on his offer. But she had to consider her mother, whose house she'd been staying at ever since they'd gotten the call about Erica's death. They were both still trying to cope with this loss and really needed each other at this time.

Upon departing the cemetery, Sheila left with Ray and his men and the rest of the Queenz, along with Ms. Davis, were back in the Denali, on their way to Stone Mountain to drop Ebony and her mother off.

"Should I go ahead and dismiss security?" Shonda asked her girls, who were both seated in the back, being that Ms. Davis was in the front passenger seat.

"I don't think we need 'em," Ebony answered.

"We don't," Theresa agreed.

Using her cell phone, Shonda dialed Ant's number and told him everything was stable for the weekend and they were free to go.

"You wanna stop and get something to eat, Mama?" Shonda asked Ms. Davis.

"I'm fine, baby," she answered. "I just wanna go home and rest. I'll eat later."

Shonda's heart churned as she glanced over at Ms. Davis, who was doing all she could to hold it together. She did not deserve this. Neither did Ebony. She was not surprised to hear that the police department had no lead on any suspects. But she would wager anything that Erica was an innocent bystander, who got caught up in the middle of some drug beef someone had with Ted.

"We'll be back to check on y'all," Shonda said, once she'd pulled into the driveway of Ms. Davis's house.

"Tonight?" asked Ebony

"Of course."

"You need me to bring you something back from the house?" Theresa asked Ebony.

"Another pair of pajamas," she answered, then indicated the bag the FBI had given her. "And put this in my room."

Upon leaving the cemetery, Poppo dismissed Hot and Stone, and they were off to Canton, Georgia. Sheila had literally cried herself to sleep and was lying across the back seat, with her head in Ray's lap. He could admit this was the saddest birthday he'd ever had. He didn't know Erica, but his heart went out to her and her loved ones. Considering how she and her boyfriend were murdered, Ray knew it had to be a hit on his behalf and she was just in the wrong place at the wrong time.

"Come on, baby." Ray awakened Sheila, once Joe pulled the truck up to the house.

"What the word is?" Joe asked.

"I'll let y'all know," Ray answered. "Just keep y'all ears to the streets."

Ray and Sheila dismounted and went inside the house. He escorted Sheila to his bedroom, where she flopped down on the bed still exhausted from a day of mourning. He helped her out of her heels and coat, then tucked her up under the covers.

"Where are you going?" she asked in a tiring voice.

"To change clothes and make a few phone calls," he answered.

"Don't leave me!"

"I'm not leaving you, baby." He kept his patience. "I'll be in the living room. I'll be back to check on you."

Her eyes were closed. She didn't respond, so assuming she'd dozed off, he exited, closing the door behind him. Getting to the living room, he sat down on the sofa and dialed Poppo's number on his cell.

"Talk to me," Poppo answered.

"I need you and Joe to get at whoever y'all can get at," Ray told him. "Find out whatever y'all can about, Ted. If he had beef with anybody, I want names."

"Is there a bounty?' Poppo asked.

"You know it is," Ray answered. "Eighty thousand, no proof, no profit."

It was almost seven o'clock when Shonda awakened from her catnap. Keeping her word, she phoned Theresa and told her to be ready when she pulled up. After freshening up and donning fresh clothes, Shonda grabbed her pocketbook, set the alarm, then made her exit. Still moved by Erica's demise, Shonda was indeed paranoid, which was why she approached her car with one hand inside her pocketbook, clutching her .380. She started her Mustang and quickly pulled out of the driveway, not allowing the engine any amount of time to warm up. Her gun in her lap and her eyes pretty much glued to her rearview mirror, she made it to Riverdale in one piece. Pulling up to Theresa and Ebony's house, she blew the horn. Seconds later, Theresa exited the house with her pocketbook and a carry-all bag.

"They want some chicken," she said when she slid into the passenger seat. "Have you checked on, Sheila?"

"Not yet," Shonda answered. "I'll do it later."

When they'd made it to Stone Mountain, Shonda stopped at KFC and ordered the family meal. Then they rode out to Ebony's mother's house, where she and her mother were seated in the living room, with only a lamp on. Being that the Family Meal came with four plastic plates, Theresa took the initiative to fix everyone a plate. They ate in silence.

"Where's Sheila?" Ms. Davis finally asked.

"Oh." Shonda placed her plate on the coffee table. "She's with her boyfriend. I forgot I'm supposed to check on her.'

Shonda wiped her hands with napkins, pulled out her cell phone and dialed Sheila's phone, to no avail. She tried again, still getting no answer. She tried Ray's phone.

"Yeah?" Ray answered, sounding as if he'd been asleep.

"Did I wake you?" Shonda asked.

"Yeah, you did."

"I'm sorry," she stated. "I called Sheila's phone and got no answer."

"She may still be sleep."

"May?"

"She's in my bedroom," he explained. "I fell asleep on the living room sofa. She was asleep the last time I checked on her."

"Can you make sure she calls me when she gets up, Ray?"

"Yeah, I can do that," he said, ringing off.

"She's still asleep," Shonda announced, placing her phone on the table, retrieving her plate.

"Was Ted dealing drugs?" Ms. Davis asked.

Ebony, Theresa, and Shonda, all exchanged glances, not knowing what to say, being that neither of them had ever lied to her.

"Mom, why would ask that?" Ebony inquired.

She answered, "Because the news reporter said it was possibly drug or gang-related."

"They say that about every murder, Mama," Ebony told her. "I guess they do that, because ten times out of twelve, it's one or the other."

They ate and made small talk until Ms. Davis announced that she was ready for bed. Ebony tucked her in, then returned to the living room and curled in the recliner that her mother had sat in.

"Are those my pajamas?" Ebony asked, now noticing the bag Theresa had brought in.

"Yeah," Theresa answered. "I brought two pairs and some underwear."

"Ebony, you don't have to make that ride tomorrow, if you don't want to," Shonda told her. "Hell, I can do it myself. All I have to do is drop the money off."

"She may not have to go," Theresa intervened, "But I am, you know the rule. And considering what just happened, we need to be extremely careful. We don't know who did it or why. But if it was done as a message to us, God forbid, then we can pretty much believe it's far from over."

Shonda's phone vibrated atop the coffee table. Figuring it was Sheila, she grabbed it and regarded the number on the screen. It was not Sheila's.

"Hello?" she answered.

"Ms. Shonda Watson?' a female voice inquired.

"Who is this?" Shonda asked, not liking the fact that some stranger was calling and referring to her by her full name.

"I'm an operator at Brink's Home Security," she answered, then informed Shonda that there was a break-in at her home and that the police department was there now, awaiting her arrival.

Ray figured Sheila would be hungry when she awoke, so after getting off the phone with Shonda, he set out to the kitchen to see what he could put together. While he was rummaging around in the dry goods pantry, Sheila, still in the black skirt she'd worn to the funeral, as he was still in his black pants and shirt entered the kitchen, carrying a small black box.

"Happy birthday," she said, handing him the box.

"Thank you." Ray opened the box to a gold Movado watch.

"You like it?"

"I love it," he said, kissing her on the lips. "You hungry?" She nodded. "I'm trying to find something," he told her.

"I'll cook," she insisted.

"You sure?" he asked, considering what she'd been through.

"It's what I do when I'm upset," she admitted.

"Okay," he complied. "I'll be in the living room."

"What do you want?"

"Whatever you feel like cooking."

Leaving the kitchen, Ray entered the bedroom, placed his new watch with the rest of his jewelry and found a pair of pajamas to surrogate what he had on. As he re-entered the living room, his cell phone was ringing on the table.

"Yeah?" he answered it, switching on the monitors.

"Don't you know I just realized it's November twenty third," his mother said through the phone. "Happy birthday."

"Thank you," he replied. "Although it's almost over with."

"That's my fault," she admitted. "So, how did you spend it?"

"At a funeral."

"Whose funeral?'

"My girlfriend's friend."

"Who is your girlfriend?"

"Her name is, Sheila, Mama," Ray said. "And could you please not hit me with a million and one questions? You'll meet her, one day."

"April said happy birthday," his mother told him.

"She's there?"

"For the Thanksgiving holidays."

Ray really wanted to talk to his baby sister. He just wanted to hear her voice. But clearly, she didn't feel the same way, because she'd told his mother to tell him happy birthday. He couldn't believe she was still pissed at him for what happened to Raymond. He was starting to feel as if she'd much rather he'd died instead.

Theresa insisted on riding with Shonda back to her house. As she drove fast, but as cautious as she could, all Shonda could think about was the stash room, where they kept their money and drugs in the closet, stashed away in piles of shoe boxes. She was hoping like hell it was a random break-in, where thieves made off with TVs, DVD players, stereos, clothes, and even the kitchen sink. Anything but their money and product.

They were expecting the whole Crime Scene Unit to be in front of the house, illuminating the whole neighborhood with their flashing strobe lights. But there was only one police car sitting in front of the house. Two cops got out of the vehicle as Shonda pulled into the driveway.

"Leave your gun in the car," Shonda told Theresa.

She pulled her driver's license from her pocketbook, shut the car off and they both dismounted as the two male cops approached shining flash-lights.

"Ms. Shonda Watson?" one of them asked.

"Yes."

"May I see some identification?" asked the same one.

Shonda handed over her license.

He scanned it with the flashlight and handed it back. "Brinks did con-tact you, right?"

"They did," Shonda answered. "Said I had a break-in."

"You did," he assured her. "The front door was breached. My partner and I visually searched the house for any victims or suspects. A crime scene tech looked around. Right now, I have to make an initial report, so I'll need you to do a quick survey of the house and tell me what's been taken."

The door was standing wide open. Shonda entered the house with both officers behind her and she assumed Theresa was behind them. Everything looked normal, except for the door to the stash room, which was normally closed. It was standing wide open. Shonda couldn't help it. It was like some instinctual force was pushing her towards the room because she was definitely headed in that direction. But once she'd made it to the door, it seemed as if her legs had become paralyzed. She didn't even have to cross the threshold. The empty shoeboxes that were strewn about the room, was like a picture with no words but told a tragic story.

Sheila made a dish of Hamburger Helper, corn and rolls. When she'd taken Ray's plate to him, she immediately sensed he was in a bad mood. Therefore, not knowing what had sparked this mood, when she returned to the living room with her plate, she curled up in a recliner and ate in silence. Periodically, she would glance over at him to see that he was mechanically consuming his food as if he'd lost his appetite.

"Shonda said to call her," he finally intoned, as he got up with his plate and left the room.

Sheila didn't know what to make of Ray's abrupt change of attitude, but it was starting to bother her. She finished her meal, then journeyed to the kitchen to wash the dishes. Once she finished, she went into the bedroom, where Ray was already in bed and under the covers. Evidently, he was not in the mood to talk, so she grabbed her cell phone from her pocketbook, sat on her side of the bed and called Shonda.

"Hey, baby," Shonda sounded somber.

"You okay?' Sheila asked in a hushed tone.

Shonda sniffed. "I um—I don't even know how to tell you."

"Tell me what?" Sheila was fully alert, silently praying that no one else had been harmed.

"I'll wait until you get back," Shonda insisted. "I don't want you—"

"Tell me now, Shonda," Sheila demanded, cutting her off.

Shonda sighed. "Somebody broke into our house."

"What!" Sheila exclaimed. "Did they hurt you?"

"I wasn't here," Shonda told her. "We were all at Ebony's mom's house. The security company called and told me about it. They hit our stash room and took everything. They even got my personal stash from my room. They went through your room, also. I didn't go in there to see what's missing." Sheila just listened. "They damaged the locks on the front door," she resumed. "I probably can't buy new ones until Monday. I'll just push a chair up to the door and sleep in the living room."

"Shonda, you can't stay in that house like that," Sheila said, now concerned about the safety of her cousin.

"I'll be alright," Shonda avowed. "They done cleaned us out. I don't see any reason why they should come back."

"At least—" Sheila stopped mid-sentence. She was about to suggest Shonda call Ant over for night duty, but that thought alone sent chills up her spine. Instead, she asked, "What about, Vincent?'

"I'll have to explain to him what happened," Shonda answered. "You don't have to go, I already told Ebony. Theresa's going with me." Sheila was quiet. "I'll be alright, baby," Shonda assured her. "Right now, I'm tired. Plus, I need to do some serious thinking. I'll call you tomorrow."

"Okay."

Sheila could not believe what she'd just heard. It seemed as if her life was becoming an ongoing nightmare. If the burglars had been in her room, then it was incontestable that they'd made off with her personal savings, also.

Needing something to relax her, Sheila took an extremely long and hot shower. Her body ached, her mind was cloudy, and it seemed as if everything around her was beginning to fall apart. She began to cry. For, this was too much for her to bear. She knew that the game had its pros and cons, but now she'd come to the conclusion that it's not even worth it.

After pulling herself together, she concluded her shower, donned one of Ray's shirts, then climbed into bed beside Ray, who had his back to her. She really needed to feel his arms around her at this time, but she knew it wasn't going to happen. Therefore, she held herself and rocked herself to sleep.

It seemed as if Sheila had only been asleep for a few minutes when she was awakened by the sound of thunder. She glanced up at the monitors and saw that it was pouring down outside. Then, feeling a little chill, she decided she would scoot closer to Ray, to contract body heat from him. But she looked over to see that he was not in bed. She sat up. The bathroom door was open, and she could tell he wasn't in there. Getting out of bed, she left the bedroom, going directly to the kitchen, thinking he'd gotten hungry and decided to fix himself a snack. He wasn't there.

Leaving the kitchen, she was in route to the living room, when she saw that the door to the King's room was ajar when it was usually closed. Assuming Ray was in there, she pushed the door open to see Ray standing at the dresser, wearing a Crown, robe, and Kingz necklace. The light was off, but there was adequate light coming through the window for her to see, Ray appeared to be staring at himself in the mirror. His facial features were distorted as if it had taken on another shape. That's when she noticed the mannequin which bore James' crown, robe, and necklace was completely naked. Ostensibly, Ray felt her presence, because he turned his head and her direction. The look he was giving her was so terrifying, she had to wheel herself to stand there, and not run like her mind was telling her to.

130

Chapter 16

Shonda felt a sharp pain in her back as she threw the blanket off her and set up on the sofa. She looked over at Theresa, who was still asleep in the recliner with a blanket over her and was glad she considered staying with her last night. Seeing that the chair was still pushed up to the door, Shonda set off to the bathroom to take her shower.

While she showered, Shonda thought about the loss they'd taken last night. Technically, they were back to square one. Ebony and Theresa still had their personal savings, although Ebony was only one smart enough to deposit hers in a bank account. But their money combined, was nowhere near the two hundred eighty thousand Vincent was expecting at twelve noon. She was already aware of what happens when one comes up short or fails to pay a loan shark, but Vincent was gonna have to hear her out and bid them more time to come up with something.

Being that it was a few minutes after eleven when Shonda had gotten out of the shower, instead of having to drive out to Theresa's house, she insisted Theresa shower there and gave her some clothes to put on. Brunch was ordered via the drive-thru of Checkers, then they were off to see Vincent. Momentarily, Shonda pulled her Mustang into the parking lot of the establishment and got a chance to park closer to the building, being that there were only a handful of cars.

"You think we should take our guns in with us?" Theresa asked, not favoring the idea of going in there unarmed at this time.

"I think we should," Shonda answered. "But nine times out of ten, his men are gonna pat us down again. And guns found on us may sway him from having a little compassion on our predicament. That won't look too good."

Pondering this, they both stashed their guns under their seats, got out and entered the building, where a blonde-haired woman sat at the front desk. They figured they would just go on up like they'd done their last visit, but she stopped them.

"May I help you ladies?" she asked.

"We're here to see, Vincent," Shonda told her.

"And you are?"

"The Queenz."

After looking through a logbook, she told them which floor to go to and picked up the phone as they were walking off, perhaps to announce their arrival. When the elevator made it to the sixth floor, the same four men were waiting for them, to conduct their routine search. Once that was complete, two of them led Shonda and Theresa to Vincent's office and threw back the double doors, where Vincent was seated behind his desk, talking on the phone. He waved them in. By the time they made it to his desk, he concluded his call.

"Have a seat, ladies," he told them. They did. "I appreciate you ladies for being true to your words," Vincent asserted, leaning back in his chair. "To be honest, I thought I'd have to pay you all a visit. Well, I feel like that with everybody I deal with. I mean, people have borrowed from me, with the intention of not paying me back. That makes it hard for the next client. But like I said, I appreciate the Queenz for being true to their word."

"Well," Shonda started, really hating to burst his bubble. "We have a slight problem."

"Slight?" he asked, leaning forward, resting his elbows on his desk. "Shouldn't I be the one to determine if the problem is slight or not? I should hope so. Now, what's this slight problem?"

"Our house was broken into last night," she told him. "Our whole stash was taken."

"And what does that have to do with my money?'

"Your money was a part of that stash," she explained. "We had—"

"I don't see how you could consider that a slight problem," he cut her off. "Me not receiving my money, is never a slight problem, on anyone's behalf. I don't mean to sound unprofessional, but where they do that at?"

"Look, Mr. Vincent," Shonda tried with a little respect. "This is not something we expected. We took a big loss. All we're asking for is some more time to figure something out."

He looked as if he was considering this, then said, "One week."

"One week," Shonda exclaimed.

"You have one week to have my money," he explained. "Do I need to have my men escort y'all out?"

Shonda called an emergency Queenz meeting. She set it for six o'clock, to make sure the girls had enough time to get themselves together and be there on time. Now, it was a few minutes after six and the Queenz were already assembled at the kitchen table of Shonda and Sheila's house, trying to figure out how they were going to come up with two hundred eighty thousand dollars in one week.

"I should have, like, thirty-two thousand," Ebony answered Shonda's question.

"About the same amount," Theresa said.

Sheila, who found out that her stash had been taken, just shook her head.

"The money we're generating from the salon is peanuts," Shonda said. "The money we have to collect from our workers won't help much, but it's better than nothing. We can put all that money together and cop some weight, but we still won't meet the deadline, which is highly impossible. Anybody have any other logical ideas or solutions?"

"I was thinking of one," Ebony said. "I would hate to get rid of the salon, but if we could find some quick buyers, we could sell that, the Denali, my Infinity, and Sheila's Cadillac."

"My Cadillac!" she exclaimed.

"Our cars are the most valuable out of the four," Ebony explained

"We already know why Shonda can't sell her car. But if you have a better idea, were listening."

"We can ask Ray for the money," Sheila insisted. "I'm quite sure he would trust us to pay him back."

"I can't agree to that one," Shonda declined, shaking her head.

Sheila asked, "Why not?"

"We're still in a no-trust zone," Shonda answered. "I don't know about y'all, But I don't think that was a random break-in. Whoever did it, knew for a fact that we kept our stash here and not in Riverdale. Now, Sheila, I'm not saying Ray had something to do with it. I'm saying we shouldn't trust or even mention this to anybody until we find out what's what."

"I agree," Theresa stated. "We should keep this between us and carry on as if it never happened. I had an idea, but I think Ebony's is way more logical than mine."

"We would still like to hear it," Shonda said anxious to hear what kind of evil thoughts Theresa had brewing in her head.

"Well," Theresa started, "I already know we won't meet the deadline. And we should all know that if we don't, Vincent is gonna send someone at us. I feel we should go after him, first."

"And how do you suppose we do that?" Shonda was now interested.

"We make the appointment," she answered. "We go in as if we got the money. Being that his men are gonna search us as soon as we get off the elevator, we need to already have our guns in hand, before the elevator doors open. And we're gonna need bigger guns. Probably three more Uzis."

"You're right," Shonda told her. "Ebony's plan is way more logical than yours. But I believe we should definitely keep that as a Plan B."

Playa Ray

Chapter 17

Ray awoke, thinking about Sheila. They didn't have much of a conversation on the phone last night. He figured she was still upset about the death of her friend, but knew it was more than that. Saturday, he overheard her phone conversation with Shonda. From the portion he heard, he concluded that their house had been broken into and Shonda may have gotten hurt. Then he heard Sheila asked about Vincent, which made him wonder if she was referring to the loan shark he constantly heard about. But Sheila hadn't mentioned anything to him about it, so he figured they didn't take much of a hit.

After feeding his dogs, Ray showered, then cooked himself some breakfast. Joe had to be at JP customs in Conyers, to inspect a shipment of rims that were coming in today, so Poppo was coming over to the house to help Ray sort out the product for their clients and workers.

After breakfast, Ray pulled his records book from his safe, and took it to the living room, placing it on the table as he sat on the sofa. He viewed his monitors for a while, before turning on the TV, and turning it to the news channel. To his surprise, they were talking about a body being found in Athens, Georgia last night, that fit the description of an Atlanta man, who was allegedly kidnapped from his residence in East Atlanta, almost three weeks ago.

"Yeah, that's that bitch," Ray said to the TV, before cutting it off and seeing Poppo's Lexus pull up to the house.

Minutes later, Poppo entered the living room, handed Ray a wad of folded bills, doffed his coat, then sat on the other end of the sofa.

"How's the weather?" Ray asked.

"He was small-time," Poppo answered. "Grew up in Thomasville Heights. Prior to dealing with the Queenz, he was dealing with, Drop Squad. He wasn't known for beefing with niggas or no shit like that. He just got to the money and fucked a lot of hoes."

"So, he was buying from, Drop Squad?'

"Yeah," Poppo answered. "Before fucking with the Queenz."

"I was thinking about doing what y'all suggested," Ray told him.

"What's that?"

"Fall back and let that shit be," he answered. "Well, at least until I come up with some valuable information."

****

Once again, Shonda had slept on the living room sofa, staying close to the front door, where she had the back of a chair pushed under the door-knob. She pulled her aching body off the sofa, grabbed her blanket, pillow, and gun that was under the pillow and made for her bedroom. After getting her things together for her shower, she went to Sheila's room, tapped lightly on the door, then stuck her head in to see that Sheila was still asleep.

"Sheila?" she called, causing Sheila to stir. "We gotta go ahead and get ready. I'm about to take my shower."

They'd all agreed not to call the Queenzmen to accompany them to-day, as they went around and collected from their workers. Last night, Shonda called most of their clients and told them there was a problem with their shipment, and she didn't know how long it would take to straighten things out.

Ebony and Theresa had shown up in the Denali, a little after eleven. Shonda and Sheila were already dressed, and ready to go. Sheila set the alarm and pull the door up as they left out. As they neared the truck, Theresa got out of the passenger seat, and climbed into the back, followed by Sheila. Shonda sat upfront.

"Where to, first?" Ebony asked.

"The first hardware store we come across," Shonda answered. "Then, find us a spot to get something to eat."

They found a hardware store, where Shonda purchase new locks for the front door, they order lunch from Burger King's drive-thru. Then they were off to East Atlanta, the first collect was from Travis and Quent. Eb-ony pulled the truck into East Lake Meadows. Automatically, Shonda looked over to where Trent was always standing with his cronies. There were four guys standing about and neither one was Trent. This made her wonder if he was dead, or if someone was holding him for ransom, because she hadn't heard anything on him, although she had not watched the news, since Friday.

Being that those four guys seem to be the only somebody's out, Shonda knew she had to call for Travis and Quent. She pulled her small note notepad from her pocketbook, found their numbers and call Quent.

"What's up?" Quent answered.

"Is Travis with you?' Shonda asked.

"Shit, he's right here," he told her. "Who is this?"

"The Queenz," said Shonda. "We're outside."

She hung up. Seconds later, they both emerge from an apartment and approached the passenger side of the truck. Shonda rolled the window down, expecting them to hand over the money, but they were regarding her as if they were expecting something.

"What's the problem?" Shonda asked, figuring there had to be one.

"Y'all supposed to be dropping the packages off, right?" Travis asked.

"We came by to pick up our money," Shonda said. "Is there a reason why you're not handing it over?"

"Ant collected that money from us, yesterday," Quent informed her. "He said y'all would drop the packages off, today."

"We had a problem with the shipment," Shonda told them, trying to contain her anger. "We'll call y'all once we get everything situated."

She rolled the window up as they walked off.

"You think they were telling the truth?" Ebony asked.

"Yeah," Shonda answered, dialing Ant's number, only to get the automated operator, informing her that the number she dialed was no longer in service.

"Call y'all security," she told them, as she dialed out to one of their workers in Carver Hills.

"Hello?"

"Demetrius?"

"Yeah," he answered. "Who dis?"

"Queen Shonda," she replied. "Has our Queenzmen been by to collect that from you?"

"Yesterday," he told her. "I'm waiting on y'all now."

"We had a problem with the shipment," she told him. "We'll contact you once everything is situated."

"Hakeem's not answering," Ebony informed, once Shonda had concluded her call.

"What about you, Sheila?" Shonda asked.

"No answer."

"Theresa?"

"No answer."

"Drive back to the house, Ebony," Shonda said. "We really gotta come up with something now. These niggas robbed us, and I have a strong feeling that Tino is behind all this."

"Are you calling a Queenz meeting?' Sheila asked.

Shonda sighed. "Yeah."

Sheila pulled out her cell phone and dialed Ray's number.

"Yeah?" he answered.

"Are you busy, baby?"

"At the moment," he answered. "What's up?"

"I really need you, right now," she told him. "We're calling an emergency King and Queenz meeting."

The Queenz retreated back to Sheila and Shonda's house, where Ray promised to meet with them. Shonda had fixed the locks on the front door and since Ray wouldn't show up until after six, they all lounged around the living room, not saying much, being that everyone was in their own thoughts.

Shortly after six, the doorbell rang. Shonda, gun in hand, got up and peered through the window to see Ray, his lieutenants and the same two guys that were with them at Sheila's birthday bash. Shonda opened the door and the two lieutenants entered, followed by Ray, then the other two.

"Y'all don't mind if my men search the house, do y'all?" Ray asked.

"Not at all," Shonda answered, closing the door.

The lieutenant with the New York accent, stayed with Ray, while the others drew guns and went off to search the rest of the house. Moments later, they returned, re-holstering their weapons.

"It's clear," announced the stocky lieutenant.

Ray and the Queenz made for the kitchen. Being that there were only four chairs, Shonda chose to stand. She leaned against the counter, facing the living room.

Sheila who was seated beside Ray took the initiative, "Our house was broken into Saturday and our whole stash was taken. Today, we found out that our Queenzmen are the ones who did it. They won't answer their phones and we were told by our workers that they'd been around, collecting our money from them. We didn't call you to ask for any handouts. We called you because we're at the end of our wits and don't know what to do, or what actions to take."

"Okay," Ray said, standing.

They all watched as he reentered the living room. He said something to his men, then they all left leaving the Queenz regarding each other with addled looks.

Chapter 18

Ray didn't like the looks Shelton gave him at Sheila's party, which was why, that following week, he had his lieutenants follow the Queenzmen from Sheila's house until they found out where Shelton laid his head. He'd already figured Shelton was going to give him a reason to drop in on him.

Well, last night's meeting with the Queenz, had confirmed his thesis, which is why he was now seated in the back seat of a Chevy Impala that Joe rented, accompanied by Joe and Poppo and stationed across the street from Shelton's red brick house in Lithonia, with B.J. and Rick parked further up the street in the same van Trent was abducted in.

It was already dark, and the driveway of Shelton's house was deserted. He was already informed that Shelton had a girlfriend and daughter, but didn't know if the girlfriend had a job, or what time she got home.

"Car!" Joe said and they all ducked down in their seats.

The car, which approached from the rear of them, pulled into Shelton's driveway. It was a dark-colored Toyota. They watched as a woman and a little girl with a book bag on her back got out and headed for the front door.

Poppo looked back at Ray. "Plan?"

"Hell, yeah," Ray said, donning his mask. "Rush that bitch."

Once all masks were on, they bolted from the car and crossed the front yard, making it to the house, just as the mother and daughter entered and was closing the door back. Ray, being the first to reach the door, tackled the door with his shoulder, knocking the female to the living room floor.

"Don't even think about it," Ray told the woman, who was about to scream. "Get up!'

"Mommy!" the little girl started crying.

At this time, Joe and Poppo, with their guns drawn, surrounded the woman, who was slowly getting to her feet. As soon as she picked up her pocketbook, Joe snatched it from her and rummaged through it, before handing it back.

"Lock the door back," Ray told her, she did. "Now, take your daughter to her room."

"Come on, baby," she told her daughter.

They followed her and her daughter to the bedroom, where Ray made both of them have a seat on the bed. Then he told Poppo to watch the front door and Joe to search the house.

"What time does Shelton get in?" Ray asked the woman.

"Whenever he feels like coming in," she answered. "Sometimes he don't come in until the next day."

"Is your phone in your purse?" Ray asked, concocting a way to speed up the process.

"Yeah," she answered.

"Call him," Ray told her. "Use the speakerphone. Tell him that your daughter is sick, and you need him to drive y'all to the hospital because your car won't start."

She pulled out her cell phone and dialed Shelton's number. *Fabolous' 'So into You'* played until he picked up.

"Hello?"

"Are you on your way home?" she asked.

"Not right now," he answered. "Why?'

She looked up at Ray as if she was thinking of doing something other than what he'd instructed. Ray had no choice, but to point his gun at the little girl, to let her know now was not the time to try some shit she'd seen in a movie.

"Camille is sick," she told Shelton, clearly making a decision between him and her daughter. "I need you to drive us to the hospital because my car won't start."

"Damn," he swore. "I'm on my way, be ready when I get there."

She concluded the call, just as Joe entered the room, carrying a Nike shoe box. He pulled the top off, showing Ray the stack of bills and three Ziploc bags containing ecstasy pills, weed and several ounces and half-ounces of cocaine.

"That's all you found?"

"That's it," Joe answered.

"Watch them."

Ray entered the living room, where Poppo was standing on the side of the window, peering through the blinds.

"He's on the way," he told Poppo, then dialed B.J.'s number.

"What up?" B.J. answered.

"Everything's good?"

Fa' sho," B.J. replied.

"Well, stand by," Ray told him. "He should be here shortly."

"They gotta dispose of their own body, right?" Poppo asked when Ray was off the phone.

"Of course," Ray answered, taking a seat on the edge of the coffee table. "Or they could pay B.J. and Rick to do it."

"I don't think those niggas are qualified for these kinds of missions," Poppo asserted. "You should have them niggas running errands or some-thing—" he paused. "—I wondered what them niggas will do if they got caught by Five-O? Every nigga that look, scream, or act solid, ain't solid, yo."

"So, you don't trust them?" Ray asked, thinking about what James had said about B.J. being his downfall, which prompted him to think about the female smoker who'd described B.J. and Rick as if they were standing in front of her.

"Man, forget what I said," Poppo told him. "It's not even my place to be talking like that."

"Shit you got a right to—"

"Here he is," Poppo cut him off, spotting Shelton.

Ray rushed off to the bedroom.

"You," he said to the woman. "Let's go, hurry up!"

To Joe, he said, "Watch the girl." As he escorted the woman to the living room, he said, "If you care anything for your daughter, you better act like it. Cut the TV on and sit your ass on the sofa."

She did as she was told. Poppo and Ray went into the kitchen, turning off the light. Seconds later, Shelton entered the house, moving as if she'd told him his daughter was dying. He stopped, facing her, with his back to the kitchen.

"Y'all ready to go?" he asked, hands held out. "Where is she?"

Before she could answer, Ray and Poppo rushed from the kitchen. Poppo struck Shelton in the back of his head with his gun, knocking him into the coffee table, breaking it. His glasses fell off as he tried to put up a struggle. Poppo hit him twice more, this time, forcing him into submission. Frisking him, Poppo found a chrome .38 Revolver. He handed it to Ray, who slipped it into his pants pocket.

"Get up," Ray told the woman. "Leave your pocketbook on the sofa." Ray escorted her back to the bedroom. "Sit down." She did. "If y'all come outta this room, I'll kill everybody."

He nodded for Joe to step out, then closed the door behind them. They made it back to the living room, where Poppo was standing over Shelton, who was pleading for his family's lives. Wasting no time, Ray dialed B.J.'s number.

"Yeah?" he answered.

"Let's do it," Ray told him.

"On the way."

Putting up his phone, Ray grabbed the shoebox from Joe. "Help that bitch up."

Once Joe and Poppo helped Shelton to his feet, Ray doffed his mask. Shelton may have been near-sighted, but that was all the range he needed, to see the face of the man standing before him. Ray saw the apprehension in his eyes.

"I guess you already know why I'm here?" Ray said. "Let's take a ride."

Poppo and Joe took off their masks. Ray holstered his gun and they escorted Shelton out the front door, just as the van pulled up in front of the house. B.J., who was already in the cargo area, slid the door open. Poppo forced Shelton inside and climbed in behind him.

"Right behind y'all," Ray asserted as Poppo was closing the door.

When the van pulled off, Ray and Joe crossed the street to the Chevy. Once inside, Ray placed a call to Sheila.

Sheila, as well as the other Queenz, were still confused about the laconic King and Queenz meeting last night. As if his abrupt exit wasn't enough, Ray had the nerve to not answer his phone, nor return her call when she tried to contact him to see if she could make some sense of his actions.

Earlier, they place for sale signs in the windows of her Cadillac, the Denali, and Ebony's Infinity, then park them at different stores. Being that they'd left the number to their business phone, Sheila and Shonda stayed in the house, hoping someone would become interested in one of the 3, or all of them. Plus, they had to answer their client's calls, and inform them that they had a problem with their shipment and would contact them once everything was situated.

Theresa and Ebony spent the day with Ebony's mother. They periodically called to check on Sheila and Shonda. In fact, Theresa was the one who'd call to tell Shonda to turn their TV to the news station. That's how they found out Trent's body was found, two days ago, in Athens, GA.

"I think I know who had Mario killed," Shonda had asserted, after watching the news, but never elaborated anything to Sheila.

Now, it was well after eight o'clock, and Sheila was exhausted from sitting around all day, watching TV. Shonda had retired to her room, about twenty minutes ago. Sheila cut off the TV in the living room, grabbed her phone off the table, and made for her bedroom. The moment she stepped through the threshold, her phone vibrated in her hand. She was relieved to see the number that was displayed on her screen.

"Yes?" she answered, concealing her excitement.

"I'm calling an emergency King and Queenz meeting." Ray asserted.

"Right now?"

"Yeah."

"Where?"

"At the Palace."

"Where's the palace?"

"Shonda knows where it is," Ray told her. "Y'all need to be on the way out the door, right now."

Ray disconnected. Sheila relayed this to Shonda, who called and informed Theresa and Ebony. Being that Theresa's car was more capacious than Shonda's, it had been designated as the new company's car.

It was after nine when they made it to the Palace. When Ebony pulled the car up to the fence, they saw that the security booth was occupied by the dark-skinned guy who was with Ray last night. He gave them a once over, then activated the gate. Ebony pulled the car up to the building, parking between the Chevy Impala and a black van that looked highly familiar to Shonda. They got out and before they could reach the door, the stocky Lieutenant met them, let them in, then led them to the office, where he knocked and stuck his head in, announcing their arrival. Seconds later, the other Lieutenant emerged from the office and gestured for them to enter. Ray was seated in one of the four chairs, with a Nike shoe box sitting on the table in front of him.

"I would ask y'all to have a seat," Ray said. "But this won't take long." He slid the shoebox across the table. "I believe this belongs to y'all."

Shonda lifted the top to see the stack of money and the three Ziploc bags that contained the Ecstasy pills, weed, and cocaine.

"Where'd you get this?" Shonda asked, knowing the stuff belonged to them.

"That's not it," Ray replied, standing. "I have something else for y'all."

They followed him out of the office to the loading area of the warehouse, where his lieutenants and the other guy awaited. Being that the warehouse was warmed by the heater control unit, they had their coats off, which gave Shonda a chance to get a glimpse of the light skin, stocky guy's arm. She couldn't see the whole tattoo, but the four legs indicated it was a dog. The red stuff that seemed to drip into a puddle showed that the dog had something in its mouth, which she was almost sure was an arm, just as Olivia had described.

Shonda was so preoccupied with the guy, she didn't notice Ray had stopped until she bumped into him. She was about to offer her apologies when her eyes landed on Shelton, who was strapped into a wooden chair. He didn't have on his glasses, so he was squinting his eyes, apparently trying to see who the new arrivals were. Sheila didn't wait for an introduction. She marched up to Shelton and slapped him so hard, he let out a loud grunt.

"How could you do that to us, Shelton?" she yelled. "Where's the rest of our stuff?"

He just looked at her.

"Shelton?" Shonda approached, keeping her voice calm. "Did Tino put y'all up to this?"

He gave her the same look he'd given Sheila. Theresa had left her patience in the car. She pulled her gun from her pocketbook, pushed Shonda out-of-the-way, and shot Shelton in his right knee. The report echoed throughout the building, accompanied by Shelton's scream.

"We have very important questions to ask you," Theresa said, pressing the barrel of her gun against his crotch. "Every time you refuse to answer, I'll put a slug in one of your limbs. This is my next target. Go ahead, Queen Shonda."

Shonda proceeded. "Did Tino put y'all up to this?"

"Yeah," he answered, not taking his eyes off Theresa.

"Do you know where he lives in LA?"

"He's not in LA," Shelton told her. "He's in Georgia."

"Where 'bout in Georgia?"

"Y'all need to get me to a hospital."

"Where 'bout in Georgia, Shelton?" Shonda rehashed.

"Savannah," he answered.

"Don't play with us," Theresa warned, pressing her gun harder into his crotch.

"I'm not," he avowed. "I swear!"

Figuring they'd gotten the information they needed it, Theresa squeezed the trigger. Shelton was screaming louder this time. but she quickly silenced him with two slugs to the chest.

Shonda looked back to see that Ray and his Lieutenant with the New York accent were talking and headed for the office. Telling her girls she would be right back, she quick-stepped and caught up with just as they made it to the door of the office.

"Ray, can I talk to you in private?" she asked.

Saying nothing, Ray pushed the door open, allowing her to enter first. He entered, closed the door behind him and sat in his chair.

"Have a seat," he told her.

144

Shonda sat down and took another look inside the shoebox she'd left on the table.

"I only had tabs on Shelton," Ray told her. "I couldn't tell you where the other three are. But my lieutenant got some people in Savannah. If the nigga y'all looking for is down there, I'll have his ass signed, sealed and delivered to y'all."

"And we appreciate your help," she told him. "But I wanted to talk to you about something else. Remember the guy I told you I was dating? The one who was murdered a few months ago?"

"I remember."

"His name was, Mario," she said, studying him for any telltale signs. "I promised myself I would retaliate on whoever was responsible. Like I said, his name was, Mario."

Ray furrowed his eyebrows. "Am I supposed to know him?"

"You should."

"And how's that?"

"Your men murdered him."

"My lieutenants?"

"The other two," she answered. "From what I was told, Mario ran off with a kilo of cocaine. I couldn't put two and two together, until I talked to, Olivia. Then I saw your two men at Sheila's birthday bash. That's when I realized it was you, he'd stolen from. You ordered the hit."

"I guess I did," Ray said, leaning back in his chair. "But that's a part of the game. He brought that on himself."

"I understand that now," she admitted. "That's why I can't retaliate. But I do have to give you a heads up."

"I'm listening."

"I think Drop Squad is looking for your men."

"Was Mario a part of Drop Squad?"

"No," Shonda answered. "But Olivia's brother is one of the head guys in Drop Squad."

"And who is, Olivia?"

"The lady they killed Mario in front of," she said, refraining from referring to her as a smoker. "The same one they went and murdered."

She could tell Ray was in deep thought, so she didn't bother to ask him about Trent, which was really none of her business. Therefore, she grabbed the shoe box and exited the office, closing the door behind her.

The Queenz ended up paying B.J. and Rick to dispose of Shelton's body. After they left, Ray pulled B.J. to the side and told him that he and Rick needed to report to his house, as soon as they dumped the body.

B.J. and Rick showed up at Ray's house, shortly after one am. Ray had just concluded his phone conversation with Sheila and was about to call and check on them when he saw B.J.'s Chevy pull up to the gate. He activated the gate for them, then let them into the house, where they all assembled in the living room.

"I'ma make this real brief," Ray started, "I was told y'all may be on somebody's hit list."

"Whose hit list?" B.J. demanded.

"It doesn't matter B.J.," Ray told him. "As far as I know, y'all got a price on y'all head. All I can do is advise y'all to skip town."

"And go where?" asked Rick.

"As far away from Georgia as possible," he answered. "Hell go to India or Mexico. Y'all need to be gone, like yesterday."

Ray was hoping like hell he could get these niggas to take his advice and get the fuck out of Georgia. After what Shonda told him about Olivia's brother, he would bet his life that B.J. and Rick had a gigantic price on their heads. Plus, a composite sketch of them was probably hanging up in the briefing room of every police department. Ray couldn't risk the chance of them getting caught by either one of the two, leading them back to him, which is what Poppo had been insinuating to him at Shelton's house.

Chapter 19

It had been four days since Tino got a call from Ant, informing him that three men in ski masks kidnapped Shelton from his home. He figured King Ray had his hand in that, he was sure that the Queenz had figured out the Queenzmen were the ones who made off with their stash. But why hadn't they intruded upon Ant, Blue, or Hakeem?

Shonda's a smart girl, so he was sure she'd already pegged him as the one who made the call and probably had somebody looking for him. But there was no way in hell she would know that he'd been hiding out in Savannah for the past two weeks. Hell, he'd only found out that King Ray was still alive because he was inquisitive and a bit jealous, when Ant told him Shonda had a date at some fancy restaurant, with some dude. He'd sent Ant back to the restaurant, the following day, to ask the manager to view the roster. To his surprise, Ant reported back, saying her date was, none other than King Ray. He'd actually used King Ray.

Now, accompanied by two other men, he was exiting Shady's Store on West 41st Street after purchasing junk food and blunt wraps. They stopped just outside the store and were looking around. What caught Tino's attention, was the old rusty colored, four-door Buick that sat in front of the store with the trunk up. Leaning against the car, was some dark-skinned, bald-headed dude, who Tino figured to be death struck. He was wearing burgundy pants, a large burgundy coat and a red bandana tied around his head, in a predominantly Crips area.

Tino couldn't help but lock eyes with the nigga, who was attentively staring back at him. Before he could ask the nigga if he had an eye problem, he almost magically produced two Chrome handguns and came off the car, firing both. First gunning Tino's men down, before putting a bullet in Tino's right leg. Tino screamed out in pain, which was really a cry for help because he was screaming as loud as he could, hoping to get someone's attention. Perhaps some Crips.

"Get in the trunk," the gunman ordered.

Tino, holding his wounded leg, looked from the guy to the trunk of the Buick, thinking he was not about to voluntarily get in no damn trunk. Fuck that! His gun was tucked in the waistband of his pants, and it seemed to be his only resort. As if the dude was reading Tino's mind, he tucked one of his guns, searched Tino's waistband and confiscated his Glock. Tucking that gun, he grabbed Tino by the back of his coat and forced him over to the trunk. Once again, Tino looked around. He could not believe this nigga had deliberately killed two men and was attempting to abduct him, in broad daylight. He knew the nigga was dead ass serious, so he sagely climbed into the trunk.

"If you make any noise, I'ma shoot through the back seat," the man threatened, before slamming the door, leaving Tino in total darkness.

It was Saturday and the Queenz hadn't had any luck selling either of the cars or the salon. Ebony had even called Charles and asked him if he wanted to buy the salon back, he didn't. They had only recovered $30,000 from Shelton's share of their money, in which they paid B.J. and Rick to dump Shelton's body. Even if they would have got all the product from the shoe box and combined every cent, they owned, it still wouldn't add up to what they owed Vincent.

Now, it was after eight o'clock and the Queenz were all assembled at the kitchen table of the stash house, trying to come up with last-minute solutions.

"We may have to do that," Shonda said after Theresa had rehashed her plan of knocking Vincent off before he could order a hit against them. "Or, we can start packing and be in another state by tomorrow night."

"We'll have to take grandma and Ebony's Mama, too," Sheila pointed out. "I think we should just ask Ray for the money."

"This is something we have to handle on our own, Sheila," Shonda said. "I respect your suggestion, but this is our problem. We ran this operation on our own. Now, we have to handle this problem on our own. He helped us get some of our stuff back, and I appreciate that. But we can't run to him every time we have a problem."

"She's right, Sheila," Theresa cosigned.

"So, we're going after Vincent, tomorrow?" Ebony asked, already having a bad feeling about it.

"We have to," Shonda answered. "This is where we really have to think logically. It's either him or us, I choose him."

Sheila's phone vibrated atop the table, getting everyone's attention. Answering phones during the Queen's meeting was prohibited but Ray's number appeared on the screen.

"It's Ray," she announced, looking around the table. Once everybody nodded their consent, she answered it. "Hello?"

"Y'all meet me at the Palace," Ray said, then disconnected.

Once Sheila had conveyed this to her girls, they concluded their meeting and we're out the door, making it to the Palace minutes before ten o'clock. There was a different man in the security booth. He activated the gate and Ebony pulled up to the building, parking between the Lincoln Navigator and an old four-door Buick.

148

Again, Ray's lieutenant met them at the door. This time, he led them straight to the landing area, where Ray, his other Lieutenant and another unfamiliar man with a red bandana around his head, awaited. Then there was—they could not believe who was strapped into the hot seat this time. Absolutely disregarding Ray and his men, the Queenz briskly approached Tino, who's right pants leg was soaked with blood, as if he'd been shot. He had his game face on as he regarded no one but Shonda.

"I'm not gonna even ask you where our shit is," Shonda spoke through clenched teeth. "All I wanna know is why?" Tino just stared at her. "Okay." Shonda pulled her gun from her pocketbook and shoved the barrel into his stomach. "You can answer the question or die!"

"You ain't pulled the trigger, yet?" he defied her.

Shonda pulled the trigger.

"Ahhh!" Tino yelled out in pain. "Stupid ass bitch. Don't worry, all y'all got it coming! Even ya' lil' boyfriend over there."

"That's Sheila's boyfriend!" she yelled, taking her gun by the barrel and holding it in the air, anticipating a strike.

"Hey!"

They all looked back to see Ray approaching and moved out of his way so that he was standing in front of Tino.

"I assume you know who I am," Ray asserted, apparently hearing what Tino had said.

"You didn't think you were that hard to spot, did you?" Tino replied.

"Cut the shenanigans," Ray told him. "Do you really know who I am?"

"According to the public," Tino answered, "You're the last King standing. Or, do you prefer LKS?"

"I prefer to know who killed the other, Kingz." Tino just stared at him. "If you can assist me on that," Ray went on. "I'll see to it that you get patched up and walk out of here alive. That's on my crown."

Tino looked as if he was considering, then said, "It was a ghost, kinda like yourself. It's like the Pac Man game, with no Pac Man. Just the ghosts, ghosts chasing ghosts."

"Get this over with," Ray told the Queenz. "I'll be in my office."

"That was dumb," Shonda said to Tino after Ray walked off. "He gave you a chance to walk out of here, alive, and you fucked that up."

"I gave him a clue," Tino said. "It's not my fault he's too slow to figure it out."

"Fuck you, Tino," Shonda voiced, shooting him in the chest.

The Queenz stood there looking at Tino's limp body for what seemed like an eon, before heading for the office. Sheila tapped on the door and they entered upon Ray's bidding.

"Have a seat," he told them, getting up so one of them could use his chair. Of, course, it was Sheila, who'd kissed him before taking a seat.

"So, what the move is?" he asked.

"We thank you for keeping your word," Shonda told him. "But we didn't get any useful information out of him. Plus, we don't have any money to pay your men to get rid of the body."

"I'll get it done," he promised. "Anything else?"

The Queenz all looked around at each other. Sheila was thinking that this was the best time to tell Ray about Vincent, while Shonda was hoping her cousin wasn't thinking of doing such a thing. Ebony was hoping like hell somebody—anybody, mentioned the situation with Vincent, so they wouldn't have to go on a killing spree tomorrow. But Theresa was thinking about a good night's rest, because her trigger finger was itching, and she couldn't wait to use the Uzi.

"That's it, for now," Shonda finally answered. "But we really do appreciate your help."

"No doubt," Ray replied. "If y'all don't mind, I'd like to speak with Sheila for a minute."

When the rest of the Queenz left the office, Ray pulled Sheila out of the chair by her hands and wrapped his hands around her waist as she threw her arms about his neck.

"I know we haven't been having much of a relationship, lately," he said, looking into her eyes, "But once we get everything situated on both our ends, I want us to leave Georgia."

"And go where?" she asked.

"Wherever you wanna go," he answered. "I'll let you pick. I just want us to be in a comfortable environment. A place where we can live and raise kids."

"Kids?" Sheila exclaimed with excitement. "You wanna have kids?"

"I mean. If you don't want—"

"Yes," she cut him off. "I would love to have your kids."

Chapter 20

The next day, The Queenz all met up at Shonda and Sheila's house. Their first mission was to meet with Tommy, a local gun dealer in Atlanta, which was why Ebony had just exited the expressway and was now driving the GMC Denali down Ashby Street. They'd taken the for sale sign down and switched the license plate for a dealership tag.

Ebony pulled the truck into the parking lot of Club Seven Twenty and parked across from the black Dodge Durango that belonged to Tommy, also known as Usher. They dismounted and walked around to the front of the club, where Tommy was standing, talking to another guy. Seeing them, he dismissed the guy and permitted them inside the club that was empty, with the exception of his girlfriend, who was stocking the bar. She nodded at the Queenz as they followed Tommy to a back room that resembled a miniature gun shop, with several shelves containing all kinds of guns and ammunition.

"I've stepped it up since the last time y'all fell through," Tommy said, locking the door. "Y'all still got the AK and Uzi?"

"Yeah," Theresa answered, looking around. "We need three more Uzis."

"I ain't got no more of those," he responded. "I don't come across them quite often. But I got a couple of pistol grips, a Mac-ten and a bunch of handguns—plenty of those."

"Let me see the Mac-ten," Theresa told him.

"Okay," he said, taking the gun off a shelf handing it to her. "It's not loaded."

Theresa looked the gun over, then handed it to Shonda. "I know you can handle this."

"I may not have a choice." Shonda ejected the cartridge, then slid it back on.

"The pumps are too big," Theresa told Tommy. "Show me some handguns."

Tommy went from shelf to shelf, pulling handguns and laying them out on the only table in the room. Once he was done, Theresa and Sheila didn't waste any time. They were like kids in a toy shop, as they perused the weapons.

"Y'all remind me of those girls from *Set it Off*," Tommy joked. "If y'all need an extra man I'm in."

"I'll remember that," Shonda replied, not in the mood to joke.

"Is King Ray still alive?" he asked, now getting their full attention.

"What made you ask that?" Shonda was thinking about what Tino said about the public knowing Ray as the last King standing.

"I heard that shit 'bout two days ago," he answered. "The dude I was just talking to outside told me the same shit. According to the streets, he survived the shooting and is the one who put y'all on. I mean, I hope he did survive because that's my nigga! I've been knowing that fool since I was twelve. We met in juvy, Four Forty-Five Capital Avenue."

"So, why didn't we see you at the funeral?' Shonda asked, throwing a curveball. "Everybody was there."

"I didn't hear anything about it," he claimed.

"Exactly!" Shonda said. "It wasn't publicized, so a lot of people didn't hear anything about it, which is why a lot of people don't believe the Kingz are dead. There were four people buried on that day and we still visit their graves."

"I guess y'all would know better than anybody," he said, accepting what Shonda asserted.

Theresa paid for the Mac-10 and two Glocks and they were back on the expressway, on their way to their meeting with Vincent. Shonda, who was in the front passenger seat, donned her Japanese wig and a pair of dark sunglasses, while the others wore ball caps and sunglasses, although Ebony would remain behind the wheel and only enter the building if needed.

Ebony pulled the truck into the building's parking lot, where there were only four cars. As planned, she pulled the truck right up to the entrance, where she would keep watch, with the engine running.

Y'all be careful," Ebony told them. "And make it back."

"We'll make it back," Theresa promised, stuffing the Uzi into her large pocketbook. "Everybody gotta stick to the plan. Don't think about killing anybody. Just do it. A second hesitation could cost you your life. Ebony, keep the phone line clear. Sheila, don't touch shit. You know what to do when you see us get off the elevator, if we're not down in ten, make the call."

Understanding the instructions, Theresa, Shonda, and Sheila dismounted, donning their black trench coats. Shonda and Theresa were the only two carrying large pocketbooks, being that they had the bigger guns. When they entered the building, the only somebody present was the blonde-haired white woman at the front desk. They approached.

"May I help you ladies?" she asked, regarding them with an awkward look.

"The Queenz," Shonda took the initiative.

The blonde flipped open her logbook. "He's expecting you all, sixth floor."

"No need for that," Sheila said, pulling her Glock out on the woman, who'd reached for the phone. "Place your hands flat on the desk."

"Keep that bitch in line," Shonda said, as she and Theresa made for the elevators.

Shonda and Theresa donned their gloves before Shonda pressed the button for the elevator, which only took about ten seconds to arrive. Thankful that it was empty, they got on and Shonda pressed six, looking at her cousin as the doors closed. Once they were closed, she and Theresa extracted their guns from their pocketbooks but kept them out of view of the camera that was mounted in a corner, at the back of the elevator.

It was a matter of seconds when the elevator reached the sixth floor. Once the doors opened, wasting no time, they stepped off the elevator, side by side, with guns ready. Two of Vincent's men were seated in foldable chairs, playing Checkers on a foldable table, while the other two were just sitting around.

Clearly, they'd heard the elevator's bell before the doors opened, because they were looking in that direction. Of course, the second they surveyed the situation, they tried to go for their weapons. But the Uzi and Mac-10's rapid firing abilities immediately put an end to all movement.

The second their bodies hit the floor, Theresa and Shonda headed for Vincent's office, switching their clips for fresh ones. They figured Vincent had heard the shots and was probably armed and ready for them. Therefore, when they made it to the double doors, Theresa didn't give it a second thought. She turned the knob and kicked the doors open. They had their guns aimed and ready to turn Vincent's fat ass into Swiss cheese. But he was nowhere to be found, although the scent of his cologne was lingering in the air. They approached the desk, where his chair was turned as if he'd left in a hurry. Shonda doffed one of her gloves and touched the seat with the back of her hand. It was still warm.

Downstairs, Sheila had been constantly checking her watch, which now indicated that Shonda and Theresa had been upstairs for seven minutes. If they're not back in three more minutes, she was supposed to call Shonda's cell. If Shonda didn't answer, then she and Ebony were to leave immediately. But Sheila didn't fully agree with that part of the plan. If they didn't show up in the next three minutes, she was going to kill the white bitch and make her way up to the sixth floor.

She cast another glance out at Ebony, who was still waiting out front, with the engine running. Then, she heard the ding from the elevator and looked in that direction, ready to shoot anybody who didn't look like Shonda or Theresa, which was also part of the plan, but it was them. They stepped off the elevator with their guns in hand, moving fast. Sheila knew what she had to do, so she didn't hesitate. She shot the blonde in her head and watched her collapse to the floor. Shonda grabbed the logbook off the desk, and they were out the door.

"Sheila, did anybody get off the elevator before us?" Shonda asked once they were back in the truck.

"No."

"Did you see anybody out here, Ebony?"

"No," Ebony answered, speeding across the parking lot. "What happened?"

"His ass got away," Shonda said, shaking her head. "We don't know how, but he did."

"Fuck," Ebony exclaimed, her bad vibe from last night, confirmed.

Sheila, who was shaking from fear, asked, "So, what'll we do now?"

"Well," Theresa took the initiative. "Considering that Ant, Hakeem, and Blue are still out there, I think we should all be under one roof. Y'all need to move in with us. As far as this situation with Vincent, I think this is one of those times where we really need Ray's help. Shonda, I know you may not agree—"

"I agree," Shonda cut in. She'd already deduced that their chances of surviving Vincent now, was highly unlikely. "Make the call, Sheila."

Chapter 21

For some reason, Ray didn't feel like being cooped up in the house all day. He needed to make some phone calls and do a lot of thinking and planning, but for some reason, he couldn't do it in the house. Therefore, he called and informed his lieutenants that he would be at the Palace, which was where he was stationed at the office.

He'd phone Eric and told him that he'd swing by the house later, to discuss the dealership. He called and checked on Nikki, then called his suppliers to let them know he wouldn't be needing anything else. Ray was serious about leaving all this stuff behind, so once the rest of his product was sold and he tied up a few more loose ends, he was going to take Sheila and move as far away from Georgia as possible. First, he wanted to make sure her family and friends were not in any immediate danger.

Now, he was looking at the small note pad on the table in front of him that contained the names of the people he'd suspected of committing regicide against his fellow Kingz, which were: Drop Squad, Akbar, Norris, and the Kingzmen. A side of him still wanted to kick down doors, until he found everybody on his list and wipe them off the face of the earth. The other side of him knew God had spared his life for other unknown purposes and that he needed to take advantage of it. As much as he hated the true nature of that fact, he knew he had to abandon his zeal for retaliation and move on.

His cell phone vibrated atop the table, bringing him out of his abstract thinking. Sheila's number was on the screen. "Hey babe," he answered.

"Hey," she replied, sounding sad.

"What's wrong," he asked, hoping she was only sounding that way because she'd just awakened.

"We need to talk," she told him. "As soon as you're available."

"I'm available now," he said. "What's the problem?"

"Can I come to your house?"

"I'm not at home, I'm at the Palace."

"Well, can I come there?" she asked. "As a matter of fact, we're not too far from there. Ebony can drop me off."

"Okay," Ray concurred. "Call me when y'all get to the gate."

Getting off the phone with Sheila, Ray didn't know what to make of her inflection. It was new to him. She didn't sound like she was about to tell him she was pregnant, but more like she was about to tell him that she was pregnant by someone else. He did not like that inflection. It took almost twenty minutes for her to call back and tell him they'd arrived. Ray got into his Mercedes and drove up to the gate, where their truck was wait-ing. Before he could bring his car to a complete stop, Sheila emerged from the rear of the SUV, in a long, black trench coat. The lock and chain wasn't affixed to the gate, so Ray pulled it open, just wide enough for her to pass through. Ebony, who was driving the truck, blew the horn and they all waved. He nodded in return as they backed out. He was surprised that was the only form of greeting he'd gotten from them. He was even more sur-prised that Sheila didn't greet him at all, as she passed him and climbed into the passenger seat of his car.

'*Yeah, this gotta be bad,*' Ray thought as he pushed the gate up and got back into the car.

Sheila was looking out the window as if she was attentively avoiding his gaze. Of course, she was quiet for the short ride to the building. Upon entering the building, they made for the office, where Ray sat in his chair and Sheila sat in Fred's. Ray placed his cell phone and keys on the table, leaned back in his chair and silently waited for Sheila to speak her mind.

"Have you found Fred's key yet?" Sheila finally spoke, eyeing his set of keys.

"Nah," he answered slowly, noting how suddenly her mood had changed, which induced him to think of Sylvia.

"What do they go to?"

"A safe," he answered, not wanting to lie to her.

"They all go to a safe?" she sounded doubtful.

Saying nothing, he got up and pressed the button on the side of the wooden box that clicked the door open, then sat down as she eyed the safe.

"Oh!" she said. "Now I see, you need all four keys to open it."

"Yeah," he answered, studying her while she studied the safe.

He couldn't deny that he was in love with her. She was a really good woman, not the kind of woman one would expect to be caught up in the things she was caught up in, which was why he was determined to get her away from the life she had no business living.

"So, what made you think Theresa had Fred's key?" asked Sheila.

"I spoke to Fred's brother," Ray explained. "He said he'd spoken to Fred that night, while they were on their way to the D.J. battle. Fred told him to tell me that somebody named Lisa had the key. I thought he might have said Theresa instead of Lisa."

That's when it dawned on him that, in order for Fred to send him such a message to him through Eric, then he had to have known they were going to die that night. It was as if he'd made preparations, which is why his key wasn't on the keyring. Now, Ray was vividly reliving that night. He remembered how extremely quiet Fred was when they arrived at his house. In fact, Fred had a worried look on his face.

The last thing Fred said to Ray as they were leaving was, "God works in mysterious ways. Just don't take it for granted."

"Fred must've had some kind of vision of that shit," Ray now spoke, regarding the Mona Lisa Painting. "He figured me being sick that night was a gift. He knew that shit was gonna happen. He prepared for it. That's probably why he wanted to stop by the Palace, that night. But why would he—" That's when he realized who Lisa was. "Shit!"

Ray got up and leaned the large picture forward. Just as he'd suspected, Fred's key was taped to the back of it. He pulled it off and regarded it as if he'd found some kind of buried treasure.

"You found it?"

Ray looked over at Sheila, who he'd almost forgotten was in the room. "Yeah," he answered. "Mona Lisa had it all this time."

Relieved, Ray grabbed his keys off the table and added Fred's key to his keyring, then used the keys to unlock the safe. He opened the safe and took a few seconds to evaluate the bills that filled up more than half the safe with their record book sitting on top. Grabbing the record book, he took his seat and opened it up on the table. According to the book, the safe contained a little over six hundred thousand dollars.

"Have you thought about where you wanna move to?" Ray asked Sheila.

"I haven't even had time to sit down and think," she answered, shaking her head. "We still have a lot going on, right now."

"I understand," he said, leaning back in his chair. "What was it you needed to talk to me about."

She hesitated for a few seconds, before asking, "What do you know about Vincent?"

"The loan shark?"

"Yeah."

"Only that he is a loan shark," Ray answered. "I've never met him."

"He said he'd dealt with, King James," she informed.

"That's not true," Ray told her. "We didn't have money problems."

"Well—" she started. "—when you turned us down, we ended up dealing with him. We owed him two hundred and eighty thousand. We had his money—"

"But y'all house was broken into," he finished for her. "The Queenzmen made off with his money in the process. When's the deadline?"

"It was last Sunday," she answered. "Shonda and Theresa went to see him and asked for more time to come up with his money. He only gave us a week. We knew if we didn't come up with his money, he was going to send somebody after us. So, we went after him."

"Y'all what?" Ray sat up in his chair, not willing to believe what he'd just heard.

"We went after him, earlier," she said. "But somehow, he got away."

"Why didn't you just ask me for the money?"

Sheila just dropped her head. Now, Ray knew he had to find out everything he could on Vincent, find him, and try to pay off the Queenz debt. Nine times out of ten, being that they'd attempted to take his life, money was no longer an interest to him.

He wanted their heads!

After dropping Sheila off at the Palace, the rest of the Queenz rode out of Norcross, to get some of Shonda's and Sheila's things from their house, being that they were all going to be staying with Ebony and Theresa for the time being. Once they'd packed enough clothes and hygiene products, Ebony and Theresa tailed Shonda in her Mustang, to their house.

After getting Shonda situated in the guest room, Ebony made for the kitchen to find something to cook, while Shonda and Theresa retired to the living room to scan the logbook Shonda had taken from the front desk of Vincent's establishment, to see if they could find something that avails them in locating Vincent. All the book contained were names, dates and the time of appointments. Not one name was familiar to them.

"This is not gonna help us," Theresa stated. "We don't know one name in here, except ours."

"Let me start from the front," Shonda flipped the book closed, then opened it from the front.

"Well, I gotta piss," Theresa announced, getting up.

She journeyed off to the bathroom, while Shonda proceeded to peruse the book that dated back to June of two thousand two. A lot of names seemed to be government names, while some were so distant, like, Milk-Man, OP, Skully, etc. She ran her index finger along the list of names as she sifted through the pages that gradually went into the next year. Almost immediately, she came across the name she'd been looking for. King James, according to the book, James had visited Vincent on the twenty-eighth of January in two thousand three. It was not that Shonda doubted Vincent's assertion of dealing with James. She just wanted to see if his name was still in the book. Other than that, like Theresa said, the book was no help to them. She closed it, just as Theresa entered the living room.

"Find anything?" Theresa asked, peering out of the curtains, before taking her seat on the sofa.

"Nah," Shonda answered. "The only hope we have now is Ray."

"Beef stew and rice, y'all," Ebony announced, upon exiting the kitchen.

"That'll work," Theresa said. "I haven't eaten since breakfast."

"Yeah, I skipped breakfast myself," Shonda admitted.

"Well, it should be ready in a minute," Ebony said, retreating back to the kitchen.

Just as promised, the meal was done in less than five minutes. They all assembled at the kitchen table, though it was done in silence. After they'd eaten, Shonda volunteered to wash the dishes, Theresa returned to the living room to watch the front of the house and Ebony headed to her bedroom to prepare for her shower. While Ebony was looking through her drawers, the large brown paper bag sitting beside the dresser, caught her attention. It was the bag the FBI agent had given her at Erica's funeral. She'd forgotten all about it. Disregarding what she was doing, Ebony picked the bag up and sat it atop the dresser. It was sealed by four, large staples, so she ripped the bag open. Inside was Erica's Gucci pocketbook, brown Prada boots and Baby Phat jean suit that was neatly folded.

Ebony laid the items out on the dresser. Then, looking through Erica's pocketbook, she pulled out Erica's cell, to see that the battery was dead. Placing it on the dresser, next she pulled out Erica's diary. Feeling something bulging inside, she opened it up and saw that it was Erica's pen she'd apparently forgotten to return to its clasp. As she put the pen where it belonged, she noticed the date at the top of the page, which was the date Erica was murdered. Plus, Erica had already written on that page.

Ebony read:

Guess what? I am soo excited! Right now, I'm leaving the clinic, on my way to tell my baby that I'm having his baby. This time, everything's legit. Now my mom can stop harassing me about a grandbaby. I haven't told her or Ebony yet, I'll tell them after I tell my baby daddy. I'll have to come back, later, and explain how happy he was...

Tears filled Ebony's eyes, she already had to live with the fact that her sister was murdered in cold blood. Now she had to live with the fact that her sister died with a seed inside her.

"You alright, baby?"

Ebony, who didn't remember taking a seat on the bed, looked up to see Theresa standing in the doorway. She couldn't even form half of a word to respond. Instead, she held the diary out to her. Theresa read the passage, then sat down beside Ebony, wrapping an arm around her waist. She didn't know what to tell her friend, so that was the only form of comfort she could come up with.

"What's wrong?" Shonda appeared in the doorway.

Theresa handed her the diary.

"Damn," Shonda said after reading it.

Then as if she'd missed something, Shonda read it again. That's when she noticed something written at the bottom of the page in the corner. The words were small but decipherable. They read *Rico Drop Squ—*

Then, there was a crooked line that seemed to run off the page, as if Erica was interrupted in the process.

"Did y'all see this at the bottom of the page?" Shonda asked them.

Chapter 22

B.J. and Rick had taken Ray's advice and chose to move to Nevada, which was why B.J. was now waiting for Rick to show up with his girlfriend, Keeby and their two-year-old son. They'd purchased an RV, in which he and his girlfriend, Krystal were sitting in, parked in the parking lot of Piggly Wiggly's, where they'd decided to meet up in lieu of pulling the camper into East Lake Meadows, which would've pretty much announced their decampment.

"They need to come on," BJ asserted, looking at his watch, then through the large wing mirror at his car that sat up on the trailer attached to the camper. "I'm already feeling sleepy."

"You want me to drive, first?" Krystal, who was seated in the passenger seat, asked.

"I got it." Just then, he spotted a taxicab pulling into the lot. "This better be them."

The taxi, that was a caravan, pulled to the right side of the camper. Once Rick and Keeby transferred their things from the cab to the camper, B.J. pulled out of the parking lot, heading for the expressway.

"Las Vegas here we come!" Keeby, who was holding her son, exclaimed.

"I can't wait to hit the casino," Krystal said.

"Oh, don't think y'all finna be gambling up our money," B.J. informed.

"Ah, earth to B.J.," Krystal replied. "Clearly, you must've forgot that we had jobs and managed to save a whole bunch of money—our own money."

"Yeah," Keeby backed her up. "And if we go broke, then we'll start gambling y'all money. Rick, you'll be babysitting."

"Man, nobody's gonna let y'all alley asses in their casino," Rick joked.

"So, I'm an alley now?" Keeby faced Rick.

B.J. was laughing.

"I'm glad you find that funny," Krystal took it out on B.J. "And you just sat there and let him call me alley."

"Shit, that's between y'all," B.J. said, keeping his eyes on the road as he traveled the highway.

"Okay," Krystal said. "When that lil' thing gets hard and you need some, that'll be between you and Rick."

"Damn, baby," B.J. said. "You just went left field on a nigga. I was just fucking wit' cha."

Krystal smacked her lips, folded her arms over her chest and pretended to be interested in the road ahead. But B.J. didn't sweat it. He knew he could get the pussy, right now, if he wanted it. To show her he wasn't fazed by her façade, he turned the radio on and flipped through the stations until he found V-103, where *Keyshia Cole's 'I Should've Cheated'* was playing. Now, he was regretting he'd done that. It put a smile on her face, but he didn't expect her to join forces with Keeby and turn into the '*World Class Wrecking Crew*,' because they were definitely wrecking a nice song.

"Who sings that song?" B.J. asked.

"Keyshia Cole," Krystal answered.

"Well, y'all need to let her sing it," he said. "Y'all sound like some drunk ass old women at the bootleggers' house."

Krystal punched him in the arm as they all laughed, but their laughter was interrupted by what sounded like multiple firecrackers being set off. It only took half a second for them to realize it wasn't firecrackers, as a hail of bullets perforated the right side of the RV. On instinct, B.J. stomped the gas pedal as he glanced over into the right-wing mirror.

It was dark and the expressway was lit by headlights and taillights, but he could make out some four-door, dark-colored car, driving alongside them, with the back window down which was where the gunman was firing from. Even with the pedal to the floor, the camper didn't seem to have picked up any kind of speed. The gunfire seemed to cease as if the shooter was reloading. The car moved closer to the front of the camper. B.J. knew if the gunman was reloading, it wouldn't be long before it started up again. Seeing that he didn't have a chance of outrunning the car, he came up with the only solution he could. The second he'd thought it, the shooting resumed. A bullet to the arm, galvanized B.J. to initiate the plan he'd concocted.

B.J. snatched the steering wheel to the right, plowing the RV into the car and forcing it towards the shoulder of the interstate. This maneuver pushed the trailer that carried B.J.'s car into a fishtail, which spiraled to the left of the camper, caught a gust of wind under it and went into a flip taking the camper with it.

****

"I've always wanted to visit the United Kingdom," Sheila told Ray.

They'd just finished making love and were lying on their sides, facing each other. They were still naked, with the covers pulled up to their waists. Before leaving the Palace, Ray burned the Kingz record book but brought the money back to the house. All the money plus his record book wouldn't fit into his safe, so he had to stash some of the money in a shoebox, in the closet of his bedroom. Plus, he'd given his lieutenants another mission, which was to find out all they could on Vincent.

"Is that where you wanna go?" Ray now asked Sheila.

"It seems like it might be a nice place to live," she replied. "They just talk funny as hell." Sheila giggled.

"They do," Ray insisted. "But if that's where you wanna go, I'm cool with it. If it's not what we like, we can always migrate."

"Somebody's at the front gate," Sheila told him, regarding one of the monitors.

"I know damn well—" Ray said, looking at the monitor, seeing B.J. standing outside of a taxi, waving his hands at the camera.

Ray got out of bed, slid into his pants and shirt, grabbed his 9mm Beretta and left the room. Getting to the front door, he punched in the code on his alarm pad to activate the gate. Then, tucking his gun into his pocket, he stepped outside where the wind had to be doing at least fifty miles per hour.

When the taxi pulled up to the house, B.J. climbed out of the passenger side. For a second Ray thought B.J. and Rick had stolen the damn cab.

"I need some money to pay the cab driver," B.J. said, approaching. "I'm fucked up."

Ray almost hit him with a million questions but noticing the minor cuts and bruises on B.J.'s face, parried the thought. Instead, he asked how much the fare was. Then went inside to retrieve the money. Once the cab driver left, Ray followed B.J. into the living room, where B.J. turned to face him, with an angry expression on his face.

"What?" Ray asked, annoyed by his posture.

"Who just tried to kill me?"

"How the fuck would I know," Ray let out, not liking the fact that his friend was accusing him of such a feat. "What happened?"

B.J. peeled off the snug fitted coat he was wearing, letting it fall to the floor. The whole right sleeve of his sweater was drenched in blood. There was an Ace bandage wrapped tightly around his biceps, which was also bloodstained.

"We were on our way," B.J. spoke, shaking his head. "We had bought a camper and everything. We were on our way to Nevada. Me, Krystal, Rick, Keeby and their two-year-old son. We hadn't even been on the expressway for ten minutes when some car pulled up beside us. Somebody was bussin' from the back seat. I couldn't outrun the car, so I rammed the camper into it. the fucking camper flipped over."

"Where's the rest of 'em?" Ray inquired when B.J. paused.

B.J. just looked at him, pretty much confirming what he'd already figured.

"And how'd you get away?'

"The windshield was already shattered," B.J. explained. "I kicked the rest of it out and ran across the expressway. That's when I saw the car. It had crashed into the guardrail. I didn't stop to see who was in it. I jetted through the bushes and still don't know what street I came out on. Some nigga saw me and thought I was running from twelve. His mama got the bullet outta my arm."

"Then you called a cab," Ray finished for him. That's when he noticed Sheila standing in the threshold, wearing his housecoat. "Go back to bed, baby." When she left, he turned back to B.J. "We gotta get you on a bus, tonight."

Sheila returned to the bedroom, what she'd heard from Ray's friend gave her the notion that she needed to call and check on her girls, so she retrieved her cell and dialed Shonda's number.

"I was just about to call you," Shonda answered. "Is everything okay?"

"I'm fine," Sheila responded. "But somebody tried to kill Ray's friend."

"Which one?" Shonda seemed concerned.

"The chubby, light-skinned one," Sheila said, then told Shonda everything she'd heard.

"Girl, we're watching that shit on the news, right now," Shonda exclaimed. "It was Drop Squad."

"Did they say Drop Squad?"

"No, but I'll explain that some other time. What did Ray say about, Vincent?"

"He got his lieutenants on it," Sheila answered. "But he said his brother never dealt with Vincent."

"King James' name is in Vincent's logbook," Shonda begged to differ. "I won't speak on what I believe, right now. Plus, we have another matter on our hands. Tell your King we need to arrange a meeting, as soon as tomorrow."

"What kind of matter?" Sheila asked, preparing herself for another dose of bad news.

"I'll tell you at the meeting," Shonda replied, then hung up, just as Ray entered the room.

Sheila watched as he put on some boxers and threw his pants back on. After putting on socks and shoes, he put on his twin-gun holster, checked his guns, then donned a light jacket.

"Where are you going?" Sheila asked, regarding his actions as rude.

"I gotta drop B.J. off at the Greyhound station," he answered, as he counted bills out of a shoebox, onto the dresser.

"And you plan on leaving me by myself?"

"I'll be right back."

"Negative." She took off his robe and began putting her clothes on. "I hate to intrude, but I'm not staying here by myself. If it's a problem, then I'll just—"

"I didn't say you couldn't go," Ray cut her off, then left the room.

Ray went to the garage and started his car before returning to the living room, where B.J. was standing in front of the TV, watching the news that was doing a report of his incident. Ray wasn't too much interested in the TV, he had a mission to complete.

"This is fifty thousand," he said handing B.J. a stack of bills. "This should last you a long time in Mexico."

B.J. accepted the bills, just as Sheila entered the living room.

"Let's ride," Ray said, then led the way to the garage.

When they climbed into the Benz, *Letoya Luckett's 'Torn'*, was playing on the radio, which was the only sound in the car, as they made for the bus station in Atlanta.

"Do you mind waiting in the car?" Ray asked Sheila when he pulled into the parking lot that accommodated the Greyhound station, Marta transit station and Pretrial detention Center.

"How long will you be?"

"I really can't say," he answered. "At least until he's on the bus. But I'll try to stand where I can see the car. Okay?"

"Okay," she replied, leaning over and kissing him.

Leaving the engine running, Ray and B.J. dismounted and made for the bus terminal. Ray let B.J. walk the rest of the way to the ticket booth, while he stood in a spot that allowed him to see the roof of his car and the ticket booth.

There was a light crowd, so Ray had a good panorama of the booths. Plus, it wouldn't be too hard for him to spot any potential threats. He just wished he'd worn a bigger coat to parry the strong wind that assailed him. His only solution was to shove his hands into his pockets, as he looked back and forth from the ticket booth to his car and periodically surveyed the crowd. B.J. was the third in line at one of the booths.

A bus pulling into the station caught Ray's attention. He was hoping like hell it was B.J.'s bus, but it wasn't. It was going to New York. Ray looked over at his car, then back towards the ticket booths. That's when he thought his mind was playing tricks on him. His eyes were watery, induced by the cold air. He wiped them with the back of his hand and tried again. The lady who was in front of B.J. was now at the window and the man who was standing behind B.J. was now standing behind the lady.

Ray eyed the crowd, hoping to spot B.J. by the light blue coat he was wearing, but didn't see him. He knew damn well B.J. didn't give up his spot in line, to run to the restroom. That didn't make any kind of sense, although it wouldn't be the first time B.J. had done something that didn't make sense, Ray glanced back at the booth, as if B.J., may have magically reappeared. That was not the case. After surveying the crowd once more, realization kicked in. Now he knew he was going to have to do something he should've done in the first place.

Chapter 23

The following day, Ray called a Queenz and King meeting at the Queenz behest, after Sheila relayed Shonda's message to him, which was why he and Sheila were sitting in the office of the Palace, waiting for the rest of them to arrive.

Ray had not mentioned anything to Sheila about what happened, last night. Neither had he mentioned it to his lieutenant, this morning. But as much as he didn't want to, he knew he was going to have to bring it to Poppo and Joe's attention, right after his meeting with the Queenz.

"What do you plan on doing with this building?" Sheila asked, pulling Ray from his thoughts.

"First, I thought about turning it into a club," Ray answered. "And leaving it to my lieutenants to run, but I might just sell it and be done with it."

"What would be the name of the club?"

"The Palace," he answered, as Joe stuck his head in, announcing the Queenz arrival.

"Send 'em in," Ray told him.

They entered the office and Ray relinquished his seat to Ebony and sat on the wooden box containing the safe.

"I already know about y'all situation with, Vincent," Ray started. "I got my lieutenants on it. As soon as I can reach him, I'll see if he'll let me pay the debt, which I seriously doubt. If that's the case, then I'll take other actions. Queen Shonda?"

"First, I wanna show you proof that King James dealt with, Vincent," Shonda stated, handing him the logbook. "Page eight."

Ray opened the book to the eighth page and ran his index finger along the list of names until he came across his brother's. According to the book, King James met with Vincent on January twenty-eighth of two thousand three. Now, this had Ray thinking about the amount of money and cocaine he'd found at James' house after James' death, which was more than he'd expected his brother to have in his possession. So, he had no choice but to accept all this as true.

Then, realizing there had to be another meeting date for James to pay what he owed, Ray slowly flipped through the pages until he found it. James had returned on March twenty-fourth, but this didn't add up to him. If James had not paid Vincent what he'd owed, then why would he wait almost five months to take action? The checks by each name had to indicate the clients making their appointments, so, if James didn't plan on paying Vincent back, why would he even attempt to make his appointment? It just didn't add up.

"Can I keep this?" Ray asked Shonda.

"We don't need it."

Ray placed the book on the box beside him. "What else?"

"I think we know who killed Erica," Shonda said. "Give it to him, Queen Ebony."

Ebony handed him an open diary. Ray read what was written on the page but saw no indications of Erica's killer.

"I don't get it," he said, looking from Shonda to Ebony.

"Look at the bottom of the page," Shonda told him. "Being that Ted's body was found in the living room and Erica's body was found in the bedroom. We figured she must've heard them arguing in the living room and may have witnessed his murder. Somehow, she knew Rico's name and knew she was going to die. To make sure she was avenged or that her killer was caught, she wrote his name in her diary. She didn't know his last name, but she knew the name of his organization. But, in the midst of jotting that down, she was discovered."

Looking at the words at the bottom of the page and how the words were abruptly cut off, Ray couldn't help but concur with Shonda's assessment. It made perfectly good sense.

"Do you know him?"

"I've heard of him," Ray answered, handing the diary back to her. "I can already sense y'all are on the road to revenge. What do y'all have in mind?"

"We haven't run it by, Queen Sheila yet," Shonda spoke up. "But the rest of us have decided to attack Drop Squad until we catch Rico, Then, we'll skip town."

"That would clearly be suicide," Ray voiced. "But who am I to speak on that? When do y'all plan to go on this ride?"

"Tonight." Shonda turned to Sheila. "Are you in?"

Sheila locked eyes with Ray, as if she was expecting him to answer for her, then turned back to Shonda. "I'm in."

"What kind of artillery do y'all have?" Ray inquired.

"Do you know a guy by the name of, Tommy?' Shonda asked.

"Yeah, I know Tommy, aka Usher."

"We bought some handguns off him, today."

"Handguns!'

"That's all he had," Shonda avowed. "He'd already sold the pistol grip pumps he had."

"Y'all are already outnumbered," he explained. "Look, at least I can do is get y'all some real guns."

Ray knew he couldn't stop Sheila from taking that ride, but he was going to make sure they were well equipped. He wasn't just worried about Sheila, he was worried about them all. When the four of them left, Ray called Poppo and Joe into the office.

"What's the word on, Vincent?" Ray asked Poppo, once they'd sat down.

"I sent my girl out there to make like she's looking for a job," Poppo answered. "She said the Feds wasn't letting nobody inside the building. I guess they're still investigating."

"Well, stay on that," Ray said. "I got a few more tasks to lay on y'all. First, I need y'all to find out the names of every major nigga in Drop Squad. Find out whatever y'all can on, Rico of Drop squad. Then put an APB out on B.J."

"Word?' Poppo asked as if he'd been waiting for Ray to say that. "Is it a hit?"

"Yeah," Ray answered. "It's a hit."

Ray never thought it would come to this, but B.J. had forced his hand. He only had two choices, which were to persuade B.J. and Rick to leave the States or take them out himself, before they were caught by Drop Squad or the authorities and brought heat his way. All B.J. had to do was board that bus to Mexico and never look back. '*Well*,' Ray thought. '*If you make your bed, you gotta lay in it.*' He knew Poppo was dying to be the one to tuck him in.

Upon leaving the Palace, Ray placed a call to Eric and insisted they needed to talk. Eric told him to stop by after six. Joe and Poppo had runs to make, so Ray told them to go ahead, instead of following him home. He didn't tell them that he wasn't going straight home. In fact, he told them to meet back up with him, tomorrow.

Hungry, Ray had a taste for Burger King and ventured to the restaurant. Instead of the drive-thru, he went inside, ordered his food and sat back at the not too crowded burger joint, where he slowly consumed his food and mulled over his thoughts. Mulling over his thoughts seemed to put him in a state of agitation. All he wanted to do was take Sheila and relocate to a better environment. It seemed like, as soon as he thinks he's close to doing that a new situation arises.

Speaking of new situations, one had just entered the restaurant. She was carrying her son, who Ray knew to be almost three years old. He watched as she approached the counter to order their food, then put her son down to pay for the order. Ray's attention fell upon her child, who was looking around. Considering the boy's facial features, Ray could pretty much tell who fathered him.

Receiving her order on a tray, Kim turned and was headed in Ray's direction. She'd only taken a few steps when she spotted him. She immediately stopped in her tracks. For a second, Ray thought she was going to drop the tray. He motioned for her to have a seat across from him. After a second of lingering, Kim, followed by her son, approached the table. She set the tray down and her son, who hadn't paid Ray an ounce of attention, climbed into the seat, clearly ready to eat. Kim sat and laid his food out on a tray for him, in which he immediately attacked.

Now, Kim regarded Ray. "I thought—"

"Everybody thought that," he cut her off, then explained why he's the last King standing.

"Some guys in my apartments were talking about you, the other day," Kim told him. "They were saying you were still alive and that you were the one who put the Queenz on. As a matter of fact, I stay in your old apartments."

"Maple Creek?"

"Yeah."

Ray nodded at the kid. "And who is this?"

"My son, James," she answered, looking at Ray as if she knew he was about to controvert that.

"Who's his dad?" Ray tested.

"James Young."

"Are you sure?"

"Mark took a paternity test," she answered with a hint of attitude. "He's not the father. There was no one else and Mark is paralyzed from the waist down. He and some dude got into it over some girl and somehow, the dude shot Mark in the back."

Ray was not surprised to hear that. He'd already said that, somehow, pussy was going to send Mark to his grave. Ray didn't care to dwell on him, nor his condition. The nigga brought it on himself. After exchanging numbers with Kim, Ray made his exit. He really didn't care if she told anybody he was still alive because it seemed like everyone already knew.

Ray gassed his Benz up and made it to Eric's house, minutes after six. Eric let him in, and it seemed as if they were anticipating his arrival, because Sharonda was already seated in the living room, with the deed to the dealership on the table.

"I'm not ready to discuss that yet," Ray told Sharonda as he took a seat beside her on the sofa. "I need to talk to Eric about something else, in private."

Sharonda didn't bother to contend. She grabbed the deed off the table and left them alone. Eric took a seat on the sofa.

"What's up?"

"Do you know any names of any major niggas in, Drop Squad?" Ray inquired.

"Nah," Eric answered, shaking his head. "That's who you suspect of that shit?"

"I still got them at the top of my list," Ray told him. "But that's not why I asked. That's not why I'm here, I need some artillery."

"What kind of artillery?"

"The kind the US troops had in Desert Storm."

The Queenz were all dressed in black and assembled at the kitchen table, where there were eight handguns, extra clips, and boxes of bullets sitting in front of them.

"Like I said," Theresa was speaking. "It's shoot on sight. Don't think, don't blink, just shoot. We don't know how this'll turn out, but I'm counting on my basic training skills and my fear no man attitude to get us through this. I just hope we make it through this alive."

"We all do," Shonda said, checking her watch, seeing it was a few minutes after seven. "Sheila call Ray and ask him what's the hold-up."

Sheila dialed Ray's number from her cell phone.

"I should be fifteen minutes out," Ray answered his phone, apparently checking the caller I.D.

"Okay," Sheila relayed this to the others.

"Anybody feel like they can't go through with this?" Shonda asked, looking around the table at her colleagues. No one spoke. "We have to also be on the lookout for Ant, Hakeem, and Blue. They're definitely on our list, shoot on sight."

"We've gone from drug dealers to killers," Ebony said.

"Which is something we were forced into," Shonda replied. "I don't know what kind of life we'll live after this, but I don't think I can go back to the dope game."

"I'll go back to doing hair," Ebony said.

Sheila felt this was the best time to reveal what she and Ray had planned. "Ray and I are moving to the U.K.," she announced.

"The U.K.?" they all exclaimed in unison.

"We decided on that, last night," she told them. "If we like it there, that's where we'll raise our children."

"That's a damn good plan," Shonda said, nodding. "Maybe I can come visit y'all sometime."

"It would be nice if all of y'all could come and visit."

The doorbell rang, startling everyone except Theresa, who'd immediately grabbed her two handguns off the table and marched out of the kitchen. The others did likewise and were right behind her. Getting to the door, Theresa peered through the transom and almost didn't recognize Ray for the black skull cap he was wearing. She tucked one gun, unlocked and opened the door for Ray, who was also clad in black clothing under his trench coat and carrying a large duffle bag on his shoulder.

Saying nothing, Ray entered the house and went straight to the kitchen. The Queenz followed. Opening the duffle Ray, one at a time pulled out AK-47s, handing one to each of them. After pulling out a fifth one, which was his, he turned the bag over on the table, pouring out boxes of ammunition and eight more extended clips that were bound together in twos by duct tape, just as the other clips were that were sticking out of the AKs.

"Now if I'm not mistaken," Ray spoke. "Y'all wanna go around bussin' on anybody who's wearing a Drop Squad chain, until y'all catch, Rico. Am I right?" No one spoke. "Well, I have a less risky plan. I know three dope houses that are operated by Drop Squad. Y'all want Rico and y'all need some get out of town money. This could work both ways. Once we get inside the houses, we put everybody on the floor and search 'em for weapons. One stay in the truck, two search the house and two stay with the hostages. That'll be the time to ask questions. We don't really need masks, because we're not leaving any witnesses. Any questions?"

"I don't know how to work this kind of gun," Sheila admitted.

"I'm lost, too," Ebony confessed.

Theresa stepped in and gave them AK-47 one on one. Once that was done, they all exited the house, following Ray to a dark blue Chevy Suburban parked out front. He made sure to crank the truck up via the left side of the destroyed steering column, with a screwdriver, before climbing into the rear, followed by Theresa, who climbed into the third seat and Sheila who sat beside him. Shonda got into the front passenger seat and Ebony into the drivers.

Their first house was in Decatur, off Flat Shoals Road. As they rode, Ray delegated chores to each of them, so everyone would know what to do once they were in. At Ray's directions, Ebony pulled the truck across the street from the house, which had two cars in the driveway.

"Do I need to turn the truck around?' Ebony asked.

"Nah," answered Ray. "This street leads to other streets. A bunch of back streets, we'll definitely need to use. Just watch our backs."

The rest of them dismounted and crossed the street to the house, looking around, AKs concealed under their trench coats. Making it to the front door, Ray eased the screened door open and tried the knob on the main door, it was locked. Gesturing for Shonda to hold the screen door, Ray backed up and fired a few rounds into the side of the wooden door, then was able to kick it open with ease. Wasting no time, they rushed inside with guns up. There were three men and one woman sitting in the living room, where two scales, a stack of bills and Ziploc bags of cocaine and weed cluttered the table. The stereo was playing and weed smoke was in the air. The three men and the woman. Who were all wearing Drop Squad chains, were clearly caught off guard. Their eyes bulged with fear, they looked as if they didn't know if they should flee or go for their weapons.

"On the floor, now!" Ray barked.

They all complied, as Sheila and Theresa branched off to search the rest of the house. Shonda searched the four affiliates, finding two guns. Seconds later, Sheila ushered another female into the living room, who wasn't wearing a Drop Squad chain. Once she was on the floor, Sheila set off to resume her search.

Shonda cut off the stereo. "Anybody wanna tell me where Rico is?"

No one answered. "So, don't nobody know, Rico?"

She still didn't get a response. Ray was impressed. A lot of people would give up their own mothers when put in situations like this. These people were clearly showing their loyalty and devotion for whoever they'd pledged their oaths to. Sheila and Theresa returned to the living room, both carrying black trash bags that were loaded. Sheila cleared the table, placing everything but two scales into her bag.

"We gotta be out," Ray announced. "Do what y'all gotta do."

Theresa and Shonda executed the members. Then, they were out the door, moving quickly to the Suburban. People were standing outside their homes. Plus, the sound of sirens could be heard in a distance. As soon as they were back in the truck, Ebony sped off and by Ray's instructions, made it back to the expressway, driving towards East Point.

"How many were in the house?' Ebony finally asked.

"Five," Shonda answered.

"Did y'all ask them about, Rico?"

"Yeah, they wouldn't talk."

"Y'all killed all of 'em?"

"Yep."

After a few seconds of silence, Ebony said, "I should've gone in. That was my sister, from now on, I'm going in. I'm not staying in the truck."

Ray felt her pain. "Sheila, you'll be staying in the truck. Ebony, you'll have to take on Sheila's task."

Ebony pulled the truck across the street from a red-bricked house that had two cars in the driveway and one parked at the curb. Before they could get out, the front door opened, and a man emerged from the house. Despite the large coat he was wearing they couldn't tell he was wearing a Drop Squad chain, as he neared the car at the curb.

Clearly, he wasn't the observative type, because not once did he look around before getting into his car and driving away. Once he was gone, they dismounted the truck, Sheila taking Ebony's place behind the wheel and made for the house. Getting to the door, Ray tried the knob, it was unlocked. He nodded to them before thrusting the door open. The living room was empty, but one man was found in the kitchen, weighing up cocaine at the table. Seeing them, he froze.

"Get up,' Ray ordered, gun aimed. The man cooperated. "In the living room."

Ray and Shonda followed him to the living room, while Ebony and Theresa searched the rest of the house, finding another man in one bedroom, sprawled out on the bed with one hand tucked down the front of his pants while watching a pornographic movie on a flat-screen TV.

"Get your desperate ass up," Theresa demanded.

The man snatched his hand from his pants, clearly embarrassed, but did as he was told. Theresa told Ebony to search the room, as she escorted the man to the living room, where Shonda and Ray were stationed. Ray ordered him to lie on the floor beside his friend, as Theresa retreated. Neither Ray nor Shonda endeavored to question the men. They agreed to leave that to Ebony. It wasn't long before Ebony and Theresa had returned, carrying large trash bags full of weed, cocaine, and money.

"Theresa, grab that stuff off the kitchen table," Ray said, then grabbed the bag from Ebony. "They're all yours," he told her, indicating the men on the floor.

Ebony walked over and pressed the barrel of her gun into the back of the man they'd found in the kitchen. "I'm not gonna ask but one time," she spoke slowly. "Where's Rico?'

"Never heard of him," the man replied.

174

Ebony was true to her word, she did not ask again. Instead, she pulled the trigger, surprising Shonda, Ray and even Theresa, who'd just entered the living room. She pressed the barrel of her gun to the other man's back, but she didn't have to repeat her question.

"Man, Rico don't have a stable address," the man offered. "He be staying with different women. He drives a turquoise Monte Carlo on gold Ds. I don't know about none of the women he fucks with, except Duchess. She dances at Strokers, tall, light-skinned bitch with blonde hair."

"Felicia!' Shonda exclaimed.

Ray looked over at Shonda, again surprised to hear her speak Felicia's name. But now he was remembering that Black had told him about encountering a Rico at Felicia's house, who was a member of Drop Squad. The same Rico he'd been hearing about since Drop Squad had surfaced.

Theresa was now remembering Rico. He was the one who approached her and Ebony at her birthday party at Club Strokers. In fact, he'd actually told them his name. "We need to pay Felicia a visit."

Playa Ray

Chapter 24

Ray wasn't against the Queenz visiting Felicia, but he couldn't chance them confronting her all gung-ho and harming her for something she hadn't taken part in. Therefore, upon leaving the house, Ray immediately called a meeting. At that point, no one was interested in the third house that was on Ray's list, so they ditched the Suburban where Ray left his Mercedes, then rode back to Riverdale.

Now, they were all assembled in the kitchen, where the money and drugs from the two houses were laid out on the table. Everybody was seated, except Sheila, who was standing behind Ray, with her hands rested on his shoulders.

"I know how eager y'all are to catch this nigga," Ray was saying. "But y'all need to sit down and come up with some kind of plan. Felicia is not to be harmed in no kind of way. Not even accidental."

"We already know about the ties you have with her," Shonda replied. "I'm hoping we can catch him by himself. But if she's around when we do, then I'll do everything in my powers to make sure she's not injured in the ordeal. That's my word."

"Y'all want me to buy the drugs from y'all?" Ray asked, changing the subject, now regarding the drugs on the table.

"We can handle it," Shonda said. "We still have a handful of clients we can make a few quick plays to."

"Not quick enough," Ray insisted. "Once y'all kill, Rico, y'all got to get out of town. Asap! As a matter of fact, y'all need to be already packed. Tie up all loose ends and leave nobody behind, but Sheila. She'll be under my care, so y'all don't have to worry about her at all."

"He's right, Shonda," Ebony pitched in. "Let him buy the drugs. We gotta work on selling our cars and the salon."

"I'll buy all that," Ray prompted. "Just let me know what everything adds up to."

"I can't sell the Mustang," Shonda protested. "James bought that for me."

"That's cool," Ray said, admiring her consideration. He stood and kissed Sheila. "Y'all know my number."

Ray made it back to his house in one piece. He pulled into the garage and waited until the garage door had closed, before getting out and carrying Vincent's logbook into the house, where he left it on the kitchen table, then went out to feed his dogs.

"I know y'all missed me," he said to his furry friends as they approached, happy to see him, but extremely happy to see he'd brought food. "I gotta introduce y'all to the girl I was telling y'all about," he said, as he filled their bowls. "I love y'all but if y'all leave one scratch on her, I'ma bury y'all under y'all dog houses. She'll be staying here until we move to the U.K."

That's when he realized he hadn't thought about what he was going to do with his dogs when they leave. He only had one idea. After filling their water bowls, he entered the house, doffed his trench coat and skull cap, then returned to the kitchen, dialing his mother's number.

"Hello?" Robert answered.

"Just the man I need to talk to," Ray said, searching the refrigerator for something to eat. "How's everything?"

"Good," Robert answered. "Your mom is sleep. I'm just sitting here watching a lil' TV, Sandford and Son."

"Not that boy, Fred G. Sanford," Ray said, smiling at the mentioning of one of his favorite sitcoms. "It's been a minute since I've even sat down and watched TV—" He paused, before going on. "—look, Robert, I don't know exactly when, but I plan on moving to another country and I need you to take care of my dogs."

"Ray, you know your mama don't like dogs."

"Build a fence around the back yard," Ray said, rebutting his statement. "Sometime before I leave, I'll bring them up there. I'll leave you with some money for food. They're good dogs. They'll never bite the hand that feeds them."

"Well," Robert started. "I'll build the fence, but if your mom asks me about it, you know I gotta tell her."

"And tell her to take it up with me," Ray told him. "I appreciate that, Robert."

Ray disconnected and placed the phone on the table, then noticed Vincent's logbook. Something within him told him to go through it, he did. He didn't know what he was looking for, so he just ran his index finger along the list of names, as he flipped through the pages. He had already passed James name, when he came across it for the third time, he stopped the date was August thirteenth, two thousand three, which was a day after the Kingz were murdered.

More confused, Ray placed a paper towel between those pages, then flipped on through the book until he came across the Queenz for the second time, which were the last visitors in the book. Then he went back to the page he'd marked.

"Three visits," he said, pondering. "If James had to see him on the thirteenth, then why would he have James killed on the day before? That shit don't sound right."

Now, Ray was thinking about what Tino said about chasing ghosts. Perhaps he really did give Ray some valuable information that was up to him to decipher. Now, he had to figure out who he would consider a ghost and as Tino put it was just like him.

It took two weeks for the Queenz to get everything situated. They'd sold the drugs, Theresa's car, Ebony's car to Ray for one hundred eighty thousand. They decided not to sell the salon but would instead, have Khandi mail the weekly checks to a P.O. box they'd purchase in Florida when they got there, which was their chosen getaway spot. Plus, they were taking Shonda and Sheila's grandmother and Ebony's mother with them.

Periodically, they had scouted Felicia's house and four days ago, encountered Rico's car parked in front of it. They wanted to act, immediately, but being that they were still trying to get things in order, Rico had been pardoned. Now, they were all at the hospital with Sheila, who'd been complaining of stomach pains for three days. Shonda, Theresa, and Ebony were seated in the waiting room. Sheila had been called to the back, almost ten minutes ago.

"Sheila might be pregnant," Ebony prompted.

"I was just thinking the same thing," Shonda admitted. "I just hope it's not bad timing."

"Well, we're about to find out," Theresa said, seeing Sheila emerge from the back with a big smile plastered on her face. They stood as she approached.

"You look mighty happy for someone who just found out they're constipated," Shonda joked.

"I'm not constipated," she replied, still smiling. "I'm pregnant."

"Congratulations!" they all exclaimed, embracing her.

Exiting the hospital, they all climbed into Sheila's Cadillac, which was driven by Shonda, retrieved their guns from under the seats and placed them in their laps as they made for the car dealership, where they were to purchase a Conversion van. Thinking of Erica and how she didn't get the chance to share the news of her pregnancy, Sheila dialed her grandmother's number.

"Yes?" her grandmother answered.

"Hey, old lady."

"I got your old lady, heifer," her grandmother replied, laughing.

"How are you?'

"I'm fine, grandma," Sheila answered. "I just came from the hospital."

"Hospital!" she exclaimed. "Whatcha doing at the hospital?"

"I was having stomach pains."

"And how many weeks are you?"

"Two, Grandma," Sheila answered, hating that her grandmother had beat her to the punch.

"And why haven't I met this man yet?"

"You will, Grandma."

"Before we leave?" she asked. "It would be nice to see who I'm leaving my granddaughter in the hands of."

"In due time, old lady," Sheila responded. "I'll talk to you later. We love you."

"You're gonna tell, Ray?" Shonda asked once Sheila ended her call.

"I am," Sheila answered. "But I wanna do it face to face, I wanna see how he reacts."

****

For the past two weeks, Ray had also been trying to get things situated. He was hoping the Queenz would go ahead and do what they were going to do with Rico, because he wanted to get the hell out of the United States, no later than the first week of January. He'd sold Ebony's car to Joe and Theresa's car, along with his Mercedes to Poppo. They conducted a decent money exchange for the custom shops. Now, Joe owned the one in Conyers and Poppo owned the one on Browns Mill Road. He was still indecisive about the BMW dealership. Technically, it belonged to him, but Fred had also put in work to make that happen. So, he didn't want to just take it away from them like that.

Ray knew he had to come up with something within two weeks. Now, he was entering his house, after starting both BMWs, which he would have to have transported to the United Kingdom, by boat. Remembering the call, he had to make, he went to his bedroom and grabbed his phone off the bed. Before he could dial one digit, it rang. The number on the screen was unfamiliar.

"Yeah?" he answered.

"Hey, big brother."

"What's up?" He was surprised his sister was calling him, after over two years. Now he was feeling something was wrong.

"Nothing," she answered. "Just checking on my big brother. I was hoping to see you at Christmas, but unfortunately, I won't be granted a pass. I have mountains of exams to take—" She paused before going on.

"—I miss you, Ray. I know I was wrong for blaming you for what happened to Raymond when I was fully aware that it wasn't your fault. He was a grown man. He wasn't forced into anything he was doing. I guess I just needed someone to blame, being that he was my first and I was pregnant by him."

"Are you asking me to forgive you?'

"Um—" She hesitated. "I guess I am."

"Can I have some time to think about it?"

"How much time?"

"I don't know," Ray said, smiling. "How 'bout two years?"

April was laughing. "You know what, I deserved that one."

"Nah, I forgive you, lil sis."

"Aww, that's sweet," she cooed. "But I'm glad I finally got that off my chest. I feel a whole lot better. Anyway, I hate to rush off, but I have a ton of work to do."

"I understand," Ray told her. "Handle your business."

"Love you, big brother."

"Love you too, baby."

Ray got off the phone with his sister, feeling exuberant. He'd almost forgotten about the call to Poppo, then quickly placed it.

"Yo, what's good?" Poppo answered.

"How's the weather?'

"It's warm out," Poppo told him. "It looks like the sun is trying to come out."

"Yeah?" Ray asked, happy to hear that Poppo had found something either about B.J. or the head figures of Drop Squad. "When can I expect coverage?"

"I can't approximate, right now," Poppo answered. "But I know it'll be far later on."

"That's what's up," Ray replied. "You know where I'm at." The moment he ended the call, another call came through. It was Sheila.

"Yeah, baby."

"Hey, boo!" she greeted. "You okay?"

"I'm decent."

"Are you busy?"

"Not at the moment," he answered. "What's up?"

"The girls and I need to have a sit down with you."

Ray pondered this for a second. Seeing that he had nothing else going on, he agreed to meet them at the Palace. Strapping on his double-gun holster, he made for the garage. Being that he hadn't driven James' BMW since it had been in his garage, he decided to take it for a spin. Pulling up to the Palace, Ray removed the chain from the electrical gate, pushed it wide enough to drive through, then drove towards the building, leaving it open. Leaving the car running, he entered the building, activated the heating system, then returned to the car that he'd backed into his parking spot so that he could watch the gate.

It wasn't long before a gray Conversion Van, followed by Sheila's Cadillac, pulled through the gate and slowly made their way towards the building. Unfamiliar with the van, Ray unstrapped his Glock and watched. But as the vehicles got closer, he saw that the van was occupied by Ebony and Theresa, and the Cadillac by Sheila and Shonda.

Re-strapping his guns, he killed the engine and entered the building as they were parking. Entering the office behind Ray, who remained standing, Shonda, Ebony, and Theresa took their seats at the table. Sheila approached Ray and took hold of his hands before kissing him in the mouth.

"Ray, I'm pregnant," she plunged in.

"By who?' he asked.

Ray didn't have to look over at the rest of them to see that they were shocked by his response. He kept his eyes on Sheila, whose smile had visibly turned upside down. She looked as if she was about to cry or attack him. Ray didn't tend to find out, he smiled to show he was only joking.

"Are you happy?" she asked, reinstating her smile.

"Hell, yeah!" he answered, embracing her and kissing her on the neck. "Of course, I'm happy. I'll be even happier once we get on that plane."

"Well, if y'all can save all that emotional stuff for later," Shonda spoke. "We can discuss all of that."

Once Sheila had taken a seat, Shonda said, "I thought of this, myself, and I'm quite sure everyone will agree with me on it. Our hunt for Rico continues tonight. I think Sheila should already be with you, because, after we get him, our only concern then, should be to pick up our parents and hit the highway."

Ray looked at Sheila. "You agree with that?"

"Not really," she answered, then regarded Shonda. "Are you sure y'all don't need me?"

"I'm positive," Shonda replied. "Trying to get you to Ray once we're done, would be time-consuming. It'd be best if you go with him, tonight."

"I agree," Theresa said.

"Me too," came Ebony.

Sheila said nothing, they all got up and one at a time hugged Sheila and Ray.

"We'll call y'all once it's done," Shonda said before they made their exits.

Ray looked at Sheila, who looked as if she'd lost her best friend.

"Come on, baby," he said, pulling her up by her hand. "Let's go home."

They left the Palace, with Sheila trailing Ray in her car. As they made their way to Canton, every time Ray encountered a bump or a pothole in the road, he'd hear a loud thump in the trunk, as if James speaker box wasn't bolted down. He had never looked in the trunk but made a mental note to do so when he got home.

When they pulled up to the house, Ray activated the door to the three-car garage and parked. Sheila parked in the spot his BMW used to be, being that he'd parked his BMW where his Mercedes used to be. Still inquisitive about the noise in James' trunk, Ray let Sheila into the house, first. For some reason, he wanted to be alone when he checked it out. Actuating the alarm box, he opened the trunk and immediately saw what was making that noise.

Ray lifted the large gun from the trunk and looked it over. He had never seen one of these guns in real life. Not outside of those Mobster movies he'd seen when he was younger. But, just holding the gun sent a surge of power through him. He felt connected to the weapon. He felt the anger inside of him building up. he felt the urge to kill. He felt—he felt like James.

The ringtone from his cell phone startled him. He placed the gun back into the trunk, closed it, then answered his phone. "Yeah?"

"Ten minutes out," Poppo stated.

"No doubt," Ray replied, ending the call, then entered the house, where Sheila was in the kitchen, pulling can goods from the cupboard.

Remembering what she'd said about liking to cook when she's upset, Ray didn't bother her. Instead, he journeyed to his bedroom, relieved himself of his coat and guns, then sat on the edge of the bed to get his thoughts together. He thought it was a good idea for the Queenz to leave Sheila out of their mission. Now, they needed to hurry up and get it over with and get gone, so he could go ahead and make travel arrangements. He hadn't told Kim where he lived, but the last time he talked to her, he told her he was going to leave her with the house and Sheila's car.

The sound of the front door pulled him from his thoughts. He entered the living room, just as Joe and Poppo did from the opposite side. Joe handed him a wad of bills before they all took a seat.

"What 'cha got?" Ray asked Poppo.

"Well, despite the—" Poppo stopped when he heard noise coming from another part of the house. "You got company?"

"Sheila," Ray answered.

"Oh," Poppo said, then continued. "Anyway, despite the large number of Drop Squad members, I found out there are only three head niggas. Rico is a lieutenant. The only name I came up with, is Kenny. I had some of my dawgs gather information on him. He stays in Roswell and uses Drop Squad members as bodyguards."

"Do you know the address?" Ray asked.

"Nah," Poppo answered, "But I remember the name of the street and the description of the house."

"Fair enough," Ray replied. "Y'all feel like taking this ride?"

It was after eleven when they made it to Roswell, Georgia, in a Chevy Astro van, Ray had stolen. At Poppo's directions, Ray pulled the van into the driveway of the house that sat directly across the street from the one belonging to Kenny and shut off the engine. Then, he and Poppo joined Joe in the cargo area. Ray still had the Ak-47 he'd taken to the Drop Squad stash houses and Joe and Poppo were carrying two handguns each.

After ruling Vincent out as a suspect for killing the Kingz, Ray went with his first thought, which was Drop Squad. He figured to pull such a stunt on an elite group, such as the Kingz, it had to have been a call from one of the head figures. He definitely considered these niggas as ghosts. Now, he was determined to make sure they were just that before he got on that plane to the United Kingdom.

"One car's missing," Poppo said, looking out one of the square windows at the back of the van. "I was told he has two cars. A Corvette and a Porsche truck. The Porsche is gone."

"That's a good thing," Ray said. "That means he's out. Let's just hope he plans on coming home tonight."

"Shit, I think this him, right here," Poppo announced.

Ray stepped over Joe and looked out the other square window, to see a black Porsche truck, followed by a white mid-sized SUV. The Porsche pulled into the driveway and the SUV parked at the curb. Five men sporting Drop Squad chains, exited the SUV, carrying guns. Once they formed some kind of formation, which Ray was impressed by, Kenny, who was well dressed and accompanied by a dark-haired white woman, emerged from the Porsche.

"Murder everything on the premises!" Ray told his lieutenants. "I want, Kenny."

Wasting no time, they lunged from the rear of the van and moved at a quick pace towards the house. Before they could make it to the middle of the street, they were spotted. As Ray had expected, Kenny tried to flee, and his soldiers went into combat mode. Poppo and Joe swapped gunfire with the group. Ray could hear the gunshots, but all he could see was Kenny, who was trying to make it to the side of the house. Ray stopped, aimed and squeezed on the trigger, sending a multitude of slugs into Kenny's back, forcing him to fall forward on his face. Disregarding his lieutenants, Drop Squad and the white bitch who was screaming at the top of her lungs, Ray entered the yard and stood over Kenny, who was panting and appeared as if he was trying to coerce his dying body to respond.

"It's over bitch!' Ray said, before emptying the clip into the back of Kenny's skull.

Playa Ray

Chapter 25

It was Christmas and the Queenz still hadn't reported anything to Ray about finding Rico, which is why he had his lieutenants on it, hoping to speed up the process. He knew it was going to be kind of hard, being that Drop Squad had been on a rampage for the past week, since the demise of Kenny.

Since Sheila wanted to spend the holiday with her family Ray decided he'd just lounge around the house until she returned. He'd spoken with his mother, Robert April, Nikki, Kim, and Precious. After feeding and spending time with his dogs, he journeyed to the Kingz room and just browsed around. Coming up on the half heart pendant, for some reason made him think about Sheila, in lieu of Sylvia. He found this quite erratic. Then he came to the conclusion that he had to let Sylvia go and concentrate on Sheila, which is why he was sitting in his car that was parked at the cemetery, staring at the pendant in his hand that he was going to place on Sylvia's grave. This would be his last visit.

Ray dismounted and as he neared Sylvia's grave, saw that there was a man, woman, and child standing there. He'd heard of cases where funeral homes have buried caskets on top of caskets and were hoping like hell that this wasn't one of those cases. That thought quickly subsided, when he approached and realized who the people were. They were regarding him as if he was indeed a ghost.

"Ray?' Connie asked with a confused look on her face.

"It's me," he replied, then realized the other person wasn't a man, but Star, the female Sylvia was dating before her death.

"But how?"

Ray already knew where this was going, so he quickly gave them a brief account of the night the Kingz were murdered.

"So, where have you been?" asked Connie.

"Around."

"Did you come here on Sylvia's birthday?" Star inquired.

"Yeah."

"So, you were the one who left the flowers," she stated.

"I brought my mama some flowers, too," the little girl spoke.

That's when Ray finally looked down at her. Despite her skull cap and large coat, she appeared very small and fragile, as if the results of premature birth. Then what she'd said, finally dawned on him.

"Who's her mama?" Ray asked, now regarding Connie and Star, who just exchanged glances.

"My mama's name is Sylvia Baker and my daddy's name is Ray Young," the girl volunteered. "They both went to heaven and they can see me. They can see you too."

"Explain!" Ray demanded, ready to cause harm to Connie and Star if they even looked as if they were going to refuse.

"She survived, Ray." Connie shrugged. "When they found Sylvia and saw that she was pregnant, they rushed her to the hospital. Rachel survived, somehow, she's a miracle baby."

"I'm a miracle baby!" Rachel exclaimed, spinning around.

"Stop, before you fall, Rachel!" Star chastised, and the child obeyed.

"So, why haven't nobody told me about her?" Ray resumed his inquiry.

"It wasn't my place," Connie admitted. "Sylvia's mom was by right, Rachel's legal guardian. So, when Rachel was released from the hospital, she took Rachel to stay with her in Cleveland. I didn't know she'd died of cancer until I ran across Sylvia's aunt last year. She told me she had custody of Rachel and was having a hard time taking care of her. So, I asked her to sign custody over to me. But, in the beginning, everybody was under the impression that you didn't want anything to do with the baby after you caught Sylvia with Keyonne."

"I wasn't meeting with her at Petro for my health," Ray spat.

"So, you had always believed she was yours?"

Ray looked down at the little girl who was smiling at him. "I mean, I did, but I was still gonna take the paternity test to make sure she wasn't his."

"Who, Keyonne?"

"Yeah."

"She's not."

"And how you figure that?"

"Because she didn't meet Keyonne until she was almost two months pregnant," Connie defended. "I was there when they met."

****

"So, when are we leaving for Florida?"

Shonda looked across the table at her grandmother who posed the question. She could tell her grandmother was ready to go. Being that they were having a hard time catching Rico, she was almost ready to give up and roll out herself. She knew the delay resulted from the murder of one of Drop squad's headmen. For some reason, she had a strong feeling Ray had something to do with it. Perhaps, he too was tying up a few loose ends of his own, before he and Sheila flew the coop.

"In three days," Shonda answered her grandmother's query and disregarded the looks on the other Queenz faces.

"Well, I'm already packed," her grandmother replied.

"Me too," Ms. Davis said, who was seated beside her. "I can't wait for it to get warm. I'll be spending my time on the beach, chasing young men."

"Mama!" Ebony exclaimed with a disgusted look on her face.

"Don't mama me!' she protested. "I need to find some kind of happiness!"

After dinner, Sheila and Shonda bid their grandmother goodnight and they all made off in the van en route to Stone Mountain, where they dropped Ms. Davis off with their next stop being Canton, where they were dropping Sheila off at Ray's house.

"In three days?" Ebony, who was driving, finally asked Shonda who was seated beside her.

"Ebony, I want Rico just as bad as you do," Shonda explained. "But it seems as if a street war is about to pop off and we don't need to be caught up in it. We got tonight and tomorrow night to look for him. Saturday, we need to be on that highway. Now if you want to, once everything dies down, we can come back and try again. But we need to be gone by Saturday."

"She's right, Ebony," Sheila sided with her cousin. "It's time to go. If y'all don't get, Rico, somebody will. He'll get what's coming to him, either way."

Ebony was quiet.

"Sheila, call Ray and let him know you're on your way home," Shonda said.

Sheila dialed Ray's number.

"Yeah?" he answered, sounding gloomy.

"What's wrong, baby?"

He cleared his throat. "Nothing. What's up?"

"I'm on my way home," she informed.

"Okay," he said, then hung up, leaving Sheila with the feeling that something was amiss.

When they got to the house, the gate was already open and Ray was standing in the front yard, watching his dogs frolic around. He and the dogs approached the van as Ebony pulled up to the house.

"Girl, don't let them big ass dogs jump up in here," Ebony exclaimed as Sheila opened the side doors to get out.

"Sit!" Sheila commanded and they obeyed.

"You have fun?' Ray asked Sheila helping her down.

"I enjoyed myself," she answered, kissing him and petting the dogs.

"You could've joined us," Theresa told Ray.

"I'm really not in the holiday spirit," he told her. "I guess I'm Mr. Scrooge this year."

"Well, hopefully, that'll change by next year," Shonda said. "You'll be a dad by then, so you should have some kind of holiday spirit."

"Maybe," Ray answered.

Leaving Canton, they made it back to Riverdale and prepared for their hunt for Rico tonight. They had buried the AKs after hitting the two Drop Squad houses, but still had their handguns, which was what they intended to use. Once it got dark, they strapped on bulletproof vests, trench coats, and skullies, then climbed into the GMC Denali.

Being that they only had two potential places to look, Shonda chose Club Strokers. Just as they'd expected, the place was packed. Shonda circled the lot but didn't see Rico's car. Then it dawned on her that Felicia's car wasn't in its usual spot.

"I wonder if Felicia took the night off," she said.

"Shit, let's find out!' Theresa said from the back seat.

Shonda exited the parking lot and navigated the truck to Sylvan Road. Nearing Felicia's house, they saw that her car was in the driveway. Shonda parked the truck across the street, two houses down.

"We don't even know if she's in there," Ebony said watching the house that was well lit by the decoration of Christmas lights.

"I don't think she would leave the Christmas lights on," Shonda replied.

An hour passed and there had been no movement to or from the house. It was almost forty minutes later when a car finally pulled up in front of Felicia's house. There was no mistaking who the turquoise Chevy Monte Carlos belonged to.

"The best time to catch him is now,' Theresa insisted. "Before he makes it inside.'

"You're right," Ebony agreed. "Let's go."

"Felicia!" Shonda said, just as Felicia stepped out on the porch wearing a housecoat.

They watched as Rico got out of his car and approached the house in a menacing stride as if he was upset. He passed her entering the house, she followed, closing the door.

"We should go ahead and kick the door in and get it over with!' Ebony voiced.

"Nah," Shonda said. "We gotta think about Felicia and her son."

"But we're not after them," Ebony insisted. "I don't think she would be stupid enough to jump in front of a bullet for him."

"She may not," Shonda offered, "But she's not the type to just lay down. She got some buck in her. Then seeing us, she would definitely put up a fight, which put us in a position where we'll have to harm her. We can't take—" Shonda stopped midsentence, when Rico emerged from the house, closing the door behind him.

"This is our chance, right here," Theresa voiced. "It's now or never."

"Hold on," Shonda said. "I think he spotted us."

Rico stopped half-way between his car and the house and was looking in their direction.

"Yeah, he's looking right at us," Ebony said in a low tone as if he could hear them.

"It's now or never, y'all!' Theresa reiterated, then lunged from the truck.

Just as she did, Rico turned and broke into a run, almost tackling the front door. One gun out, Theresa fired two shots, just as Rico got the door open. Shonda and Ebony were out of the truck now.

"Back door!" Theresa said when the front door slammed shut.

She broke into a run approaching the side of the house as Shonda and Sheila endeavored to keep up. Theresa came up on the back of the house, just as Rico emerged from the back door. He spotted her and leveled his gun attempting to flee. Theresa stopped and leveled hers. Rico fired, Theresa, fired, both guns discharged multiple times. Rico went down, Theresa went down.

"Theresa!' Ebony cried out, reaching her friend.

"I'm good," Theresa claimed, feeling the pain in her chest where bullets had slammed into her vest. "He's still alive, finish him off."

"Come on, Ebony," Shonda said, ushering her towards Rico, who was now on his hands and knees feeling around for his gun.

Using all the strength she could muster, Shonda kicked Rico in his chest. He yelled out in pain, rolling onto his back. Blood was spilling from his mouth, he was panting and staring up at them wide-eyed.

"Man, I thought y'all were the fucking police," he spoke in a raspy voice.

"Nah, you're just gonna wish we were the police," Shonda told him. "Handle your business, Ebony."

"That girl you killed at Ted's house," Ebony said, pointing her gun at his face. "Was my sister."

Apprehension spread across Rico's face. Clearly, he thought he'd gotten away undetected. He didn't know Erica had given him up before he committed the act.

"We gotta go, Ebony," Shonda prompted, and Ebony deliberately squeezed the trigger until her gun was empty.

The following morning, Ray got up real early. He had so many things on his mind, he could hardly sleep. His main focus was on his daughter, Rachel. When he told Sheila about her, she insisted that Ray get custody and take Rachel to the U.K. with them. At first, he felt it would be wrong for him take Rachel away from Connie and Star, who were a couple, but after realizing Rachel was his child and not theirs, Sheila's suggestion had gradually grown on him, which is why he and Sheila were now on their way to see Connie and Star, who were now staying in Monroe, Georgia.

Finding the house, Sheila parked her car in front of it, being that Connie's Range Rover and Star's Pontiac Grand Prix were parked in the driveway. Dismounting, they approached the front door. Ray rang the doorbell. Moments later, Connie let them in, then led them to the living room, where Star was seated on the sofa and Rachel was on her knees at the coffee table, coloring in a coloring book. Ray made the proper introductions before he and Sheila took a seat on the sofa beside Star. Connie sat in the recliner.

"We're all here," Connie said, perhaps ready to hear what Ray wanted to talk to them about.

"I didn't tell y'all I plan to move to another country," Ray said.

"Another country!" Connie exclaimed.

"Yeah," he answered. "And, being that I'm her father, I feel I have the right to take her with me."

Tears streamed down Connie's face.

Seeing this, Rachel ran over to her and held Connie's hands. "Auntie Connie, what's wrong? I haven't done anything. I've been a good girl."

"I know, baby." Connie hugged and kissed her on the cheek.

"Well, why are you crying?" Rachel persisted.

"Come here," Connie pulled Rachel into her lap. "You see that man, right there?" she asked, pointing to Ray.

"Yes, he gave me this," Rachel said, indicating the half-heart pendant pinned to her shirt.

"That's your, daddy," Connie told her.

"My daddy?" she asked, regarding Ray with a look that reminded him of Sylvia. "You said my daddy went to heaven with my mama."

"He came back."

"Did my mama come back, too?" she asked, now regarding Sheila.

"No, your mama didn't come back."

"Why not?"

"I have no idea, sweetheart," Connie answered. "Go and say hi to your daddy."

Rachel got down out of Connie's lap and gingerly approached Ray, regarding him with the same eyes he was regarding her with. She stopped in front of him, interlocking her hands behind her, in a shy manner.

"Hey, Daddy."

"Hey, baby." Ray picked her up with extreme caution, being that she was so small and light. "This is my wife, Sheila."

"Hey, Sheila."

"Hey, beautiful." Sheila greeted, rubbing Rachel's chin. "You look just like your daddy."

"I look like my daddy and my mama," she rectified with a hint of attitude.

"Ray, would you really take her away from us?" Star finally spoke.

"She's my daughter," Ray pointed out. "I'm leaving the country. I would be less than a man if I left my child, now that I know about her."

"But she's all we have, Ray," Connie protested. "I feel I owe it to Sylvia to raise her child and see to it she makes something of herself. And I really have my heart set on that. Had Black not wanted to wait until after I graduated, I would have my own child. But Rachel is the closest thing I have to that. She's my heart."

Everyone was silent. The only sound that could be heard, was Connie's crying. Ray's heart went out to her. He could already imagine the kind of pain he would cause her if he extracted Rachel from her life. Lord knows he didn't want to push her into attempting suicide. This made him think of Nikki, who told him she thought she'd seen Connie with a child that favored him and not any of Black's children.

"Daddy, why is my Auntie Connie crying?" Rachel asked.

Ray had only one answer for his daughter, "Because she's gonna miss you."

Theresa, Ebony, and Shonda had got a jump start on their last-minute chores. The first thing Ebony had to do was report the Denali stolen, although they'd taken it out to Dunwoody last night and set it afire. Leaving the house, they went to retrieve the trailer they'd purchased, which matched the van. As they did last minute shopping for traveling supplies and food, they could tell Drop Squad was still touchy about the ongoing slaughter of their members, because each one they'd encountered, looked as if they were ready to go to war with God, himself.

"You okay?" Shonda asked Theresa as they were exiting a grocery store, carrying bags of junk food and drinks.

"I'm good," she answered. "The redness went down on my chest, but I still feel a lil' pain. That should be gone in a couple of days."

"You need to get a job as a bodyguard," Ebony said. "The way you moved last night, surprised the hell out of me. But I was scared as hell when I saw you go down."

"I'm just surprised Felicia didn't come running outside with some big ass Dirty Harry gun!" Shonda joked.

"I was damn sho' expecting that," Theresa admitted.

"I just hope she didn't see us," Shonda said, as they climbed into the van.

Ebony's phone vibrated. "Hello?"

"Are you feeling better?" Phillip asked.

"A little," Ebony answered, starting the van. "How's it going with you?"

"Business, as usual," he told her. "I was hoping we could get together."

"Hold on." She covered the phone. "Phillip wants to get together."

"We leave at ten, tomorrow," Shonda replied. "Just be back before then. And don't tell him we're leaving town."

"It's a date," Ebony told Phillip. "Just have me home by nine, tomorrow morning."

Ray and Sheila grabbed something to eat at a soul food restaurant, headed back to the house and pretty much ate in silence. Shonda had called and informed them that it was done and they were making last-minute arrangements before they headed out at ten in the morning.

Bored, Sheila busied herself with the laundry and tidying up the place, while Ray went through his books and waited for his lieutenants, who'd arrived shortly after five o'clock and joined him in the living room.

"People think LKS is going broke," Joe told Ray. "They don't believe you're just retiring from this shit."

"Let 'em think what they want," Ray responded. "What're we looking like?"

"We done sold all the product," Joe answered. "Once we make these few pick-ups tomorrow, that'll be it. You won't have nothing left in the streets."

Ray nodded. "That's what's up."

"And I found out another name of a head nigga in Drop Squad," Poppo stated.

"I'm listening," Ray said.

"Some dude named, Phillip," Poppo said. "He owns a limousine company, PLS Limousine or some shit like that."

Now, Ray was thinking. This name sounded real familiar. Perhaps this was the name of the dude who was with Ebony at Sheila's birthday party, who he thought looked familiar. He got off the sofa and went into the kitchen, where Sheila was wiping the counter with a rag.

"Baby?"

"Yes?" Sheila stopped what she was doing.

"That dude who was with Ebony on your birthday," Ray inquired. "What's his name?"

"Phillip."

"He deals drugs?" Ray ventured.

"Not that I know of," she answered. "He owns a limousine company. That's all I know about him."

Ray's mind automatically went back to the night his comrades were murdered. When they were leaving his house, he remembered looking out at the stretched Cadillac Escalade, where the chauffeur was waiting with the rear door open for them. Now he was remembering the chauffeur's face.

It was Phillip!

Now, he was sure Drop Squad had made the hit.

Playa Ray

Chapter 26

Being that the only vehicles they owned were the van and Shonda's car, Ebony decided to let Phillip pick her up. He showed up to the house, fifteen minutes before six. Now, they were en route to The Royal Suite, in his gray Aston Martin.

"I thought you'd given up on me," Ebony said to Phillip.

"I was just doing what I felt was best," he told her. "I wanted to be there for you, but some people heal better when they're left alone."

"I guess you're right," she said regarding Phillip, who'd been over supportive and patient with her. She knew she and her friends had to leave Georgia, but she did not want to leave him.

"Any idea who may have done that to your sister?" Phillip finally asked.

I assume it was Drop Squad," she answered.

"Why would you assume them?"

"I don't know," she replied, keeping the Queenz promise of not revealing what they'd found in Erica's diary. "I guess they were after Ted, and she just happened to be home at the time."

"Is that a strong assumption?"

"It is."

They'd made it to the hotel and Ebony thought they were going to the same room, but they didn't. In fact, they went to a different floor. Plus, the room was in no way as elegant as the last one.

"I got some of that soothing bubble bath solution," he told her. "I want you to soak for a while. Then we'll order room service. How's that sound?"

"It sounds good."

Joe pulled the stolen Chevy Yukon into the parking lot of PLS Limousine Service and up to the small building, which was the office. Ray, who was in the front passenger seat, donned his black cap, got out and entered the office, where a young white female was seated behind the desk.

"How may I help you, sir?" she asked.

"I'm here to see, Phillip," Ray told her.

"You're here about the night job, right?"

"I am," he went along.

"Mr. Lakes tried to wait on you," she said. "But something came up and he had to rush over to the hotel."

"What hotel?"

"The Royal Suite," she answered. "He owns that, too."

The Queenz had two more tasks to complete for the day. They had to collect the week's pay from the salon and Shonda had to go by the house in Norcross to pack the rest of her things. Being that they had done more than enough driving for one day, Theresa insisted they split the chores, which was why Shonda had driven out to Norcross and Theresa pulled the van into the plaza. Parking, she crossed the almost empty lot and entered the salon, where Khandi and one of her clients were the only ones present.

"Girl, you stay working late," Theresa said, taking a seat in the waiting area.

"I know," Khandi replied. "I might start charging late fees."

"Don't start today," her client protested. "I ain't got it like that."

"Well, you better raise the price on that coochie," Khandi joked, sparking laughter from Theresa and her client.

Once Khandi was done, she let her client out, then went to the restroom to clean up. That's when Theresa directed her attention to the TV, that was turned to the news. They were saying something about a woman being found dead in her home by her six-year-old son, and her assailant, who'd actuated a knife for his murder weapon, was found dead in her backyard, with multiple gunshot wounds to the face. Then, they showed Felicia's house.

"Damn!" Theresa reflected. "That's why he exited the house expeditiously, he murdered Felicia."

At this time Khandi emerged from the restroom. Standing, Theresa followed her to her station and waited as she counted the money out. Then, a vehicle pulling up in front of the store caught her attention. Realizing the make and model of the vehicle, she took no chances.

"Khandi, get down!"

Theresa was digging into her pocketbook for her gun as the front and rear passenger doors of the black H-2 Hummer swung open and two masked men got out, both holding sub-machine guns, in which they were now aiming at her. Her gun was out, but knowing she couldn't take them both, she aimed at the one who'd gotten out of the front seat and immediately opened fire, just as their guns erupted. Glass shattered. Khandi was on the floor, screaming. Theresa didn't have on her vest, so their bullets seemed to go straight through her body. She collapsed on the floor, just as her gun discharged its last round. Her eyelids were heavy, but they didn't close until she'd watched the Hummer speed off, leaving one of their men lying in front of the store.

Ebony had been soaking in the bathtub for more than twenty minutes. Phillip promised he'd be back in a few, but she was under the impression he'd left the room because it was way too quiet beyond the bathroom's door. Feeling as if he was planning to surprise her with something special, she decided to be patient.

As she relaxed, her mind wandered. Now, she was thinking of Theresa, which made her horny as always. She'd never met a man, who could stand up against Theresa when it came to oral sex. Ebony had never believed in same-sex relations, but Theresa made it seem as if it was meant to be that way. It had started on the night of Theresa's birthday, after they had the run-in with that Hummer on the expressway, upon leaving Club Strokers. They ended up sleeping together in the guest room of Shonda and Sheila's house.

Ebony was so shaken up, she couldn't sleep. Theresa held her close and whispered to her while planting soft, extremely soft, kisses on her neck and cheek, which despite her mental state at the time, turned her on. The next thing she knew, she was locking lips with Theresa, who, subsequently, gave her body the best *sexual healing* she'd ever experienced. She just felt bad they hadn't disclosed their relationship to Sheila and Shonda.

The sound of the hotel's room door brought her out of her reverie. She was relieved because she was ready to get out of the tub. Then, suddenly, the bathroom door was pushed open and two men entered. Moving on instinct, Ebony grabbed her pocketbook off the toilet seat. They rushed her, one wrested the pocketbook from her grasp, then they both forced her under the water. She tried to put up a fight, but her arms were restrained. She kicked her legs out, but only incurred pain as her feet thrashed against the faucet and knobs. The soap stung her eyes, the water burned her lungs. The fight in her subsided, as her strength waned. She silently hoped Phillip would come to her rescue, it never happened.

"Are you sure you got it?" Poppo asked Ray from the back seat.

They were parked in the parking lot of the Royal Suite. Neither one of them knew what kind of car Phillip was driving, so Ray insisted they hang out until they spotted him.

"Yeah, I got it," Ray now answered Poppo. "If it's more than three or the police pull up in the process, I'll accept y'all assistance."

"So, you don't want to snatch his ass up and make him give the other head nigga up?" Joe inquired.

"He wouldn't do it," Ray answered, keeping his eyes on the entrance of the hotel. "I don't know him like that, but I can tell he wouldn't bitch up at the sight of a gun. He's a cowboy. You'll have to drag that iron on his ass. And that's what I intend to do."

"Well, I hope it's more than three of 'em," Poppo said. "Cause I'm in the mood to drag some iron tonight."

"Shit, I want some action, too," Joe said.

"Y'all gotta put that on pause," Ray told them, seeing Phillip emerge from the building. "Watch my back."

Ray got out, tucked his Glock with the extended clip in the back of his pants and moved through the parking lot at an even pace, trying to match Phillip's stride and direction, so he could meet him head-on. The sound of a car's alarm being disarmed, startled him, probably because he'd just passed the car, which was an Aston Martin. He regarded the car for a quick second, then looked back at Phillip, who'd changed directions and was headed back towards the building.

Ray quickened his steps, in an attempt to catch him before he made it back inside because clearly, he'd recognized Ray or just detected danger. Figuring Phillip was close enough to the entrance, Ray decided to put an end to this cat and mouse game. He pulled his gun from his pants and just as he did, Phillip did a quick half spin and held his hand out. Ray saw the chrome handgun and ducked behind a car as the gun barked and bullets slammed into the metal and glass of the vehicle. As soon as the firing ceased, Ray swung around the car, gun first and saw Phillip running for the entrance.

Having no time to give chase, he secured a proper aim and sent a hail of bullets at Phillip's back, making sure each one was accounted for. Phillip made it to the entrance, but his nervous system had already been damaged, which caused his body to slam into the glass doors, shatter them and fall back onto the concrete, where he laid stationary.

Shonda entered the house with the intent to grab the rest of her things and leave as quickly as she'd come. They'd already moved most of the furniture to storage, where they would meet the movers tomorrow and hit the highway from there.

The only piece of furniture left in Shonda's room was a dresser. She placed her pocketbook on top of it, opened her large black trash bag up on the floor and began pulling clothes from the drawers. Once that was complete, she moved to the closet and began taking down the clothes she had hanging up. Then, she thought she'd heard a strange noise coming from another apart of the house.

Taking no chances, she rushed over, closed the door and turned the lock on the knob. Then, she pulled her gun from her pocketbook and stood facing the door. Seconds later, a shadow appeared at the bottom of the door. Shonda raised her gun, the intruder tried the knob. Shonda fired a round through the door. The shadow disappeared. Shonda maintained her stance. It was quiet for a few seconds. Then, the reports from a gun sounded and a salvo of bullets penetrated the door. Standing her ground, Shonda returned fire. Unlike Theresa, she'd worn her bullet-proof vest, so she was able to sustain a good amount of hits. But the bullet that went through her neck, barely missing her windpipe, is what brought her to her knees. The gunfire ceased, but despite the blood exuding from the side of her neck, she was still vigilant.

Holding one hand over her wound, she sat back on her haunches, pulled her pocketbook off the dresser and dumped the contents onto the floor. Seeing her extra clip, she placed the gun between her knees for a firm grip and ejected the cartridge, while keeping a wary eye on the shadow at the bottom of the door. It appeared motionless. Painfully inserting the other cartridge, she flipped the gun over and using her knees again, cocked the chamber, which took her several tries to accomplish. Then, crawling on her knees and the one hand that held the gun, she got to the door and paused long enough to take a deep breath. Leaving the gun on the floor, she unlocked and opened the door. Yes, her intruder was, indeed motionless.

Then his head lifted, and he smiled revealing blood-stained teeth. This gesture angered her more than the fact that he'd broken into their home and robbed them blind, which had gotten them in their current predicament. Apparently, he'd been casing the house and waiting for an opportunity to retaliate on the count of Tino and Shelton.

"I got you good," Ant managed in a feeble voice.

"Not good enough," she responded in a voice parallel to his, before injecting two slugs into his skull.

Then, she closed and locked the door back. Leaving the gun by the door, she again, handicap crawled over to the dresser and planted her back against it, with her legs stretched out. The blood from her wound was seeping through her fingers, incessantly, and she knew she was dying. She grabbed her phone off the floor and abstractedly punched in numbers.

Ray and his lieutenants wiped the Yukon down, before ditching it and were now back in the Navigator, on their way to Ray's house. Ray was hoping the Queenz wouldn't be too mad, once they put two and two together and realize he's the one who'd murdered Ebony's boyfriend. Things would, indeed, get ugly. Now, he was wondering about the third head figure of Drop Squad. For some reason, Norris and Vincent popped into his mind. He would not be surprised if one of them turned out to be the third guy, especially Norris.

His cell phone vibrated in his lap. He regarded the familiar number on the screen for a second, before answering. "Yeah?"

"Is she with you?" Shonda's voice was almost a whisper.

"What's wrong?" Ray asked, already sensing it.

"I've been shot."

"What!"

"Calm down, Ray," she told him. "Don't alarm, Sheila."

"She's at the house," he replied. "Where you at?"

"It's too late to save me, Ray," she stated. "Right now, I just need you to listen. Would you please listen?"

"I'm listening."

Shonda continued. "I was fourteen and Sheila was twelve at the time. I had a boyfriend, she was scared of boys. Both of our mamas died in a car wreck when I was five and our grandmama took us in. When I was twelve, she took on a second job and left us at home at night, being that I was old enough to watch Sheila. Most nights, I would sneak out with my boyfriend and we would have sex in the back seat of his dad's car. One night when Sheila was asleep, I snuck out with my boyfriend. While I was gone, a man entered our apartment." Shonda took a deep breath. "Sheila was asleep, she had never hurt nobody. He hurt her, Ray. He hurt my baby and it was all my fault, I left her alone."

"And where is he now?" Ray asked as tears welled up in his eyes and anger stirred up inside of him.

"He was killed in prison," Shonda answered. "That's why, till this very day, I never liked leaving her alone."

She fell silent.

"You there?" Ray asked as Joe pulled the truck up to the house.

"Ray, promise me you'll take care of her."

"You don't have to worry 'bout that," he assured her. "Me and God'll have it out 'bout shawty. Are you sure you can't be helped?"

"I'm positive," she answered. "I had a shootout with, Ant. He's already dead, I'll see his ass in hell."

"You can probably still make it, Shonda," Ray told her, unwilling to believe she was dying. "Tell me where you are."

She sighed. "I've already lost too much blood, Ray. My vision is blurry and I'm—" She was quiet.

"Shonda!" Ray bellowed through the phone to no avail. He was about to try again when he heard a thud that may have been the sound of her phone falling from her hand.

Ray leaned his head back on the headrest, closed his eyes and drew a breath. He did not want to be the one to disclose this to Sheila, but there was no way to avoid it. He knew she was going to be crushed and it was going to take the help of God and at least forty days and forty nights to console her. Plus, this was really going to complicate their traveling plans.

"Fuck!" he let out.

Playa Ray

Chapter 27

It was February, two months since the deaths of Shonda, Ebony, Theresa, and Felicia. Since then, it seemed as if the violence in the south had died down. Plus, every police department in Georgia, was strongly enforcing their curfew laws, in an endeavor to decrease the violence.

Since attending all four funerals, Ray and Sheila had been spending most of their time at the house, periodically dropping in on Ms. Davis, Sheila's grandmother, his daughter Rachel and even his nephew, James. Ray had also maintained contact with Nikki and Ace, who'd undergone an impromptu marriage, in order to adopt Kevin. He hadn't heard anything on B.J. and being that he was done with the drug game and didn't really have any use for Poppo and Joe, they'd retired and were both active managers at their establishments.

Despite all that's happened, Ray still had a few scores to settle. He was still hunting the third head member of Drop Squad and trying to ascertain the whereabouts of Vincent, which is why he told Joe and Poppo to keep their ears to the streets. He was sure that Vincent still had it out for Sheila, and being that he was well aware that Sheila's life could still be in danger, he wouldn't dare let her leave the house without him.

Neither of them said a word to each other about leaving the country and Ray could pretty much tell that Sheila who seemed distant at times, did not intend on leaving her grandmother, nor Ms. Davis behind. Ray still felt it'd be best if they executed that move. If she was worried about the well-being of her grandmother and Ms. Davis, he was willing to come to some kind of concord with her, which is why he entered the bedroom, where she was lying across the bed, on her side, watching TV.

Ray climbed into bed behind her. "How ya' feeling, baby?' he asked, rubbing her protruding stomach, which was attributed to her two months of pregnancy.

"I'm okay," she answered, placing her hand on his.

"I wanna talk to you about something," he told her.

She rolled onto her back, regarding him.

"It's about us moving," he went on. "We made plans and I really believe we should stick to that. I don't think we'll ever find happiness here."

"I still wanna leave," she replied, "But I don't wanna leave Grandma and Ms. Davis. I can't leave them like that. I'm all they have."

"That's what I wanna talk to you about," he said. "They can come with us if that's what you want. You think they'll go?"

"I don't know, I'll have to call and ask."

"Well, the sooner you do that," he said. "The sooner I can make arrangements."

"I can call now," she said with a hint of excitement in her voice.

"Gone and check on that," he said, kissing her. "I gotta feed the dogs."

Ray got off the bed and left the room, feeling a whole lot better. As soon as he entered the kitchen, his cell phone vibrated on his hip.

"What up, P,'" he answered.

"Bout ten minutes out," Poppo said. "We got a three-card draw."

"I can't wait to see it,' Ray said, then concluded the call.

He was insensible of the mischievous grin on his face as he grabbed the dog food and exited the back door. Poppo's call was right on time because Ray thought he'd be in the U. K. by the time he'd found out who the third head member of Drop Squad was. Now, as soon as Poppo arrived, it would be revealed. He'd been prepared because he'd bought ammunition for the Tommy gun he was dying to use. It seemed as if Poppo had miscalculated, because as soon as Ray returned to the house, Poppo was entering the kitchen.

"I thought you got lost back there," Poppo joked.

"Who is he?" Ray asked, not wasting another second.

"Some dude named, Miles," Poppo answered.

"Don't ring a bell," Ray said. "What's the four one-one?"

"He owns that bowling alley in East Point," Poppo informed. "He's always there on Fridays and Saturdays, betting big money on the pool tables. He also uses Drop Squad members as bodyguards."

"So, he'll be there tonight," Ray stated. "What y'all got planned?"

"Not a damn thing," Poppo answered. "We got a couple of AKs on deck, with Drop Squad written all over 'em. I already got Stone and Hot Ru looking for a van. You don't mind if they tag along, do you?"

"Nah, we may need them."

"Oh," Poppo said as if remembering something. "I just found out Murda Ru got caught with that body."

"What body?"

"The nigga he snatched up in Savannah," Poppo answered. "He got caught on Fulton Industrial."

"Damn!" Ray exclaimed? "What about, Vincent?"

"Nobody's seen or heard from him."

Poppo, Hot Ru, and Stone picked Ray up in a dark blue GMC van, around ten and they made it to the bowling alley, close to eleven o'clock, where they parked in the parking lot, watching the building. The place was packed, but there was no sign of anyone who matched the description

Poppo had given of Miles. Around eleven-thirty, a white Bentley GT Coupe pulled into the lot, followed by a blue Chevy Caprice. The Bentley parked in a vacant spot close to the building and the Caprice parked close by. The occupant of the Bentley didn't get out until the four occupants of the Chevy surrounded his car.

He had on a black trench coat and what appeared to be orange dress pants and matching dress shoes. He greeted the members standing out front as one opened the door for him.

"What's the word?" Hot Ru asked, who was seated in the driver's seat, being that Ray let Joe sit this one out.

"Not yet." Ray who was in the cargo area with Poppo, said, as he watched Miles congregate with the group of men at the pool table by the entrance, before proceeding on to another part of the building.

"I guess he'll be back, once he do a quick survey of the place."

Ray was right, about twenty minutes later, Miles returned with his coat off and a small black bag in his hand. Some of the men at the table began pulling out money. Once it was decided who was going to be the first to battle with Miles on the table, the first game had begun. Ray wanted to get it all over with but chose to wait until everybody was all into the game. Miles had won the first game. Another opponent stepped up and the second game commenced. The members outside, who were standing around like guards, now had their backs to the parking lot and were watching.

"Y'all know the plan," Ray prompted. "Kill 'em all, let God sort 'em out."

Hot Ru started the van and pulled out of the parking spot. He drove towards the edge of the lot as if he was leaving, then circled around, moving towards the building. Once he'd rounded the horseshoe and the rear of the van was facing the building, he stopped. Ray and Poppo lunged from the rear doors of the van and Stone from the passenger seat. Stone and Poppo were armed with AK-47s and Ray with the Tommy gun. Ray's focus was on Miles, as his gun raised. The members at the door, turned and appeared to be going for their weapons, but were too slow. Guns erupted, bodies fell, glass shattered, and more bodies fell. Miles' body was forced back onto the opposite pool table by the rounds of the Tommy gun. Then Ray maneuvered the barrel, trying to hit as many people as he could before the drum went dry. Once it did, they were all back in the van and speeding out of the parking lot.

The following day, Ray left the house to make travel arrangements, being that they'd planned to leave in a few days. Ms. Davis and Sheila's grandmother, both said they'd be more than happy to leave the country and were still packed. A part of Sheila didn't want to leave, because she wouldn't be able to visit the graves of Shonda, Theresa, and Ebony. But she knew she had to put all of this behind her, which was why she was packing some of her and Ray's clothes into suitcases.

While she packed, she reflected on her girls and how they'd died. There was no doubt in her mind that Phillip had killed Ebony. She didn't understand why, until Ray had told her what side Phillip was on. He didn't have to tell her, he'd murdered Phillip, right after he'd murdered Ebony because she'd already known he was after the head members of Drop Squad. Besides he'd left the house that night, with his lieutenants, just as he'd done last night. She'd seen the shooting of the bowling alley this morning.

Shonda and Theresa had both went out in a blaze, taking their killers with them. "Sistah Soulja." From what Ray had told her, had taken another Kingzmen out and "Jane Bond." Had murdered Ant, in the process of him murdering her. Sheila felt a lot better knowing these men didn't get away with the deaths of her comrades. She had all of their tiaras and planned on acquiring four mannequins when they got to the U.K. and housing the Queenz with the Kingz.

"Hello?" Sheila answered her cell phone that was on the dresser.

"I'm having severe chest pains," her grandmother informed. "I don't think it's a heart attack, but I called nine-one-one and they're sending an ambulance. I assume they'll take me to hospital."

"Which hospital?' Sheila asked, hoping her grandmother wasn't about to die on her.

"I don't know which one," she answered. "Probably Grady."

"I'll find out," Sheila assured. "As a matter of fact, I'm on my way out the door, now."

Getting off the phone with her grandmother, Sheila shed her pajamas, got dressed and made for the garage, where she climbed into her Cadillac. She was thinking about her grandmother so much, she didn't even think to call Ray and inform him of her movement.

She made sure the electrical gate had locked into place, before pulling away from the house. While visibly breaking the speed limit, Sheila kept a wary eye out for the law as she traveled the highway, swerving in and out of lanes. She made it to her Grandmother's house in no time. Using her key to get in, she searched the house to find her grandmother wasn't there. Calling Grady Memorial Hospital, she was informed that a Dorothy Hines was en route at that very moment.

Leaving her grandmother's house, Sheila made for the hospital. When she came upon a traffic light at an intersection, the thought finally occurred that she should call and inform Ray of her whereabouts. She pulled her phone from her pocketbook on the passenger seat, but before she could dial a single number, the driver's door window came crashing in and glass shattered all over her. All she saw was gloved hands reach inside the car.

The assailant grabbed the seatbelt and was trying to wrap it around her neck. Trying to fend him off with one hand, she reached for her pocketbook, retrieving her gun. As soon as she'd swung it around to get an aim at her attacker, it was snatched from her grasp. Then, on instinct, she smashed down on the gas pedal in an attempt to flee, but only crashed into the back of the car in front of her. Clearly, that pissed her attacker off, because he punched her in the face, puzzling her, almost rendering her unconscious. A second blow immediately supervened the first one. This time she lost consciousness.

Playa Ray

Chapter 28

Ray managed to get four plane tickets to the United Kingdom and made arrangements to have both BMWs brought over by boat. Now, he was on his way back to the house to feed the baby. Hell, it seemed as if all he and Sheila had been doing for the past couple of weeks, was having sex. But he was doing it more for her, than for himself, because she was the one in need of the healing. Well, he just hoped she was in need at this very moment, because he was. His desire for sex decreased, once the garage door opened and he saw that her car was missing.

'*I know damn well she ain't left this house,*' he thought as he pulled into the garage and pulled out his phone, dialing her number. Her voicemail picked up. He tried again, getting the same results.

He didn't know what to think until he entered the bedroom and saw the packed and half-packed suitcases on the bed. That's when his mind conjured the silly idea that Sheila had run away. He didn't want to believe that, but after reflecting everything she'd been through, he reluctantly accepted it as the case.

Heartbroken, Ray sat on the edge of the bed. threatened by tears, he closed his eyes and laid back on the bed, taking deep breaths. At the same time, he was silently praying this wasn't so. He didn't know he had fallen asleep until he was awakened by his cell phone. The number on the screen was unfamiliar, but sensing it might be Sheila, he answered.

"Ray, this is Ms. Dorothy," Sheila's grandmother announced. "Is Sheila home?"

"No, she's not, Ms. Dorothy," Ray answered, concealing his anger as much as he could.

"I spoke with her earlier," she said. "I told her I was having chest pains and on my way to the hospital. She told me she was on her way out the door. I still haven't seen her and she's not answering her phone."

Now, Ray's mind had shifted into overdrive. The thought of Sheila running away had immediately been ruled out. Her grandmother called and informed her she was having chest pains, which could have been a heart attack. Knowing Sheila, a tornado in the middle of the blizzard wouldn't keep her from seeing about her grandmother, this only left Ray with one deduction, somebody had harmed his baby, both of them.

"Are you still at the hospital, Ms. Dorothy?' Ray asked.

"Yes."

"Are they releasing you?"

"If someone comes to pick me up."

"I'm on the way."

Getting off the phone, Ray took another glance around the room, before leaving out. Making it to the hospital, he received Ms. Dorothy and they were on their way to Decatur.

"You don't think she was hurt, do you?' Ms. Dorothy asked.

"Do I think she was hurt?" Ray asked, keeping his eyes on the rear-view mirror. "Nah I don't think she was hurt. And you shouldn't stress yourself with that thought."

"She's the last of my babies, Ray."

"I understand that, Ms. Dorothy," Ray said, glancing over and seeing the tears stream down her face. "She's okay.

When they'd pulled up to her house, Ray said, "I'll go in with you, check the house and make sure everything is okay before I leave, okay?"

"Alright."

Ray did just that, once he made sure she wasn't in any immediate danger, he was back in his car and on his way home. He'd been on the expressway ten minutes when his phone rang. Sheila's number was showing on the screen.

"I hope you have a good explanation, for all this," Ray answered, not trying to hide his anger.

"Of course, she does," a familiar male voice came back at him.

"Who the fuck is this?" Ray barked.

"You might wanna calm down a little," the man warned. "I have someone I assume you care about. No, make that two, because she's with child, you may want to think about that. In fact—"

"How much?" Ray cut him off, already figuring it was about money if Sheila was still alive.

"This is not about money, King Ray," the man replied. "This is far bigger than money. I thought my mission was complete when I was told the Kingz was dead. Then, two years later, I find out that one survived. That pissed me the fuck off! And trust me, pissing me off should be the last thing anybody wants to do."

"I see," Ray said, trying to figure out who this familiar voice belonged to. "Since it's not about money, what do you want?"

"I thought you were the smartest King in the deck," he responded. "But since I was wrong, I'll break it down for you. Considering the baby is not born, I'll refer to your pretty little girlfriend as one. What I want is an even swap, your life for hers. King for a Queen, you show up, I'll let her go."

"And I'm supposed to believe you'll let her go when I show up?"

"No, you shouldn't believe that," he told Ray. "I'll admit that I'm known to play dirty, but tonight, since it's you, I'll keep my word. If anything happens to her after tonight. It won't be by me nor the hands of my men. That's my word."

"How do I know she's still alive?"

Seconds later, he heard Sheila yell, "Don't do it, Ray!"

"When and where?" Ray asked.

Once he'd acquired the time and place, he hung up and continued to his house. He'd never thought in a million years, he would have the chance to prepare for his demise. The person who ordered the hit on the Kingz had called and requested his life. Picture that! So, Ray had killed all those Drop Squad members for no apparent reason. Perhaps it was their own karma and God had chosen him to do the job, oh, well!

It took almost an hour for Ray to do what he had to do. Now, he was on his way to his meeting. The abandoned building, he was to meet them at had no lights anywhere around it, so Ray activated his bright lights as he circled around to the back. Seeing no one, he put the car in park and waited.

Almost ten minutes later, bright lights shone through his car from behind. Three black H-2 Hummers circled his car, parking in front of it. Wasting no time, Ray got out and stood in front of his car. Four men in Army fatigues, emerged from the first truck, carrying AK-47s. Four men of the same caliber climbed from the last truck. Three men climbed from the middle truck. Only two of them were military dressed. The third guy was wearing a long trench coat and Ray immediately knew who he was.

Looking at the guy, Ray thought about what Tino said. This dude was definitely a ghost because he'd actually witnessed him being murdered.

"I didn't think you would show," he told Ray.

"Fuck the small talk," Ray responded. "Where is she?"

"Oh, I'm sorry," he said, then made some gesture with his hand.

The rear passenger door opened on the middle Hummer and another military clad figure emerged with Sheila, holding her by her coat. Her hair was in disarray as if she'd put up a fight, but she wasn't bound. Then, he got a good look at her handler.

"You can let her go now, Grip," Ray said, letting it be known that he recognized the former head Kingzman.

Grip looked to his master for confirmation. Franco nodded. Released, Sheila rushed over and wrapped her arms around Ray. She was crying and her face was bruised.

"Ray, you didn't have to do this," Sheila insisted.

"Baby, you need to go before he changes his mind," Ray told her, still not trusting the setup. "There are two guns on the seat. Poppo and Joe are parked at the gas station by the expressway. They'll follow you home." He was now looking into her face. "Just make sure my baby knows everything there is to know about me—everything."

"Okay," she said, still crying.

Ray walked her to the driver's door, opening it for her. The only kiss he could muster was a peck on the lips.

"I love you, Ray!"

"I love you too," he said, rubbing her stomach. "Now go." He watched as she drove away, then turned to face the mob awaiting him.

"That was quite touching," Franco said. "If it was me, my wife would be one dead bitch. Child or no child, and let me make one thing clear for you, I hired the Kingzmen after the death of your comrades. They had nothing to do with that. I know what you're thinking, right now. Let me clear that up for you, also."

He did another gesture with his hand and guns erupted from his company. Three of his men went down. Grip was one of them, so Ray figured the other two to be the other two former Kingzmen, although he didn't get to look at their faces.

"The hit came from the Kingz," Franco went on. "But the Kingzmen were the ones who pulled the trigger. Had I not had this metal plate in my head, I wouldn't be here today, huh?" He pulled out a chrome revolver, aiming it at Ray. "Any last words?"

"Why'd you go after the Queenz?" Ray asked. "They haven't done anything to you."

Franco lowered the gun to his side and appeared to be thinking. Then, as if he'd come up with something, he said, "Strip."

"Do what?"

"Take your clothes off."

"Fuck that," Ray protested. "I'ma die with some kind of dignity."

"You asked me a question," Franco said. "If you expect me to answer your question, I have to make sure you're not wearing a wire. It's your call."

Ray had to think about this. It was damn near below zero and this white boy wanted him to get butt ass naked. '*Fuck it!*' Ray thought and began undressing until he was wearing nothing but a pair of socks.

"Before I answer your question," Franco went on, "I have a question for you. What made you go at Drop Squad like that?"

"They were the first ones I suspected," Ray said, teeth chattering from the cold.

"I commend you for the job you did on them," Franco said. "You really did a number on them. But, to answer your question, it started off as a scare tactic. When I heard there was a group of women trying to take on a male-dominated game, I figured I could scare them into returning to household chores women are supposed to be doing. But, when I found out they were the Kingz widows, it turned real. They were tougher than I thought. They wouldn't go down without a fight."

"What about, Curt?" Ray asked, remembering Poppo mentioned something about a black Hummer.

"I remember that," Franco answered. "That was a case of mistaken identity. His car was similar to—"

"What about, Akbar?" Ray cut him off. "The West End shooting."

"That wasn't me."

The Crips in Carver Homes?"

"They tried to extort some of my men."

"Who did, Spenz?"

"Never heard of him."

"What about, Yvonne?" Ray asked. "The girl King Fred was messing with. She was set on fire in her salon."

Collateral damage, my friend," Franco answered. "And so were your workers, though Drop Squad had a part in that."

"You shot their bowling alley up," Ray accused. "And they thought we did it."

"Negative," Franco contradicted. "That was done by King James and the Kingzmen."

Ray did have a strong feeling that James had something to do with that. Now, he had one more question and he knew he was going out on a limb, but he had to know. "What about, Sylvia? And don't give me that collateral damage bullshit."

"I can't really say too much on that," Franco answered. "All I know is what Grip told me. She was a prostitute and you were in love with her, she was pregnant. You caught her sucking another's man's dick. James didn't agree with her, so he had her killed. That's all I know about her."

"Bullshit," Ray spat, reluctant to believe his brother had done some shit like that. "Why the fuck would he have Sylvia knocked off?"

"I already told you what I know." Franco raised his gun. "You wanna die with your clothes on, or not?"

Playa Ray

Chapter 29

Baby Girl,

If you're reading this, then that means he kept his word. I've never told you this, but when I first laid eyes on you at the New Year's Eve party, I knew you were special. Your bitchy attitude was exceptional. I knew you were the one for me, all along. I brushed you off because I didn't want to rush into it. Just in case I was wrong. I've been wrong my whole life, but all those wrongs, which all resulted in heartbreaks, led to something right, which was you. I knew that once I got you, I would never let you go, nor let anyone harm you. Trust me this decision I'm making didn't take an ounce of a second for me to decide on. You're my Queen and my heart will always be with you. Just make sure my seed knows everything about me, whether good or bad. I trust that you'll maintain contact with Connie, for the sake of Rachel. Also, look out for Kim and Nikki. I didn't tell Joe and Poppo what I was doing, but I'm sure once you tell them what went down, they'll be there for you. There's over one point four million dollars in my safe. I trust that you'll do the right thing with it. The combination is eleven-twenty-three-seventy-nine. And make sure to see Sharonda at Posh BMWs, in Marietta. She has something for you. Look, I have to make this meeting. I love you. Your King, Ray

Sheila wiped the tears from her eyes and slid the folded letter back into the white envelope that read: *To My Queen*. She'd read the letter every day for the past two and a half years and it still brought tears to her eyes. She got off the bed and placed the letter back on top of the piles of money in the safe. Once she closed it and put the large picture of George Washington Carver back up, she exited the room that was now her bedroom, being that she'd given the main bedroom to her grandmother and the other guest room to Ms. Davis.

Sheila entered the Kingz and Queenz room, where there were now eight mannequins. The Queenz were all draped in long dresses, fur coats and topped with their tiaras. Plus, they were all standing by their respective King. After regarding them at length, she kissed King Ray, then left out, making sure to secure the door behind her, lest her two-year-old son came in and tore up something, which was pretty much all he knew how to do.

Speaking of the little devil, she entered the living room and encountered him banging one of his toy trucks on the coffee table, visibly scratching it up.

"Prince Ray, I'ma whoop your butt," she threatened, thrusting her hands on her hips.

"Stop," he exclaimed, which was something he'd always say when someone threatened to do something to him.

"You stop," she shot back, smiling at her son, who was the spitting image of his father. "Come here."

He flung the truck across the room before running over to her. She picked him up, kissing him on the cheek.

"You're going to make me put your bad butt up for adoption."

"Stop!"

"I'ma tell your, daddy."

Just as she'd expected, he regarded her with enlarged pupils, which was something he did whenever someone threatened to tell his daddy on him. Suppressing her smile, Sheila went to Ms. Davis's room and tapped on the closed door.

"Mama?"

"It's open."

Sheila entered the bedroom, where Ms. Davis stood in the mirror, doing her hair.

"You got a date?"

"I need one," Ms. Davis replied.

"Well, today is your lucky day," Sheila asserted. "Prince Ray needs his hair braided."

"You call that a date?" she asked, smiling.

"All you need is some popcorn and a belt," Sheila joked, prompting laughter.

"What are y'all in here cackling about?" Ms. Dorothy entered the room, wiping her hands on a towel.

"Nothing, Grandma," Sheila answered. "Ray's mama called me last night and wanted to know if she could come and get Prince Ray next weekend. I'm trying to get mama to do his hair, so he can stop running around looking like Charles Lee Ray."

"And who in the world is Charles Lee Ray?" Ms. Dorothy asked.

"Chucky, grandma."

"Chucky," Prince Ray repeated.

"Here." She kissed her son, then relinquished him to his great-grandmother. "I gotta get going."

Sheila rushed back to her room, grabbed her keys and pocketbook, then made for the garage, climbing into Ray's BMW. She'd gotten her Cadillac out of impound, fixed the driver's window, got it painted and gave it to Kim, who now resided at the house in Norcross. She'd given the house in Riverdale, to Nikki, who's now six months pregnant with Ace's second child.

Sheila pulled the BMW into Connie's driveway, parking behind the Range Rover. She dismounted and for some reason, just stood there, relishing the warm August weather.

"I don't recall having a statue in my front yard."

Sheila looked over and smiled at Connie, who was standing in the doorway with Rachel.

"Hey, stepmama, Sheila." Rachel beamed as Sheila approached.

"Hey, my princess." Sheila picked up Rachel, who was five years old and still smaller than average kids her age. "How're you doing in school?"

"Fine," she answered. "My teacher said I'm smart."

"You are smart," Sheila told her. "Your daddy was smart, so that makes you extra smart."

"The other kids pick at me," Rachel said sadly. "They said I'm a dwarf and I look funny."

"Dwarfs are cute," Sheila insisted. "Besides you're a miracle baby. You know what that means?"

"I'm special?"

"That's exactly what it means," Sheila replied. "They're just mad they're not special like you. Don't you forget that, okay?"

"Okay."

"Give stepmama a kiss." Rachel kissed her on the cheek, and she kissed her back. "I love you!"

"I love you, too!"

"Let me talk to, Aunt Connie," Sheila said, putting Rachel down and watching her walk away.

"Come on in," Connie told Sheila.

"I can't," Sheila refused. "I'm on my way to the dealership. We got new imports coming in. Did Ms. Mary call you last night?"

"She did."

"Are you gonna let her get Rachel, next weekend?"

"Yeah."

"So, you'll be free next weekend, huh?"

"I guess."

Sheila just looked at her.

"Why do you keep trying to get me to come out to the club?" Connie inquired.

"Because you need to get out of the house, sometimes," Sheila answered.

"I might fall through next weekend," Connie swore.

Leaving Connie's house, Sheila drove out to Glamour Girls, which she'd relocated to Marietta and still had the same stylists. After making sure everything was everything, she drove farther down the street to Posh BMWs, which was now owned by her. She went over the necessary paperwork with Eric who was still the manager, inspected the two thousand nine imports when they arrived, signed for them, then was on her way to Atlanta.

The Palace looked a whole lot better, now that it was decked out with neon lighting and a large neon sign that read: *The Palace*. Sheila entered the club and was still blown away by how the inside had been constructionally converted. There were three bars to serve drinks and one served food. There were fifty-six-inch TVs along the walls, a D.J. booth, a stage, and two VIP booths.

"How you doing, Sheila?"

Pulled from her reverie, Sheila looked to see Nikki's husband, Ace, who was one of the security guards approaching.

"I'm fine, Ace. How's everything?"

"Everything's good," he answered. "Kevin's on punishment for fighting in school. Other than that, the family's good."

"I'm glad to hear that," she told him. "Who's all here?"

"Shoot, everybody," he said. "Precious does not play. If we're not here when she says be here, that's our ass. You picked the right person for management."

Sheila was laughing. "I guess I'm glad to hear that, too. Where's Poppo and Joe?"

"Man, Precious got the whole security team back there unloading food and ice."

Sheila narrowed her eyes at him. "All except one."

"She got me running errands," he told her. "I gotta make sure the artists have what they requested in their dressing rooms."

"Well, I won't hold you up," she said. "I'll be in the office."

Sheila journeyed to the office, waving at Star, who was a bartender, before entering. The office was pretty much the same, except for the array of monitors that lined one wall and the computer on the table. The chairs, table and safe were still there. Even the Mona Lisa painting remained.

Sitting her pocketbook on the table, she flopped down in one of the four chairs and looked up at the monitors. She smiled as she watched

Precious flex her authority. Ray told her how Precious held down his weed spot in Maple creek, He'd also told her about their short-lived relationship. Putting herself in Precious shoes, Sheila felt Ray had done her wrong by leaving her when she was only trying to console him. that's why she befriended Precious and chose to let her manage the club.

Now, Sheila was studying the wedding ring on her finger, in which she'd bought, to keep men at bay. Whenever a man approached her, she just held up her left hand. She already knew she'd never find another man like Ray, so she continued to shy away from the dating game. She couldn't even entertain the thought of opening her legs for another man. She still belonged to King Ray. She figured if Ms. Davis and her grandmother could go a million years without a man, then so could she. Or, was she just hoping Ray was still alive, being that his body hadn't surfaced?

To Be Continued...
KINGZ OF THE GAME 5:
THE INVESTIGATION
Coming Soon

Submission Guideline

Submit the first three chapters of your completed manuscript to ldpsubmissions@gmail.com, subject line: Your book's title. The manuscript must be in a .doc file and sent as an attachment. Document should be in Times New Roman, double spaced and in size 12 font. Also, provide your synopsis and full contact information. If sending multiple submissions, they must each be in a separate email.

Have a story but no way to send it electronically? You can still submit to LDP/Ca$h Presents. Send in the first three chapters, written or typed, of your completed manuscript to:

LDP: Submissions Dept
Po Box 870494
Mesquite, Tx 75187

DO NOT send original manuscript. Must be a duplicate.

Provide your synopsis and a cover letter containing your full contact information.

Thanks for considering LDP and Ca$h Presents.

SOUL OF A MONSTER III
By **Aryanna**
THE COST OF LOYALTY **III**
By **Kweli**
THE SAVAGE LIFE II
By **J-Blunt**
KING OF NEW YORK V
COKE KINGS IV
BORN HEARTLESS II
By **T.J. Edwards**
GORILLAZ IN THE BAY IV
De'Kari
THE STREETS ARE CALLING II
Duquie Wilson
KINGPIN KILLAZ IV
STREET KINGS III
PAID IN BLOOD III
CARTEL KILLAZ III
Hood Rich
SINS OF A HUSTLA II
ASAD
TRIGGADALE III
Elijah R. Freeman
KINGZ OF THE GAME V
Playa Ray
SLAUGHTER GANG IV
RUTHLESS HEART II
By Willie Slaughter
THE HEART OF A SAVAGE II
By Jibril Williams

FUK SHYT II

By Blakk Diamond

THE DOPEMAN'S BODYGAURD II

By Tranay Adams

TRAP GOD II

By Troublesome

YAYO II

A SHOOTER'S AMBITION II

By S. Allen

GHOST MOB

Stilloan Robinson

KINGPIN DREAMS

By Paper Boi Rari

CREAM

By Yolanda Moore

SON OF A DOPE FIEND II

By Renta

FOREVER GANGSTA

By Adrian Dulan

LOYALTY AIN'T PROMISED

By Keith Williams

THE PRICE YOU PAY FOR LOVE

By Destiny Skai

THE LIFE OF A HOOD STAR

By Rashia Wilson

<u>Available Now</u>

RESTRAINING ORDER **I & II**

By **CA$H & Coffee**

LOVE KNOWS NO BOUNDARIES **I II & III**
By **Coffee**
RAISED AS A GOON I, II, III & IV
BRED BY THE SLUMS I, II, III
BLAST FOR ME I & II
ROTTEN TO THE CORE I II III
A BRONX TALE I, II, III
DUFFEL BAG CARTEL I II III
HEARTLESS GOON
A SAVAGE DOPEBOY
HEARTLESS GOON I II
By **Ghost**
LAY IT DOWN **I & II**
LAST OF A DYING BREED
BLOOD STAINS OF A SHOTTA I & II
By **Jamaica**
LOYAL TO THE GAME
LOYAL TO THE GAME II
LOYAL TO THE GAME III
LIFE OF SIN I, II III
By **TJ & Jelissa**
BLOODY COMMAS I & II
SKI MASK CARTEL I II & III
KING OF NEW YORK I II,III IV
RISE TO POWER I II III
COKE KINGS I II III
BORN HEARTLESS
By **T.J. Edwards**
IF LOVING HIM IS WRONG…I & II
LOVE ME EVEN WHEN IT HURTS I II III

By **Jelissa**

WHEN THE STREETS CLAP BACK I & II III

By **Jibril Williams**

A DISTINGUISHED THUG STOLE MY HEART I II & III

LOVE SHOULDN'T HURT I II III IV

RENEGADE BOYS I II III IV

By **Meesha**

A GANGSTER'S CODE I &, II III

A GANGSTER'S SYN I II III

THE SAVAGE LIFE

By J-Blunt

PUSH IT TO THE LIMIT

By **Bre' Hayes**

BLOOD OF A BOSS **I, II, III, IV, V**

SHADOWS OF THE GAME

By **Askari**

THE STREETS BLEED MURDER **I, II & III**

THE HEART OF A GANGSTA I II& III

By **Jerry Jackson**

CUM FOR ME

CUM FOR ME 2

CUM FOR ME 3

CUM FOR ME 4

CUM FOR ME 5

An **LDP Erotica Collaboration**

BRIDE OF A HUSTLA **I II & II**

THE FETTI GIRLS **I, II& III**

CORRUPTED BY A GANGSTA I, II III, IV

BLINDED BY HIS LOVE

By **Destiny Skai**

WHEN A GOOD GIRL GOES BAD
By **Adrienne**
THE COST OF LOYALTY I II
By Kweli
A GANGSTER'S REVENGE **I II III & IV**
THE BOSS MAN'S DAUGHTERS
THE BOSS MAN'S DAUGHTERS II
THE BOSSMAN'S DAUGHTERS III
THE BOSSMAN'S DAUGHTERS IV
THE BOSS MAN'S DAUGHTERS **V**
A SAVAGE LOVE **I & II**
BAE BELONGS TO ME I II
A HUSTLER'S DECEIT I, II, III
WHAT BAD BITCHES DO I, II, III
SOUL OF A MONSTER I II
KILL ZONE
By **Aryanna**
A KINGPIN'S AMBITON
A KINGPIN'S AMBITION **II**
I MURDER FOR THE DOUGH
By **Ambitious**
TRUE SAVAGE
TRUE SAVAGE II
TRUE SAVAGE **III**
TRUE SAVAGE **IV**
TRUE SAVAGE **V**
TRUE SAVAGE **VI**
By **Chris Green**
A DOPEBOY'S PRAYER
By **Eddie "Wolf" Lee**

THE KING CARTEL **I, II & III**

By **Frank Gresham**

THESE NIGGAS AIN'T LOYAL **I, II & III**

By **Nikki Tee**

GANGSTA SHYT **I II &III**

By **CATO**

THE ULTIMATE BETRAYAL

By **Phoenix**

BOSS'N UP **I , II & III**

By **Royal Nicole**

I LOVE YOU TO DEATH

By Destiny J

I RIDE FOR MY HITTA

I STILL RIDE FOR MY HITTA

By **Misty Holt**

LOVE & CHASIN' PAPER

By **Qay Crockett**

TO DIE IN VAIN

SINS OF A HUSTLA

By **ASAD**

BROOKLYN HUSTLAZ

By **Boogsy Morina**

BROOKLYN ON LOCK I & II

By **Sonovia**

GANGSTA CITY

By **Teddy Duke**

A DRUG KING AND HIS DIAMOND I & II III

A DOPEMAN'S RICHES

HER MAN, MINE'S TOO I, II

CASH MONEY HO'S

Playa Ray

By Nicole Goosby
TRAPHOUSE KING **I II & III**
KINGPIN KILLAZ I II III
STREET KINGS I II
PAID IN BLOOD **I II**
CARTEL KILLAZ I II
By **Hood Rich**
LIPSTICK KILLAH **I, II, III**
CRIME OF PASSION I & II
By **Mimi**
STEADY MOBBN' **I, II, III**
By **Marcellus Allen**
WHO SHOT YA **I, II, III**
SON OF A DOPE FIEND
Renta
GORILLAZ IN THE BAY **I II III**
DE'KARI
TRIGGADALE I II
Elijah R. Freeman
GOD BLESS THE TRAPPERS I, II, III
THESE SCANDALOUS STREETS I, II, III
FEAR MY GANGSTA I, II, III
THESE STREETS DON'T LOVE NOBODY I, II
BURY ME A G I, II, III, IV, V
A GANGSTA'S EMPIRE I, II, III, IV
THE DOPEMAN'S BODYGAURD
Tranay Adams
THE STREETS ARE CALLING
Duquie Wilson
MARRIED TO A BOSS... I II III

230

By Destiny Skai & Chris Green

KINGZ OF THE GAME I II III IV

Playa Ray

SLAUGHTER GANG I II III

RUTHLESS HEART

By Willie Slaughter

THE HEART OF A SAVAGE

By Jibril Williams

FUK SHYT

By Blakk Diamond

DON'T F#CK WITH MY HEART I II

By Linnea

ADDICTED TO THE DRAMA I II III

By Jamila

YAYO

A SHOOTER'S AMBITION

By S. Allen

TRAP GOD

By Troublesome

Playa Ray

BOOKS BY LDP'S CEO, CA$H

TRUST IN NO MAN

TRUST IN NO MAN 2

TRUST IN NO MAN 3

BONDED BY BLOOD

SHORTY GOT A THUG

THUGS CRY

THUGS CRY 2

THUGS CRY 3

TRUST NO BITCH

TRUST NO BITCH 2

TRUST NO BITCH 3

TIL MY CASKET DROPS

RESTRAINING ORDER

RESTRAINING ORDER 2

IN LOVE WITH A CONVICT

Coming Soon

BONDED BY BLOOD 2

BOW DOWN TO MY GANGSTA

Kingz of the Game 4

www.ingramcontent.com/pod-product-compliance
Lightning Source LLC
Chambersburg PA
CBHW070446260626
47161CB00004B/1224